A kiss. That was al
Hayden wanted.

And Tomara wasn't fighting him. At first he was afraid she wasn't going to respond to the light touch of his lips against hers, and he wondered how it was possible to want something as much as he wanted this woman.

And then, slowly, she unfolded.

It couldn't be any other way. Tomara had known that they would end this way. Oh, there were barriers between them. There might always be barriers. But for this moment she would turn her back on them. She clung to Hayden's warmth and strength, recklessly taking what she needed.

He might still be her enemy. She could accept that, because with his arms keeping her safe from the world, she could accept anything.

In another lifetime, she would deal with the consequences.

Dear Reader,

Welcome to the Silhouette **Special Edition** experience! With your search for consistently satisfying reading in mind, every month the authors and editors of Silhouette **Special Edition** aim to offer you a stimulating blend of deep emotions and high romance.

The name Silhouette **Special Edition** and the distinctive arch on the cover represent a commitment—a commitment to bring you six sensitive, substantial novels each month. In the pages of a Silhouette **Special Edition**, compelling true-to-life characters face riveting emotional issues—and come out winners. All the authors in the series strive for depth, vividness and warmth in writing these stories of living and loving in today's world.

The result, we hope, is romance you can believe in. Deeply emotional, richly romantic, infinitely rewarding—that's the Silhouette **Special Edition** experience. Come share it with us—six times a month! With this month's distinguished roster of gifted contemporary writers—Bay Matthews, Karen Keast, Barbara Faith, Madelyn Dohrn, Dawn Flindt and Andrea Edwards—you won't want to miss a single volume.

Best wishes,

Leslie Kazanjian,
Senior Editor

DAWN FLINDT
Prairie Cry

Silhouette Special Edition

Published by Silhouette Books New York

America's Publisher of Contemporary Romance

SILHOUETTE BOOKS
300 East 42nd St., New York, N.Y. 10017

ISBN: 0-373-09617-8

First Silhouette Books printing August 1990

Printed in the U.S.A.

Books by Dawn Flindt

Silhouette Special Edition

The Power Within #448
Prairie Cry #617

DAWN FLINDT

Having a mother and a grandmother who were teachers and growing up in rural areas without television reception paved the way to a love of reading for this Oregon writer. Her first writing attempts were comic books—with horses as the main characters! These "literary masterpieces" failed to bring her international acclaim, but the author says her sister loyally appreciated her efforts. Although Dawn has done everything from newspaper work to magazine articles, fiction remains her first love. Married to a social worker and the mother of two teenage sons, Dawn Flindt also writes as Vella Munn.

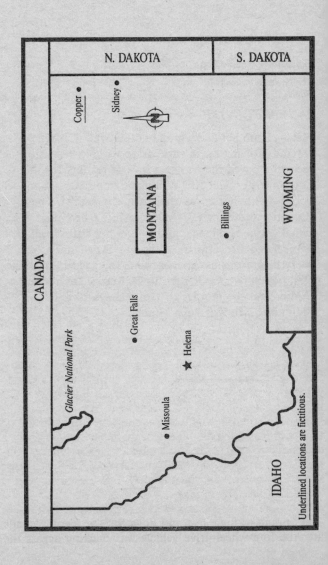

N. DAKOTA

S. DAKOTA

Copper •

Sidney •

MONTANA

• Billings

CANADA

• Great Falls

★ Helena

• Missoula

Glacier National Park

WYOMING

IDAHO

Underlined locations are fictitious.

Chapter One

At five minutes past nine in the evening, Montana game warden Hayden Conover banked the helicopter he was piloting, his eyes drawn to a spear of light on the Richland county plain below him. Hayden had been in the air since a little after dawn counting antelope before the opening of hunting season. Although it was dark, he was still at work, now looking for poachers. If he was closer to civilization he might have discounted the light as belonging to camping Sioux or Assiniboin Indians, but this particular rugged area was too remote. His "antennae," honed by five years of being a game cop, kicked into high gear.

Hayden nosed down. What he saw when he switched on the spotlight forced out a grim oath. A battered Jeep of indeterminate color with its headlights on was parked perhaps ten feet from an antelope carcass. Two men were squatting, not by the slain animal, but over a form that looked suspiciously human.

The sound of the approaching helicopter startled the men. They sprang to their feet and dove for the Jeep. Seconds later the four-wheel-drive vehicle was bucking across the

open country. Hayden could have given chase. He could
have pulled out his bullhorn and ordered them to surrender, but he did neither of those things. For one, confront-
ing two men who were probably armed on the Montana
plains wasn't the sort of thing an intelligent thirty-four-year-
old man would do if he wanted to go on living. Second, he'd
seen the fleeing Jeep's license number and committed it to
memory.

Hayden lowered the helicopter gradually until he found a
clear spot among the rocks and sagebrush and landed. He
cut the engine and stepped out of the cockpit when he was
certain the Jeep wasn't going to circle back.

He went first to the antelope. A quick look told him it had
been dead for hours. Then, knowing that tonight was going
to be different from any other he'd spent since leaving Los
Angeles, Hayden made his way slowly to the inert form that
had commanded the men's attention. The still-whirling helicopter blades stirred the night air but did nothing to dis-
sipate the cold sweat on the back of Hayden's neck. Except
for the dying sounds of the machine, the night was silent.

The man was, Hayden guessed, somewhere in his early
forties. He was clean-cut and soft in the middle. He was
wearing new boots, a flannel shirt that probably hadn't been
washed yet, jeans not yet molded to his body. One hand was
clamped around a clump of grass. He'd been shot in the
back.

After a minute spent squatting next to the man, Hayden
returned to the helicopter. He switched the spotlight back on
and pulled out his camera. Then he made contact with district headquarters. "I've got a body here," he explained
tersely. "I'd say whoever did it used a rifle. I've got a license number. I'd appreciate it if you'd get someone to run
it down for me. Yeah. I'm all right. Yes. I will."

After taking a deep breath, Hayden was able to put his
emotions on ice. He'd seen death while working in L.A. He
could handle it again. He got back out of the helicopter and
walked around the body until he had the best angle for taking pictures. It was only an educated guess at this point, but
Hayden would be willing to bet his three-year-old Bronco

hat the man hadn't known what hit him. Hayden was also willing to bet that he hadn't been dead as long as the antelope.

He'd taken his pictures and was jotting down a description of the man's clothing when his radio squawked to life. Hayden returned to the helicopter and picked up the receiver. The first time he'd called in, the night dispatcher was on the line. She'd been replaced by the regional supervisor. "You all right out there?" he asked on the tail of Hayden's brief explanation of what had happened. "Are you sure you're alone?"

"No, I'm not sure I'm alone." Again cold pricked at the back of Hayden's neck. "The only other vehicle I've seen is the Jeep that hightailed it out of here."

"They could have left someone behind."

"What are you trying to do, scare me?"

"I don't need you dead, Hayden. Look, I've got the name of the Jeep's registered owner. Metcalf. Al Metcalf."

"Metcalf?"

"You know them. Old man Metcalf and his son have been running on the wrong side of the law as long as I've been working for the state. The old man's been in jail God knows how many times and the kid one or two times himself. Cattle theft. Drunk and disorderly. Poaching. A lot of poaching. Maybe that's what this all boils down to. Metcalf shot himself an antelope out of season and then did in the joker who stumbled on them."

"Maybe." Somehow Hayden didn't think it was that simple. "How long do you think it'll take for someone to get out here?"

"Hopefully less than an hour. I've already talked to Jay and the state police. You hold tight. Sorry, Hayden. So much for peace and quiet."

"Yeah." Hayden bit down on the word.

Tomara Metcalf was getting ready to climb a telephone pole on West Sunnyside Road in Idaho Falls when the call came over the walkie-talkie. "He didn't say who he was."

The office woman relayed the message. "All I know is, he says he's a lawyer from Copper, Montana. He wants you to get in touch with him as soon as possible."

Copper. History. Dead and gone. Or at least it should have been. Although her long chestnut hair was caught in a practical braid, Tomara reached for the strands that had clung to her neck all the time she was growing up. Angry at herself for the gesture, Tomara pulled her hand away and stared at the offending limb. There was a half-healed cut at the base of her thumb, compliments of the way she earned her living. It would have been little more than a scar by now if she'd had stitches taken, but Tomara couldn't be bothered with trips to a doctor. Instead she'd slapped a tight butterfly bandage around it. The bandage was gone now, she noticed. "Do you have a number?"

The woman explained that she'd already placed it on Tomara's desk. "He said he'd be in his office until the middle of the afternoon. I thought you should know. What is it? I didn't know you knew anyone in Montana."

I don't, Tomara wanted to say. But that wasn't true. She might have been able to put hundreds of miles between herself and the past, but she couldn't exorcise that past. "Look, I'm coming in now," she said, although making that particular phone call was the last thing in the world she wanted to do.

"But you've got two more service calls to make before lunch."

"They'll have to wait. This won't take long."

Fifteen minutes later Tomara was back in the telephone company office. Because she knew the woman's curiosity would get the better of her, Tomara slipped in the back way, waiting until the linemen's room was empty before picking up the receiver. She asked the operator to bill her home phone and then waited, the years siding away into nothing while the connection was being made.

Leonard Barth, attorney-at-law. She hadn't seen the man in six years. Tomara accepted the reality of his call with the same stoicism as she would have had had the call been from the coroner's office. She doubted that Leonard's office had changed since she'd packed two boxes and caught a bus out of town. He'd still be sitting at his desk, staring at Copper's main street, watching life plod by, taking note of the changing seasons, storing up gossip to spread at the post office or in Mandy's Saloon.

"Tomara. I didn't think you'd get back to me this soon. Had a hell of a time running you down."

"What is it, Leonard?" Tomara leaned against her desk, her right hip taking most of her weight. She didn't trust herself to sit.

"You're not going to like hearing this, but I'm afraid your dad and brother got themselves into some trouble."

"They're always getting into trouble. What is it this time?"

"They're in jail."

"Jail." She said the word without emotion. "What's the charge?"

"You're not going to like this, Tomara."

"What's the charge?"

"Murder."

Tomara waited for shock, for disbelief, for anger even. She felt none of those things. She shifted the receiver to her left hand and stared at the healing wound on her thumb. She should have finished her morning's work before coming back to call Leonard. But he was on the line, and there were things she had to ask. "Are you representing them?"

"It looks like it. Tomara? Your dad doesn't know I called. He said this wasn't any of your business. But Hoagy, he managed to get a call through to me this morning from Sidney. That's where they're being held. He thought you should know."

Tomara had long ago stopped being shocked by anything her father did, but her kid brother was another story. What was it he'd told her, that as soon as he saved up his money, he'd be hightailing it out of Copper the way she had. But he wasn't leaving the little town settled on the eastern Montana prairie. He was in jail, charged with murder.

"Thanks, Leonard. Ah, what about your fee? Are they going to be able to pay you?" This wasn't what she should be talking about. There were a million more important questions, such as were they guilty? But Tomara couldn't make herself ask that. Yet.

"We haven't gotten that far," Leonard was telling her. "Of course there's the river land. I guess they could sell it if it gets to that. They were only arrested yesterday."

Tomara ran cold fingers down the faded denim covering her taut thighs. Without knowing she was doing it, she began to unfasten the tool belt hanging low on her hips. Once she was free of her burden, she dropped it, forgotten, onto her desk. "I won't be able to get there for at least two days."

"That's not why I called, Tomara. Hoagy just wanted you to know."

"Wednesday afternoon. I should be there by then."

Hayden was sitting in Jay Eagle's office, waiting for the compact Sioux Indian to get off the phone. Opening day of antelope season was only a few weeks away, but that was the last thing on his mind this hot, windy afternoon. From where he sat, Hayden could see down the narrow, sun-bleached street to Mandy's Saloon, and beyond that the weathered building that housed Leonard Barth's law practice and the clinic of nurse practitioner Waylin Saul, Copper's answer to a doctor. In about an hour, Leonard and Waylin and the other business people would be heading for Mandy's for a beer and talk. Hayden had no doubt what they'd be talking about today.

"That was someone from the governor's office. They're sure agitating to have this taken to Helena for trial. That and trying to find out where our victim came from has been a pain." Jay replaced the telephone receiver with his broad hand, reminding Hayden of countless arm-wrestling contests between the two. Hayden had lost track of who was in the lead now and doubted that Jay knew, either. What mattered was the competition, the good-natured boasts, the gathering of Copper's residents around the sturdy table in Mandy's Saloon while the area's two strongest men went at each other. "I'm not giving up that easy," Jay went on.

"Yeah, we're small, but we do have electricity in this county. We can conduct our own trials."

"Maybe." Hayden looked out the dusty window in time to see Connie Coyne cross the street headed for the post office. The divorced ranch owner's shorts barely contained her generous rear end, but the stretch of thigh didn't distract Hayden from what he and Jay were talking about. Hayden and Connie had dated a few times, not because they had that much in common, but because she was one of the few single women around. Fortunately for both of them, they'd discovered they had little in common except a commitment to the land. "Are they going to be able to get an impartial jury around here?" Hayden asked. "Unless you're hearing different things than I am, Al and Hoagy have all but been convicted."

"I know. That's why I didn't hang up. I hate losing out on the notoriety, but the Metcalfs have earned their reputations. Neither of them has enough friends to count on the fingers of one hand. Nothing they've done has ever turned out. That's why—you never did meet the girl, did you?"

"What girl?"

"Al's oldest. Tomara. The only one in the family with any brains." Jay's gravel voice softened. "I don't know why she didn't hightail it out of here the moment she got out of high school. I guess, maybe she felt some loyalty or something. After she left, Al told me she was never coming back."

Connie was cutting back across the street. She stopped as another rancher pulled his pickup alongside and called out to her. "What'd you call her? Tomara. Do you think she knows her old man and brother are in jail?"

Jay shrugged his massive shoulders. "Who knows? Neither Al or Hoagy are much for writing or calling. As far as I know, that place of theirs doesn't even have a phone. I remember her... I think I could have loved her."

Hayden was no longer interested in Connie. "Why?"

"Because, maybe because she looked like someone who needed loving. Maybe I wasn't the right one to give her what she needed, but I thought about it. She was like one of the antelope. Half wild. Quiet. Kept her opinions to herself. That kind of thing makes a man think.''

Hayden wasn't surprised to hear his friend say that. Jay cared. It was that trait that made him a good cop. And that led to his getting married in the fall to a woman with two children. ''So this Tomara isn't like the rest of the family. That must mean she doesn't have a criminal record.''

''Hardly.'' Jay blinked. His eyes strayed to the window. ''As I remember, Tomara drove her teachers crazy. When she'd gone through every book in the school's library, Mrs. Palmer sent away for college material. Mrs. Palmer tried to get Tomara to sign up for some scholarships.'' Jay leaned forward, his chair squeaking a protest. ''I can't remember what the scholarships were for. Some kind of trade, I think, because Tomara wasn't one for sitting behind a desk when she could be outside. I can remember...''

Jay's voice trailed off; his eyes became even deeper. ''I saw her once running along a ridge about dawn. She was crazy about running. Just like the antelope. Anyway, it was dawn. I was out looking for one of my dad's bulls that hadn't come in to water the night before. It had rained a little, and the sunrise was something. All red and orange with these big, brooding clouds hanging over. I was thinking maybe I'd spent the day out on the plains instead of going to school when there she was.''

Hayden waited maybe five heartbeats before realizing that Jay wasn't going to finish what he'd begun. The world beyond the window was flat, dry, timeless. Still, Hayden understood that there were times when the prairie with its ridges and valleys, sage and sparse watering holes could be magic. He had no idea what Tomara Metcalf looked like, but a girl running along the skyline at dawn—it was enough to make him forget that Connie's bed could be his and no questions asked. ''This girl? She didn't know you were alive?''

''She knew I was alive. There was no way she couldn't in a town this size. But she started riding a trail bike to school when she was twelve or thirteen, so she didn't ride the bus. Then—'' Jay's chuckle was soft and low ''—I'll bet even money she wasn't fourteen when she started driving that Jeep. The damn old thing had sat out there at the Metcalf place for years, but she got it going again. Drove it until Hoagy nearly wrecked it. She was mechanical. Fixed it again. Wasn't anything she couldn't do with her hands. Tomara Metcalf's a looker. She didn't know it, though, or if she did, it didn't matter. Built for running, with hair—oh, God, that hair. I never did know what was going on inside her. Maybe that's why I thought about her so much. I kept thinking, I kept thinking maybe she needed someone to talk to."

"And you were willing to fill that role." Hayden gave his friend a skeptical look. "The way you're going on, I'd think that talking was the last thing you'd be interested in."

"She did get the hormones going," Jay admitted. "I wonder..." His voice trailed off again. "I wonder if anyone's told her. If she comes back here, I could handle an introduction and let you take it from there."

Hayden tried to shrug off Jay's offer, but it wasn't as easy as he hoped it would be. The truth was, although Hayden had never regretted his decision to leave the insanity of Los Angeles, there were times when the solitude of eastern Montana was more than he was comfortable with. True, he could have taken advantage of Connie's suggestion that, even if bells hadn't gone off between them, there was no reason they had to sleep alone. There'd been a few times back last winter when icy winds whipped across the plains for days on end that losing himself in her arms had been more than a little appealing.

But Hayden had never made that call.

"You're dreaming, Jay," Hayden said as he got to his feet. "Even if this wild woman does come back, she and I are going to be on opposite sides of the fence."

"Yeah. I know. I was just thinking out loud. Wanting you to have what I'm finally going to have." Jay glanced at the clock on the far wall. "I've got about another hour here. You want to grab a beer at Mandy's then?"

Hayden nodded and left without bothering with a formal goodbye. His own office, if it could be called that,

consisted of one room in his house. In that room was the
communication system that linked him to the state Department of Fish, Wildlife, and Parks, but since the hookup in
his Bronco served the same purpose, there was no need to
travel the three miles to the five acres he owned west of
town.

Hayden slipped behind the wheel of the Bronco, but before he could pick up the CB, he was approached by one of
the area's old-timers. The tobacco-chewing, leathered
rancher was angry but philosophical. He'd lost a calf last
night, not to coyotes but to some of the half-wild dogs that
roamed the area. He could, he explained, have gone out on
his own and done away with the dogs, but he figured Hayden should know. Once that was out of the way, the rancher
was more than ready to shift the conversation to the biggest
piece of news to hit the county in years.

By the time Hayden finally broke free of the rancher, the
last thing he wanted to talk about was the murder of one
Bart Renfree and his role in it. The moment, however, he
stepped into Mandy's Saloon it started all over again. Three
regulars were already in the weather-blasted building. Hayden was offered a beer and invited to join the card-playing
trio. Fortunately, Mandy rescued him.

"You don't want to get trapped by them." Mandy jerked
her head at the three. "You'll never get loose. Besides, to
hear them tell it, it was them and not you who came across
the body. You want a beer?"

"Not yet. And thanks." Hayden lowered his voice. "I'd
much rather flirt with you than get taken at cards." Hayden waited while Mandy went about pouring him a glass of
ice water, marveling that anyone could move as smoothly
and silently as she did. Mandy was at least fifty, and what
last name she went by wasn't important. She'd been married three times and had buried her last two husbands. The
saloon had once belonged to her father, but the story was
that Mandy had run it since she was a teenager. Except for
the postmaster, there wasn't anyone in Copper who knew
more about what did or didn't happen in town. Mandy was
one of Hayden's favorite people.

"When are you going to get tired of playing the field and marry me?" Hayden asked after the icy liquid chased away the worst of his thirst. He'd been asking the handsome woman that question for better than four years now.

"When you get rich enough to support me in the style to which I'm accustomed," Mandy answered as she always did. "I'm surprised you have time to come in here. I thought you'd be out investigating or whatever it is you cops do."

"Game warden," Hayden corrected automatically. "And it isn't my business to investigate. If anything else needs to be done, it's up to Jay."

"I guess. I keep thinking of him as a kid. I remember—let's just say it's a good thing he grew up." Mandy lifted a glass to her own lips and crunched down on shaved ice. "You guys got it figured out where this trial's going to be held?"

"No. And don't ask me when, either."

"Figures. Nothing moves fast around here. I understand—" Mandy glanced at the trio in the corner of the room "—there's talk of bail for Al and Hoagy."

Hayden hadn't heard anything about that, but it didn't surprise him that the rumor mill had reached Mandy before it did him. "Who's going to post bail? They don't have that many friends."

"True. But Leonard was by yesterday. He said he'd gotten a hold of Tomara. She has a good job. Maybe she's working to get them out."

Hayden thought about letting the comment slide, but Jay had perked his interest about the Metcalf girl. "Jay doesn't think she'd come back here."

"She'd be smart if she didn't. Copper might be right for me. It might even be right for you, but a girl like Tomara—I don't think it'll ever be right for her."

"But her father and brother—"

Mandy's harsh snort was more telling than any words. "Her old man couldn't have cared less whether Tomara made anything of herself. And Hoagy, I don't think he's smart enough to get out himself. Still, I wouldn't mind

seeing her again. She's a maverick. And a dreamer. I'd like
to think she's found whatever it was she was looking for."

"I didn't think you had much use for the Metcalf clan."

"Not for the men. Tomara's mother, she was my best
friend. Al, he damn near killed her."

"Are you serious?"

"Not with his hands. The idea of Al killing someone . . .
But he sucked the life out of his wife. Kept her here with
nothing for her brain to do until she had to get out. And
then when she tried to take the kids with her, all hell broke
loose. Wasn't no one going to take Al Metcalf's kids from
him. He was right about that. That poor woman. I sure wish
she could have found her way out of a bottle. Well—"
Mandy's gray hair went flying as she shook her head
"—Tomara finally showed him. I don't see her bailing those
two losers out. And I don't see her coming back here."

Tomara stepped on the rusted Jeep's brakes and rose half
out of her seat. She was looking at the town she'd sworn
she'd never see again. She'd driven all day to get to the
house and then traded her car for her father's Jeep before
taking off for Copper. She hadn't expected to find the Jeep
there; somehow she thought the police would have confiscated it. But not only was it sitting just outside what passed
for a garage, but there was almost a full tank of gas in it and
the keys were in the ignition.

She hadn't taken time to go in the house. She'd do that
later, when she had no choice. Right now she'd try to locate
Leonard, and maybe, if she had to, drive over to Sidney to
see her father and brother. And then, even if it was dark, she
might head the four-wheel-drive vehicle out onto the plains.

But first, business.

Still, it was another two minutes before Tomara gathered
the courage necessary to enter Copper. The post office had
been painted, and there was a new plastic sign over the gas
station. The fabric store had closed down. The awning over
Marshall's Drugstore was new enough that the wind hadn't
torn it.

She hadn't forgotten what a town without sidewalks looked like. Or what a street that was as much dirt as pavement could do to a vehicle. Two blocks off the main street was the school, a little building with cardboard cutouts and crepe paper decorating the windows. Tomara had always wanted to get closer to her teacher, to have a gentle hand on her shoulder turn into a hug. But she hadn't known how to ask, and the moment never came.

The only woman who'd held her since her mother left owned Copper's one bar. Mandy would tell her the truth.

Leonard would have to wait.

Tomara parked the Jeep just beyond Mandy's Saloon in front of a Bronco identifying itself as belonging to the state fish and game. She barely took note of the vehicle. Tomara catapulted her body easily out of the open Jeep and landed silently on the ground. Her tennis shoes kicked up dust that had once been fertile soil; her legs were protected by the faded jeans she wore both on and off the job. She ran her hand down the mass of hair caught in its braid, stopped the gesture and stepped out of the sunlight.

Mandy's Saloon was dimly lit. If it wasn't for the small windows at the front of the building, Tomara might not have known who was inside. She kept her distance from the three men in a corner and headed toward the counter. She was halfway across the floor before she was sure. Mandy was there. Smiling at her.

Seated on a stool a foot away was the biggest man she'd ever seen in Copper. He was looking at her, his eyes bold and honest. If Tomara was going to talk to Mandy, she would have to bring her body close to the man.

All she wanted to do was run.

Chapter Two

Tomara. My God, girl. You're here."

Mandy's soft, shocked whisper propelled Tomara forward. Somehow she managed to fight off her reaction to the man sitting at the bar. She tried to smile, but the gesture felt unnatural. "I'm here." Tomara's whisper mirrored that of the saloon owner. "I didn't think anything on earth would bring me back."

"Times change, girl. Situations change," was all Mandy said on the subject. "The years have been good to you." Mandy leaned forward, blinking away the dim light. "Leonard said he was going to get in touch with you."

Tomara nodded. The gesture freed a few strands of hair that had been clinging to her throat. She took a deep breath and fought off the need to touch the thick mass that was all she'd kept of her years here. The saloon smelled of sweat, bleach, sage and wheat. Everything in Copper, Tomara remembered, smelled of what grew beyond the town.

"I was on my way to see him, but . . . I needed to talk to you first." The big man was listening to the conversation. Tomara felt his eyes on her, not bold and challenging the

way many men looked at her but in honest, open appraisal.
"It's true. Everything Leonard told me is true?"

"I'm afraid so." Mandy dipped her head in the direction
of the man. "Maybe the first thing I should do is introduce
you to the person responsible. Tomara, I want you to meet
Hayden Conover. He works for the state. Fish and game. He
came here about a year after you left."

Tomara could no longer ignore the man. With Mandy's
words turning her blood cold, Tomara turned and faced him
as squarely as she'd always faced the realities in her life. He
was wearing a short-sleeved shirt with the state insignia on
his shoulder. She should have been thinking of nothing except that. She wasn't. His eyes had found hers; for a moment there was nothing and no one in the world except this
one man.

Although he was sitting, Tomara judged his height at over
six feet. He was solid with no fat but with enough muscle to
push his weight to about two hundred pounds. His shirt
clung limply to him, letting her know he hadn't spent the
day sitting behind a desk. Yet the work hadn't stripped him
of his vitality. She could too easily picture this man putting
her father and brother under arrest.

If the word *jail* was foreign to her, Tomara would have
been filled with shame. But she knew who and what the men
in her family were. She could face and would continue to
face this man, not because she condoned what her father
and brother did, but because she could only be responsible
for her behavior, her code.

Hayden Conover stuck out his hand, not smiling, the
gesture letting her know that he would understand if she
didn't place her hand in his. She did. The man was asking
something of her; she would meet the challenge. "I didn't
arrest them. The police chief did." The words came from the
depth of his chest and rumbled through her. Her hand remained lost in his; for a moment Tomara wanted nothing
but to feel his strength. "I don't know how much of the details I should be giving you."

"I'll try not to ask," Tomara made herself say. She
shouldn't let her guard down around this man. "Leonard

didn't tell me much.'' Gathering strength, she pulled her hand free. Her flesh continued to hum with the aftershock of the contact.

"Tomara?" Mandy asked gently. "What do you need to know? It might not be the truth, but I can tell you what the gossip is."

Tomara straddled a stool and leaned her weary body on the bar. "What is the gossip?"

With an economy of words unlike Mandy, the saloon owner told Tomara the bare facts as they'd been passed on by her customers. Tomara sat with her hand gripping her icy glass, hearing words that slowly, relentlessly turned a nightmare into reality. Her father's neighbor had been out working on his truck when Sheriff Jay Eagle pulled onto the Metcalf property. Jay had knocked on the front door, and then he'd drawn his gun. The neighbor had never seen Jay with his gun out of its holster. Finding out what was going on had been a hell of a lot more interesting than putting in a new fan belt.

"Neither of them put up a fuss," Mandy went on. "Carl said Jay slapped cuffs on your dad before calling for Hoagy. Your dad was cussing loud enough to be heard in the next county, but in the end they went quietly. As far as I can tell, that was the first anyone knew there was trouble."

"I didn't know who it was when I spotted the Jeep. I found that out a little later." Hayden's voice was so low that Tomara accepted it without alarm. "It was dark."

How many times had she had to ask questions so she'd understand what her father's latest brush with the law was about? Enough times that she'd been rendered shockproof. Or at least she'd thought she could handle any shock until this time when the charge was murder. And the man she had to ask the questions of wasn't one she could dismiss. "I don't understand," she made herself say. "Where were you? Where were they?"

Hayden had no idea how he was going to tell this lean, graceful woman about finding a man with a bullet in him and her relatives speeding off across the plains. Despite the reality of the crime, he wanted to be gentle, wanted to spare and protect her. But there was no way. "I don't know the details of the case against them. The coroner's office has the bullets, but I don't think there's been a match yet."

"Bullets? That man, he was shot more than once?"

Was she going to pass out or turn hysterical? Hayden concentrated on her huge dark eyes and decided she had more self-control than that. Good. Strength might see her through this. "No. There was an antelope carcass there, too. The D.A. wants to know if both bullets came from the same rifle."

Tomara nodded as if they were discussing nothing more important than the weather. Still, when she spoke, it was with a telling catch in her voice. "My dad poached. I don't know if he still does."

Damn! How could a father do that to his daughter? Hayden understood parents who could hardly wait for their kids to turn eighteen so they could drop all responsibility for them. He understood because that was what had happened to him. But, even if his folks had never bothered to come to his football games or teacher conferences, at least he hadn't been ashamed of the way they ran their lives. There was no way in hell Tomara Metcalf could be proud of her father. He could hate the man for that.

"I'm not the investigating officer, Tomara," he said, his thoughts on the sound of her name on his lips. "That's not my role. Jay knows a lot more than I do."

"When did Jay Eagle become sheriff?"

"About the time Hayden got himself transferred here," Mandy supplied. "He's doing a good job, too. There isn't a square inch of this county he doesn't know like the back of his hand. He goes off to some training programs every year and comes back all steamed up. Thanks to him, for the first time we've got a search-and-rescue unit people can depend on. Jay'll be honest with you."

She should get to her feet, walk out the door and down the street to the tiny police department office. But she wanted to talk to Mandy some more. Gathering her thoughts, Tomara downed the last of her water and waited while Mandy refilled the glass. "I went by the house," she

said softly, aware that Hayden Conover was still listening.
"It hasn't changed much. At least it hasn't on the outside.
I'm driving Dad's Jeep. My car's not made for this coun-
try."

"You didn't go in the house?" Mandy asked gently.

Tomara shook her head. The braid felt hot and heavy on
her back. "Not yet."

Mandy poured herself a beer, accomplishing the task
without having to take her eyes off Tomara. "I don't think
it's been painted since you left. Hoagy was up on the roof a
couple of times last winter. I noticed that they don't put
their rigs in the garage anymore. Good thinking. One stiff
wind and it'll be down around their ears."

Hayden had been past the Metcalf property hundreds of
times since coming to Copper. He figured they had two,
maybe three acres. It was hard to be sure because the fence
was down in so many places. The house wasn't much more
than a shack, although someone told him it had inside
plumbing. The garage was actually bigger than the house,
but it had been built without a foundation and the years had
done irreparable damage. There wasn't much of a yard,
though Hayden had noticed a rocked-off area close to the
door that might have once been a flower garden. He didn't
have to be told to know who had been responsible for that.
She was probably also responsible for the shade trees that
doubled as a buffer against the wind. Had the trees, the
flowers kept her sane?

"Are they still in Sidney?"

Hayden was pulled out of his thoughts, not by the question, but by the resignation in Tomara's voice. He hated the
sound. He opened his mouth to answer before he realized
the question was directed at Mandy.

"I'm afraid so. Jay took them right over the day he picked
them up. You know we don't have any place to keep prisoners. Never really had to before."

Tomara blinked but otherwise didn't react to Mandy's
matter-of-fact reply. She sat hunched over her empty water
glass. Idly, she ran a finger over the healing wound on her
thumb, going back in time.

She should have driven out of town the day she graduated from high school; she would have if her father hadn't lost his job at one of the cattle ranches. Hoagy would have dropped out of school if it hadn't been for the money she promised to bring in. Guiding hunting parties out onto the prairie wasn't what she wanted to do. She hated everything about it. The stalking of beautiful, innocent creatures, being around half-drunk hunters, fending off advances. But Copper didn't have much to offer a seventeen-year-old girl with a thirst for knowledge and a rural education, and if nothing else Tomara knew the land and the animals who lived on it.

The guiding work held them together through the fall and into winter until the hunters stopped coming. Al still hadn't found a job, and she knew Hoagy wouldn't stay in school if she left, when Mandy asked if Tomara wanted to handle her books. The routine of that job wasn't what she would have chosen, either, but once she'd proven herself, Leonard asked her to do the same thing and then the owner of the grocery store approached her. Then when she took on the Copper Cafe's and the drugstore's books, as well, Tomara was making more money than her father ever had.

The job made her feel both proud and trapped. She was supporting her father and brother, cooking for them, and running for miles every morning because not running was unthinkable. Tomara was still in Copper when next hunting season came around. The calls for her service started coming again, and Tomara accepted the job. She did it for two reasons. One, if the antelope herds weren't kept within limits, the winters would kill them. Two, Tomara was putting away every penny she made on the prairie.

She remembered the day Hoagy graduated from high school. The small graduation ceremony was over, and her father had mercifully remained sober. He had gone to the grocery store for beer and was cracking open a couple of cans for himself and Hoagy when Tomara, maybe in an attempt to make him see what she'd accomplished, tossed her bankbook at him. His eyes bulged when he saw the amount, and when he licked his lips, Tomara knew she had to leave that day or he'd somehow get his hands on the money. In a moment of weakness or sorrow or what passed for love between them, Tomara promised to leave a thousand for them. "To hold you until you get a job," she told them. "Or for you to come with me if that's what you want, Hoagy. But I'm not going to stay any longer."

And now she was back again, and the only family she'd ever known was in jail charged with murder.

Hayden sat silent and unmoving. He was ready to give up a great deal to know what was going through Tomara Metcalf's mind. They'd barely said a word to each other, and all he knew about her was that she was beautiful. Beautiful and as alone as he'd felt on his twelfth birthday when his parents left him alone because work came before their son. Work came before everything. "What are you going to do now?" he asked despite Mandy's warning glare. The question was hard-edged. It shouldn't have been. He knew better than to allow himself to go back in time.

"I don't know. I've never had to do this before."

"You've had to get your old man out of jail before, Tomara," Mandy said gently, while Tomara's words took Hayden out of himself and left him hurting for her.

"It's different this time. Murder." The word sounded like an oath. "Mandy, I can't believe it. Anything—anything but murder."

"Talk to Leonard, honey. See what Jay has to say. They'll tell you the truth."

Tomara pushed herself to her feet. She reached out and gripped Mandy's strong, dry hand. "I'm glad you're here," she whispered. As she turned away, Tomara's eyes fell on the game warden. Mandy might be warmth and understanding and caring; this man was strength, nothing but strength. She sucked in an unsteady breath, but the hot, dry air did nothing to help her regain her self-control. If he wasn't who he was and she wasn't who she was— No. She hadn't thought that.

Tomara hadn't reached the front door before Hayden joined her. He opened it and stepped back to let her out. His bulk forced her to repeat her denial. She didn't feel anything around him. "Where are you going?" he asked when they were out in the sunlight.

"To see if Leonard has time to talk to me. I told him I didn't think I'd be here until tomorrow."

"I'll go with you."

"Why? So you can keep an eye on me?" The questions came out too quickly. "I'm sorry. I shouldn't have said that. You—why didn't you arrest them?"

God, she had guts. More than any woman he'd ever known. Hayden guessed Tomara had to be six or seven inches shorter than him. Despite that, her legs were long enough that she easily kept up with his stride. He wondered what she smelled like. Nothing. Either that or wherever she'd come from hadn't been able to exorcise the clean scent of the prairie. Her magnificent hair was clamped into submission. She wore jeans like nine tenths of the people in the county, and yet on her denim took on a new dimension and texture. The top she'd chosen was loose and yet limp enough that her breasts were gently outlined. He wondered how many men had held that lean and yet curvy body. Not many. She wasn't a woman to easily share herself.

She'd asked him a question. He had to answer it, not wonder why he knew certain things about her when life had taught him that knowing—caring—about another had a way of backfiring. "They were gone before I landed," he explained. "I was in a chopper. They were next to the bodies—the man and the antelope. When they knew I'd spotted them, they took off. There was no way I could follow them in the dark."

"They ran." Despite the awful reality, Tomara met Hayden's eyes. She had grown up knowing what it felt like to be judged, to not be accepted. It didn't feel like that now. Yet, Tomara was too wary to believe what she wanted to believe. "They wouldn't have run if they didn't have something to hide."

"I'm sorry."

They'd reached Leonard's office. Tomara wasn't ready to leave this man with the caring eyes. "Why should you be sorry?"

"Because they're putting you through hell."

"It isn't the first time, Mr. Conover."

"Hayden. No, I don't suppose it is."

"Did you—do you know my father and brother very well?"

"Well enough. The last time was when I tried to fine them."

"For what?" Tomara ran her hands down her sides, feeling the strength of her thigh muscles.

"Poisoning a watering hole. Don't," Hayden warned when Tomara drew away. "What I should say is, they tried to poison an irrigation ditch used by Blake Duncan's cattle and a lot of wildlife."

"Blake." Tomara didn't put any more distance between herself and Hayden; neither did she erase her earlier backward step. It was safer to remain where she was, to give away as little as she could. "There's been bad blood between Blake and my father since Blake fired him."

"That's what your dad said. He kept telling me Blake had it coming and he wasn't about to pay the fine. He was right about that."

"He didn't pay?"

She's asking questions like we're discussing the weather. Hayden wondered how many years ago she'd come to accept the way her father approached life. He wished he understood more about what held relatives together. "No. He did jail time instead."

"Was Hoagy involved?"

"Not as far as I could tell. Look, are you going to stay around for the trial?"

"I don't know." Tomara pressed a hand to her forehead. "I'm taking this one step at a time. Leonard—"

"Yeah," Hayden agreed although that wasn't what he wanted to do. "You need to see him." If he hadn't thought before taking his next breath, he would have asked Tomara to call him when she was finished talking to the lawyer. But caution returned, and he held back. She'd been civil enough around him, but he had no idea what was going on inside her. Until he knew more about her, which maybe would never happen, Hayden wasn't going to risk getting in any deeper.

But if he didn't see her again, he'd never get to know what kind of woman she was. "I'm going to Sidney in the morning. Maybe I'll see you there."

"Maybe." The conversation, if that's what it was, had come to an end. Tomara should have been walking into Leonard's office. Instead she looked into Hayden Conover's eyes and wondered if she would have left Copper if he'd been there six years ago.

"I guess..." Tomara couldn't think of anything more to say. At least the words propelled her away from the game officer and toward Leonard Barth's law office.

Leonard couldn't see her. Although he waved and shrugged helplessly, his gestures made it clear that he would be on the telephone for a long time. The attorney mouthed the word *tomorrow* and then went back to concentrating on his long-distance conversation.

Less than a minute after she'd walked into Leonard's office, Tomara was back on the street again. She stared after Hayden's broad retreating back. The moment in Leonard's office had helped. The game officer wasn't important. Only seeing her family was. Still, it wasn't until Hayden had gotten inside his Bronco and driven off in the opposite direction that Tomara returned to her Jeep. She thought about going back inside and talking to Mandy, but that would only put off the moment when she would have to face her ghosts.

The Metcalf property was some five miles outside the city limits on a dirt road that trailed off to nothing another mile and a half farther on. There was one more house on the road, but although the Purdys had been neighbors for as long as Tomara could remember, they'd never done more than nod at each other. Carl and Alice Purdy didn't have children and had little tolerance for youngsters who strayed onto their property. After a couple of run-ins, Tomara and Hoagy had learned to leave the couple alone.

There weren't any vehicles parked in front of the house Carl and Alice lived in, which meant Tomara could get out of the Jeep and enter her childhood home unnoticed. Occasionally her father got it in his head that he needed to protect his property and started locking the front door, but the door that led to the kitchen had never had a lock on it. Tomara entered the house from the rear.

It smelled of not enough sunlight. There were dirty dishes piled in the sink and spilling onto the counter. The kitchen flooring was curling up at the seams. The curtains Tomara had sewn and placed over the kitchen window were still there, now stiff with accumulated dirt and grease. She didn't have to open the grayed, ancient refrigerator to know she'd find little except beer.

Tomara made her way from the kitchen to the living room. There was a new TV across from the sofa she'd picked up at an auction; the TV was fed by the satellite dish out back. The dish was perhaps the only thing her father had bought new. Next to the sofa was Tomara's chair, still covered with an Indian blanket. A coffee table was buried under the weight of coffee mugs, empty beer cans and full ashtrays. She moved automatically toward the coffee table to clear away the debris but stopped herself in time. It didn't matter what the place looked like.

There was an old black phone on the floor next to the broken recliner, but when Tomara picked up the receiver, there was no dial tone.

In a minute, in less than a minute maybe, Tomara would walk out the back door. But first she had to see her room. She'd been either nine or ten when she told her father she could no longer share a room with her brother. Al hadn't comprehended, but Tomara insisted on stringing blankets down the middle of the room. From then on she referred to her bedroom as if it were something separate from the rest of the house.

Standing inside it this evening, Tomara wondered if anyone had been in it since she left. Dust covered the top of the dresser she'd painted white, and she was afraid to touch the coverlet she'd hand-sewn from fabric bought at the now-closed fabric store. Pictures of mountains and lakes and wildlife photos cut from *National Geographic* covered the walls she'd painted the year she graduated from high school.

This room was the past Tomara had walked away from. She still felt free from it, but the charge against her father and brother might still snare her, as well. If she didn't get in her car tonight and drive back to the life she'd made for herself, tomorrow might be too late.

But even as she thought about it, Tomara knew it was too late. She wouldn't be here now if she hadn't accepted certain responsibilities and made certain commitments. She was here because she didn't believe her father and brother capable of murder.

There was a certain peace in her room. It was here that she'd played her mail-order tapes for hours on end. When she wasn't working or tracking game or running, Tomara would lie on her single bed and read her books and dream her dreams. Most of the dreams had come true. She had learned a trade and could support herself doing work that used her muscles and brain and kept her outside. She was buying a house that allowed her to stretch her arms in all directions without feeling boxed in. She had friends and even dated occasionally.

One dream hadn't come true, the dream of finding someone to share her life with, but Tomara had waited a long time to get where she was today. She could wait a little longer.

Tomara was glancing through her diary when she heard a vehicle pull into the drive. She pushed the faded drapes aside in time to see Hayden Conover get out of his Bronco. For an instant Tomara was filled with panic. He would come inside. He would see! He would know too much about her past.

It doesn't matter, Tomara told herself as she went into the living room and opened the door in a gesture of invitation that really wasn't one. She might have taken on the responsibility of trying to get her family out of jail; she couldn't be responsible for the way they lived. And she wasn't responsible for whatever the game warden might be thinking.

"You didn't get to talk to Leonard?" Hayden asked.

"No. He was busy."

"I'm sorry. The waiting must be hard." Hayden had been on his way home when the impulse, the unexpected and un-accustomed impulse, overtook him. He thought to wait at the Metcalf house until Tomara got home, and then en-courage her to talk, if that's what she needed. But she was already there, and he hadn't had time to think beyond wanting to see her. "What are you going to do now?"

"I don't know." Tomara moved aside so he could step inside. "He'll see me in the morning."

"It's a long time until morning."

He cares! The thought had no right, no reason for being. Still, Tomara couldn't deny it. The room no longer at-tacked her senses. She could stand where she was and ab-sorb a man's words. A man's impact. "I know." He'd opened his shirt more at the throat; he wasn't wearing a T-shirt. "I wasn't going to stay here long."

"Where are you going to be staying?"

"Mandy will let me stay with her."

"Good idea. I don't like the idea of your being here."

"Why not?"

"It's so isolated."

"I grew up here."

Hayden shrugged off her comment and tore away from eyes with the power to make him forget too much. And want too much. Jay had told him that the Metcalf house was a dump, and from what he'd seen of the outside, the interior shouldn't surprise him. But Tomara Metcalf had grown up inside these walls. How had she done it and stayed sane? "Is there anything I can do before we leave?"

"We?"

"I'm not going until you do."

Tomara turned away. She didn't want his caring now. Didn't want to have to deal with it. "There's nothing for you to do here," she told him in a tight, unnatural voice.

"What were you doing when I came in?"

"Looking at my room."

Tomara still wasn't looking at him. He could reach out, take her slender arm and pull her against him. The need to do that was so strong that for a moment Hayden wasn't sure he could fight it. But he did. His parents had taught their child not to give or expect a touch; he hadn't forgotten the lesson. "I'd like to see your room."

"Why?"

Damn her hard questions. "Curiosity," he told her. He could sense her indecision and was afraid he'd never understand the urge that had suddenly become the most important thing in his life. But the fear died a quick death. With a shrug, Tomara turned away from him. He followed, watching the graceful interplay of muscle and bone, telling himself he wasn't doing that.

Her room. It wasn't even a whole room, but despite the dust and neglect, he found the warm, searching girl she'd been mirrored in the crowded bookshelf, the fading magazine pages taped to her wall, the pocket of femininity and life in a lifeless house. Her bed was narrow and close to the floor, sagging in the middle but covered with a blue-and-white coverlet. The one window in the room was on her side of the blanket wall. The curtain was lacy enough to let in the sunlight. Hayden knelt and ran his hand over an ancient set of encyclopedias. He wanted to tell her about having grown up in a lifeless home himself. He knew he wouldn't. "Where did you get these?"

Tomara was standing behind him, arms folded, fingers spread to grip her slim waist. "A teacher. The district bought a new set, and she let me have the old ones. I wasn't supposed to tell anyone."

Hayden straightened and walked over to a tiny desk crowded with rocks, a snake skin, a dried chunk of sage, half of an antelope horn. "There's a story behind all of these things. Why didn't you take them with you?"

"I didn't have room. When I left, I had two boxes. That's all they let me take on the bus."

Hayden tried to absorb the stark reality of what he'd just been told. He had no business being there. This was Jay's investigation. Jay's business. And he didn't want to be feeling certain things. "Where did you go? Did you know what you were going to do when you got there?"

Tomara could have told him about fear and excitement and feeling as if her life was just beginning and leaving everything she knew behind, but she didn't. Maybe, someday, if she knew him better. Maybe, in another world. "It was a long time ago." She indicated the room. "There isn't much to see."

"Yes, there is. Our childhood rooms tell a great deal about us."

Unexpectedly, Tomara wanted to know where Hayden had grown up and what things he'd put on his walls. Instead she told him she didn't need anything out of her room and retraced the steps to the living room. Hayden was slow to join her. "Are you ready to leave?" he asked.

"Yes." The word was both hard and easy to say. Hard because there were still things there that she needed to come to grips with and easy because she wasn't being forced into that confrontation today. She hadn't asked Mandy if she could stay with her, but she didn't want Hayden to know how rootless she was. "Jay doesn't need anything from here?"

"I don't know. You'll have to ask him."

"Tomorrow. I'll see him after I'm done with Leonard."

She should be bigger, Hayden thought. A woman with a burden such as that to carry should have more meat on her. "When are you going to see your father and brother?"

"Sometime tomorrow. It's a long drive to Sidney. I don't want to do it in the heat of the day."

"What are you going to say to them?" When she jerked her head around, Hayden knew he'd gone too far. "I'm sorry. I had no right asking that. What I'd like to know is, what are you going to do about dinner?"

"Dinner? I hadn't thought about it. Mandy—"

"Mandy isn't going to be able to leave for hours. The cafe isn't great, but the food won't kill us."

"You don't mind being seen with me?"

"No. I don't. Listen to me, will you?" He reached out, wrapped his fingers around her wrist, but didn't try to pull her closer. "Things have to be rough for you now. They're not going to get any easier."

"I know that," Tomara said with less strength than she wanted. He shouldn't have touched her. He had no right. And yet— No. There was no *yet* to it. She had come back to Copper because she was a Metcalf. He couldn't possibly understand that.

Chapter Three

One of the windowpanes at the front of the Copper Cafe had been broken and covered over with cardboard until the owner, Ralph Kemper, got around to replacing the pane. Several of Copper's high schoolers had placed bets on when that would be. His son, David, was sure the cardboard would stay in place until November or December, whenever winter pushed its way through the cracks and customers started complaining.

Hayden would have preferred to steer Tomara to the table farthest from the front door, but a couple of local ranchers were already there. David Kemper and some of his friends had taken over the large table in the middle of the room. Three of the grocery store's part-time clerks sat nearby, glaring at the teenagers. Hayden cupped his hand under Tomara's elbow and aimed her toward the table to the right of the broken window. Her flesh was soft and warm, her elbow sharp. He told himself he wasn't surprised when she put a quick end to the contact.

Tomara didn't wait for Hayden to pull out her chair but balanced herself lightly on the edge of it and then rested her elbows on the table. At her insistence, they'd driven to the cafe in separate vehicles. Tomara had had to fight down the urge to punch the accelerator and keep on going. As she found a place to park, she tried to remind herself she wasn't the one who'd been accused of a crime.

Now, with three middle-aged women taking note of who'd come in with the county game warden, Tomara was having second and third thoughts. If it wasn't for his eyes, she wouldn't have sat down. But in his eyes were strength and curiosity and something she couldn't put a name to but couldn't walk away from.

Hayden slid into his chair and leaned back, his powerful arms hooked over the wooden chair arm. The gesture held her. He took a moment to look around, nodding at the two ranchers and giving David Kemper the thumbs-up sign. "Is that Jeep running all right?" he asked Tomara.

"Better than I thought it would." Tomara wanted to relax the way Hayden had, but every breath she took, every place she went here took her down another road that led to the past. She'd done the books for Copper Cafe for over a year, but this was probably only the third time she'd come in for a meal. The reason was simple. She hadn't had the money. Tomara said something about her brother being a fair mechanic even if he didn't believe in taking care of a vehicle's exterior and then picked up the menu.

The words blurred. She attributed her light-headedness to a lack of food, and concentrated. Hayden hadn't made it clear whether he was offering to pay for her meal, but if he didn't, Tomara had the funds these days to buy anything on the menu. Knowing that she could now do what everyone else seemed to take for granted gave her a sense of power. Made her believe she could face Hayden on equal footing.

Why that was important she couldn't say.

When after three or four minutes a waitress hadn't come to take their order, David Kemper grabbed an order pad and planted his lanky body near Hayden. "Carla'll be back in a minute. She had to run an errand for Dad. What'll it be? Not the chili. Believe me, not the chili."

"All right." Hayden laughed. "Is the steak a safe bet?"

David Kemper shrugged. "It'll do. But if you want my opinion, Dad cooks a mean cheeseburger."

Hayden stuck with steak and potatoes with a salad on the side. Tomara had been trying to choose between several cold sandwiches, but when David Kemper turned his bright, seventeen-year-old eyes on her, she suddenly felt ten years younger. "I've never known a cheeseburger I didn't like," she told him. "Can we skip the fries?"

"That would be my suggestion." David wrote without looking at the menu pad. "I know you, don't I?"

"Maybe." Tomara took a breath. She wasn't going to start hiding now. "We went to the same school, but you were several years behind me. Tomara Metcalf."

"Yeah. Yeah?" David blinked but gave no other indication of what he was thinking. "I know your brother. He knows this country better than anyone else. I'm sorry he got himself in the trouble he did."

"So am I." Tomara waited until David left before easing back in her chair. It had gone more easily than she thought it would, but David was only one person. There would be others to face. She was sitting across from one of them. She looked out the window at a couple of pickups rumbling past, but the street didn't hold her attention long.

"Did my dad and brother really run when you spotted them?"

"I don't know what else to call it."

Tomara shook her head but stopped when dizziness overcame her. "They've been in trouble so many times—they're conditioned to avoid the authorities."

"I understand that." Hayden leaned forward, his voice too low to be heard by anyone else. "This isn't the first time I've had to do business with Al and Hoagy. I know what they think of me and what I represent."

"Then—"

"Then nothing," Hayden said in a tone he wished he didn't have to use. "Your father and brother, I don't think they're fools. They had to know what it would look like if they didn't stick around. Maybe they thought I wouldn't recognize their vehicle. I don't know. What I'm saying," he went on when her big eyes stayed on him too long, "is that I came across a murder and the two people I found beside the body took off the minute they heard me coming."

"You're saying their running makes them guilty, aren't you?"

"I didn't say—"

"You don't have to. If I was in your position, if it was anyone else, I would have thought the same thing. But Hayden—" she drew out his name, trying to learn what might be behind the sound "—I grew up in the same household with them. My dad's always run from reality. From—" Tomara almost stopped, but when Hayden continued to watch her with deep-set, unblinking eyes, she gave him honesty. "He hid from the reality of not holding a job. He hid from a great many things. The times he was arrested and fined for poaching, he always found someone else to blame." Tomara let the chair accept her weight. "Maybe life made him that way."

"Maybe."

Another truck rumbled by outside, the back of this one loaded down with fencing material. Tomara could hear the sizzle of her hamburger frying. She could feel Hayden's eyes still on her. "Look. I'm not making excuses for him. I'd just like you to understand that, for my father, running from a man with a bullet in him doesn't automatically mean he put the bullet there."

"That's for a jury to decide, Tomara."

"Yes. A jury. Did they have their rifles with them?"

It wasn't the first time Hayden had been asked the question. When he was in the D.A.'s office, the answer hadn't been this important. "I didn't see any. It was dark. I was trying to absorb what I'd seen and jot down a license number."

"I see." Tomara was aware that the three women from the grocery store kept looking over at her, but she was being bombarded by too many emotions to let that bother her. As hard as it was, she wanted Hayden to tell her, in detail, everything that had happened that night. But maybe she had no right. He'd invited her here because there was nothing to eat in the house, not because he wanted to talk about what it was like to come across a murdered human being.

Eating. That's what they were here for. Wasn't it?

She wasn't sure. Now, with him silent across from her, she wasn't sure of anything. Finally their dinner arrived. With their teenage waiter standing nearby, Hayden made a show of cutting into his steak and chewing a small piece. At length he swallowed and gave David another thumbs-up signal. "It'll do."

"That's what I told you." David turned toward Tomara. "When you see your brother, tell him, tell him hi for me. I'd have already gone to see him, but my old man— It's going to take a while to break free and get over there." David shrugged. "Hoagy'll understand."

Tomara bit into her cheeseburger. Yes, she acknowledged, Hoagy would understand.

"What's wrong?"

"Nothing," Tomara said without thinking. One look at Hayden told her that he wouldn't let her get away with that. "Nothing I'm not used to," she amended. She watched David return to his friends, all too aware of the difference between the easy way this self-confident young man carried himself and the boastful bragging of her brother that was, she knew, a cover-up for deep-seated insecurity. "I've been away so long," she went on softly. "Time blunts things. I'd almost forgotten what it was like." She was surprised by her ability to tell him this.

Hayden glanced up as a couple entered the cafe, and then returned to his dinner companion. "Between Jay and Mandy, I got the picture."

"I'm sure you did."

"You've had what, six years to put between you and the past."

"Six years," Tomara repeated.

"Are you sorry you're back?"

Tomara tore her eyes off Hayden. The wind was blowing down Sky Street the way it had since before the town was founded. She could see far enough down the street that she could tell when someone entered or left Mandy's Saloon.

The man pulling on the heavy handle now was Leonard Barth. Tomara was a little surprised to see Leonard going in there, but then she didn't know the attorney that well. What she did know was how the wind felt on her cheeks and hair, temperatures that could hit minus sixty in the winter, the perfection of a June morning, a summer thunderstorm, the smell of a chinook pushing the temperature up fifty degrees in a few hours.

She knew where the antelope and mule deer bedded down around the rougher hills, where white-tailed deer hid out in the brush along the Missouri River. She would never mistake the cry of a coyote for anything but what it was. "I told myself I'd never come back."

"The trial isn't going to be for a while. I have no idea how long it's going to last. Are you going to stay here the whole time?"

"I don't know." Tomara took another bite and washed it down with water. "I haven't thought that far ahead." She should be talking to Leonard or Mandy about these things, not Hayden. She shouldn't even be sharing a meal with him. "I have to meet with Leonard. And go to the jail."

Hayden nodded. "Your job. Will it cause a problem, your being gone that long?"

"It might."

"What do you do?"

It took Tomara a few seconds to switch gears. That other world seemed a million miles away. She explained that she was employed by the local utility company as a telephone lineperson. She didn't know if his question was prompted by anything more than trying to keep a conversation going. "I've been working for them for a little over three years now. It's a good job."

"It doesn't surprise me."

"What doesn't surprise you?"

"What you do for a living. Sitting behind a desk wouldn't be right for you."

The front door opened and then closed. A sage-scented breeze warred momentarily with the smell of hot grease. "How do you know what's right for me?"

"I didn't mean that. But Jay told me some things about what you were like as a girl."

Tomara tried to shrug off Hayden's explanation; it didn't work. She shouldn't be here. She should—"Jay. You and he—you're friends?"

"Probably the best friend I have."

"I have to see him." Tomara took another bite. She remembered Jay as an intelligent boy, maybe not book smart but in ways that mattered. He lived his life one day at a time. He was rough and strong. And he was someone who belonged here. "I don't know if he's supposed to talk to me."

"I think he will."

"But there might be things he can't discuss. There have to be." The air in the cafe was stale, and there wasn't enough of it. For perhaps a half second, Tomara was afraid she was going to get up and walk out. She didn't; something was holding her here. "Things that will come up at the trial."

The front door opened, and the prettiest girl in Copper stepped in. From the look on young David's face, Tomara knew this was why the teenager hadn't left when his friends did. When the girl slipped her arm around David's waist and lifted her face for a quick kiss, Tomara felt a thousand years old. She couldn't remember the last time she'd wanted to smile like that or if she'd ever smiled at a man in that way. She tore her eyes free and returned her attention to the man sitting across from her. They really were here, doing this, saying the things they were. It seemed incredible.

It felt like something that had to be done.

Hayden was speaking. "The trial. That bothers you?"

"What bothers me is having to be here. Saying the things I have to say. Asking questions." She had to stop talking. Otherwise she might tell Hayden she blamed him for everything. If he hadn't been out there— No. "I wish to hell I'd never gotten the phone call."

"Do you?"

Had she really said that, really exposed herself? "Yeah. I do. What are you doing here?"

"With you?" Hayden didn't blink. "Having dinner."

"That's not what I mean." Tomara hurried on. "I mean living here. Doing what you're doing. You didn't grow up around here."

"No." Hayden turned his attention from his half-eaten meal. "I came from L.A. A big-city cop who'd seen too many things and been stuck in too many traffic jams. I arrested people who didn't give a damn what they did to someone else, or what happened to them. One night not long before I quit, I tried to stop someone from bleeding to death just because he looked at someone else the wrong way. I had to get out while there was still something of me left."

"And you're happy here?"

"Yeah. I think I am. I don't have to look over my shoulder here. I like not having to lock my doors and being able to talk to everyone I see at the post office. Do you know what I'm saying?"

"I don't know." The sun was low in the sky now. A shadow had fallen across Hayden's face, darkening his hair and drawing his eyes into mystery. "I grew up seeing Copper one way," she told him. "I've heard people say they love living here. I don't think Mandy would ever be happy anywhere else. And Jay belongs here, too."

"But not you."

"Not me." Tomara gave Hayden a smile that lasted no longer than a heartbeat. "I love the seasons. Maybe I even miss the wind. But—I don't think I need to spell it out for you."

"No." Neither of them had finished their dinner, but Hayden wasn't interested in eating, and he didn't think Tomara was, either. "Jay's going to be glad to see you."

"Is he?" The three women had finished their meal and were getting ready to leave. Tomara nodded at the one who'd once been the president of the PTA. The older woman gave Tomara a faint smile in return but didn't say anything. Tomara didn't speak until the women had left. "Not many people are."

"Maybe. I can't answer that." Reluctantly Hayden looked at his watch. "I'm flying again tonight. I'm sorry. I need to do a few things first."

Tomara got to her feet. The girl who'd come in to see David Kemper was giggling at everything he said. Tomara couldn't remember ever doing that around a boy. She was sorry she hadn't. "Thank you for dinner."

"Thank you for agreeing to eat with me."

They were silent until they were outside. Tomara could go into the saloon now and wait for Mandy. It was the logical thing to do. The only thing. But she was reluctant to make the first step. Instead she stood looking beyond the collection of old buildings to the prairie. The gently rolling grassland stretched for another ten miles before giving way to rugged hills. It was in those hills that Tomara once led out-of-state hunters with dreams of bringing down swift antelope or large mule deer. Although she'd done what she had to to support herself, Tomara was sorry she'd ever brought men and their rifles to the beautiful creatures. "Do you hunt?" she asked Hayden.

His answer took longer than it should have. "I shot a man once, Tomara. I'll never take a life if there's any other way."

Tomara was no longer interested in her surroundings. She'd been able to accept the fact that this man wore a gun, but she hadn't thought about him pulling it out of its holster and aiming it at another human being. "Did you kill him?"

"No." Hayden was standing so close. She could see his chest expand and contract. "But it was close."

"But—" She shouldn't push; this was none of her business.

"But what?"

"Nothing," Tomara started and then decided on honesty. "Maybe I don't understand. You're not a policeman anymore, but I saw the rifle in your rig. Weapons are part of your job."

"They're part of the trappings of my job. I have to keep pace with certain elements of society. It didn't used to be like that. I wish that hadn't changed."

"You do?"

"Yeah. I do. At least I haven't drawn a weapon since I moved here. Hell." Hayden jammed his hands in his back pockets. "Maybe I'm trying to deny a certain piece of reality."

"What are you trying to deny?"

"That I've been given the power to wound or possibly kill a person. The responsibility to make that kind of decision."

Tomara couldn't speak. His words had brought her face-to-face with her father and brother.

"I'm sorry," Hayden was saying. "I shouldn't have said that."

Tomara looked into his eyes that understood too much. She had to take herself away from his understanding. Had to, somehow, find the space she needed. "Carrying a weapon, it isn't anything you can take for granted."

"No. It isn't." He shook his head. "Your father and brother—"

"I know," she finished for him. "My father and brother are behind bars." Her fingers were pressing against her thighs. "And maybe they took a human life and will have to pay for it."

"But you don't believe that."

"No. I don't." The cafe door opened, and David and the pretty girl stepped out. The girl was clinging to David's arm, smiling up at him as if he was the most powerful person in the world. Tomara tried not to look or think, but it was impossible. Love happened.

She wondered when or if it would ever happen to her. And she wondered if her world would ever feel right.

"Maybe you're right," he said.

Tomara couldn't shake off Hayden's final words. Even when she was back inside Mandy's Saloon and the sturdy woman was motioning for Tomara to join her behind the bar, Hayden's words remained. She wanted to believe him. Irrationally, insanely even, she wanted to take the scant hope he'd given her and turn it into something.

But she'd been a Metcalf too long, and Copper was where lessons had been learned.

"You aren't looking a hell of a lot better," Mandy admonished when Tomara turned down her offer of a beer. "You should be catching some shut-eye, not hanging out in here."

"I will. Soon," Tomara promised. "You don't mind if I sleep on your couch?"

"You don't have to ask that. You know what I'd say if you were thinking about staying out at the house. That place isn't fit for anyone."

Tomara explained that she'd been in the house. She didn't say anything about Hayden following her or their having dinner tonight. It wasn't because she felt she had to keep things from Mandy, but Mandy wasn't the only one listening.

For the first couple of minutes, Tomara hadn't paid much attention to the man nursing his drink nearby. But then her eyes adjusted to the dim light. Copper's only attorney had been talking to Mandy when Tomara walked in the door. Although he wasn't wearing a tie, his nearly new, well-tailored shirt set him apart from the ranchers who made up the bulk of Mandy's customers. Leonard was a little too thin; his tapered shirts and dark slacks emphasized that fact. Still, when he spoke it was with a confidence that made people forget he weighed a lean one hundred and forty-five pounds.

Leonard entered the conversation. "I'm sorry I couldn't see you earlier, Tomara. You will be able to meet with me in the morning, won't you?"

"Oh, yes," Tomara answered softly. "I have a lot of questions."

"I'm sure you do." Leonard glanced around at the nearly full saloon. "I hope you agree that our business is better conducted in my office."

Tomara had no objections to that. The truth was, on the tail of her meal with Hayden, she was in no shape to concentrate on what had brought her back to Copper.

"I was telling Mandy I went by your dad's place the day after the arrest. He'd asked me to make sure the front door was locked." Although Mandy's radio was blaring out a country and western song, insulating whatever he might say from the others, Leonard leaned toward Tomara. "I have to admit I indulged my curiosity. The front door was locked. I guess Jay took care of that. But I could see in the windows. Mandy's right. You don't want to stay there."

Tomara could have reminded Leonard that she'd spent her growing-up years inside those walls, but didn't. Instead she sat listening while Leonard and Mandy continued their conversation. Leonard was trying to convince Mandy that she could afford to hire someone to come in a couple of nights a week so Mandy would have a little freedom. Mandy, eyes flashing, wanted to know what she would be doing with all that freedom. "Where would I go? What would I do? You know what I think of TV."

"There's more a person can do with an evening than watch TV. You know what I think of your cooking."

Mandy snorted and leaned toward Leonard. "You're just looking for a kitchen slave."

"Among other things." Leonard covered Mandy's hand with his. His eyes were as full of life as hers. "You are going to get Ellie to come in this weekend, aren't you?"

Mandy flushed. Tomara couldn't remember ever seeing the saloon owner at a loss for words. "I'm thinking about it," she told the man holding her hand.

"Thinking about it? That's not what you said last night. I'm leaving for Billings as soon as I can get away on Friday. You're coming with me."

"Is that an order?"

"If that's what it takes," Leonard said before removing his hand and downing the last of his drink. He said something about an evening appointment to Tomara, leaned forward to brush his lips across Mandy's cheek, and left.

Tomara sat looking after the lawyer. She'd known two of Mandy's three husbands. Both of them were hardworking, hard-talking men, nothing at all like the cultured, soft-spoken attorney. When she heard Mandy sigh, Tomara pulled herself back into the present. "He's quite a man, isn't he?" Mandy asked.

"I don't know. I don't know him very well."

"Neither did I." Mandy was busying herself with stacking glasses. "Leonard's been coming in here for years. We kidded around. He was a lot of help when George died and George's kin tried to get their hooks into this place and the acreage over by the reservation. But that he might be interested in me—well, it just never occurred."

"I'm happy for you."

"I hope I am, too. What I mean is we're two very different people," Mandy went on when Tomara gave her a puzzled look. "Leonard's educated. His business takes him to Billings and Sidney every few days. He's had lunch with the governor. What would have me passing out from fear, he handles like he's ordering beer. The truth is, I don't know what he sees in me."

"Don't say that," Tomara pressed, although the same question had occurred to her. "You own your own business. No one's going to push you around. A professional man's got to admire you for that."

"Maybe. One thing I do know—" Mandy lowered her voice "—he doesn't have any complaints in bed."

Tomara didn't know what, if anything, she was expected to say in return. Mandy was an earthy, realistic woman. She'd always told Tomara that life was too short not to go after everything it had to offer. During the years Mandy was helping guide her into womanhood, Tomara had listened, learned, and most important, believed and dreamed.

"There's one thing that a man has to learn, though," Mandy continued. "No one but me calls the shots. I've had three husbands. I know what it's like to have to consider someone else's opinions. I'm not sure I want to do that again."

"Marriage." Tomara worked over the word. "It's a big step."

"Isn't it, though. Specially when you're as old and set in your ways as I am. It'd be easier for you."

Tomara hadn't come in here to discuss marriage. Still, now that Mandy had brought up the subject, it seemed easier to talk about than a murder charge. "I don't know," she told her friend and mentor. "I thought about it last year. But when it came down to talking about it, I got scared."

"You were seeing someone?"

"I guess you could call it that." Tomara laughed. Because it was a weeknight, the saloon was quiet. A few ranchers were nursing beers. A long-distance trucker and his wife danced to the songs blaring from Mandy's radio. The saloon had taken on a dreamlike quality. Dark corners waited for lovers to fill them.

With Johnny Cash singing about traveling men and lonely women as her backdrop, Tomara told Mandy about meeting a man through work who was as passionate about his motorcycle as Tomara was about running. Parr introduced Tomara to speed and a hint of danger. He gave her weekends devoted to exploring country roads, talking to the people they met on their travels, making love in deserted barns. Parr was an engineer for the telephone company, and although he took pride in his job and did it well, work wasn't his life. It was Parr who let Tomara dream of more than earning a paycheck and having a roof over her head.

It was also Parr who wanted her to move in with him. "We didn't discuss marriage," Tomara told Mandy. "He'd been married once. He said he wasn't ready for that scene again. That was fine with me because I—I just couldn't see myself getting married."

"Does he know why you're here?"

Tomara had picked up a toothpick while she was talking. Now she snapped the slender wood in half. "We broke up. Before I moved in."

"Why?"

Tomara was grateful for the bold question. "I don't know. I honestly don't. Parr was wonderful and attentive. But everything had to be his way. I was getting interested in photography. I wanted to take pictures while we were out on our rides. Parr didn't see any reason for weighing ourselves down with a lot of equipment. Does that make sense?" she asked. "I broke up with him because he wouldn't let me take pictures of some newborn lambs."

"If it makes sense to you, that's all that matters."

"Maybe." Tomara tried to put the pieces of her toothpick back together. The fit was almost perfect, but the seam still showed. "It was more than that. I'm buying a house, Mandy. It isn't new, but it's mine to do what I want with it. That's important to me. I asked Parr to consider moving in with me, but he wasn't interested. He has a condo. A condo." Tomara spoke the word as if it were something foreign. "He put a lot of thought into furnishing it. It was modern, airy, with white furniture and glass coffee tables and posters of the Riviera on the walls." Tomara dropped the toothpick. "It wasn't me. It would never be me."

"Don't let it get to you, honey." Mandy waved as one of her regulars got up to leave. "The right man will come along."

"I'm not sure I'm the right woman for any man."

"Now you're talking like me. You're much too young to feel that way."

"Am I?"

"I know, honey." Mandy's voice went low with love and concern. "Growing up the way you did, it wasn't easy. Look, I'm a tough old broad. I think I was born a tough old broad. And yet I found three men who saw some redeeming features in me. The same thing will happen to you."

Tomara was exhausted. She hadn't known how tired she was until this moment. "I don't know if I want to be part of someone else. With Parr, in the end, I was looking for an excuse to break it off. I felt as if he was taking me over. Being independent is the most important thing to me."

"You're thinking that way tonight because your menfolk have gotten themselves into a heck of a mess and you'd like to disown both of them. You aren't going to always feel that way."

"I'm not so sure," Tomara said softly, the words coming from the depths of her being. "I'm not very good at making compromises. Freedom. Independence. That's felt so wonderful these past six years." The song on Mandy's radio ended. For perhaps two seconds, the tavern was silent. Tomara loved the silence. "I don't want anyone trying to turn me into what I'm not."

Chapter Four

It probably hasn't changed a lick since the last time you saw it. I was always going to do some decorating, but—'' Mandy shrugged her broad shoulders. "So I'm not domestic. It isn't a crime."

"I didn't say a word," Tomara reminded Mandy. In a single glance, she'd taken in the apartment Mandy maintained over the saloon. Now she went over it again, noting the practical furniture, the small but efficient kitchen, the windows with their view of the street and alley. "How many times did I come here when I needed to unload?"

"No more times than I wanted you to. Believe it or not, you're not going to have to sleep on the couch. I finally got that other room turned into something. An office I guess you'd call it. It's got a hide-a-bed. That room and that bed's yours for as long as you need it."

"I want to pay you—"

"We'll talk about money later. Right now I bet the only thing you're interested in is some sleep."

Mandy was right. Because it was a weeknight, Mandy had closed the tavern at midnight. Still, Tomara's day had begun a little after six, and her eyelids felt heavy. "There's so many things I want to ask you about. So much to be caught up on."

Mandy grunted. "I thought you weren't interested in this burg."

Mandy had a point, but Tomara was too exhausted to question what she was feeling. "I saw the Kemper boy today. David. From what he said, he and Hoagy hung out some together."

"More than David's old man wanted him to. That David, he's going to do all right. Best damn ball player to ever come out of Copper. People get excited just talking about what he might be able to do." Mandy plopped on her couch and started to remove her shoes. "In fact, he's going to be pitching in a game tomorrow afternoon. I haven't missed one of his games this year. Think you'd like to watch it with me?"

A baseball game sounded like the most relaxing thing Tomara had done in years. She explained about needing to meet with both Jay and Leonard tomorrow, and, if she had time, running over to Sidney. But if she got back early enough, she'd join Mandy. By then Tomara had shed her own shoes and was looking forward to getting out of the rest of her clothes. She'd brought a single suitcase with her. Tucked in with two more pairs of jeans, three wash-and-wear blouses, and one dress, just in case, was the oversize T-shirt she wore to bed.

Five minutes later the two women had made up the hide-a-bed and Mandy was warning Tomara that she was on her own when it came to breakfast. "You won't see me until at least ten. Later than that on weekends if I have to stay open late. But help yourself to whatever's in the kitchen. Unless we can figure a way to get out of it, we'll go shopping in a day or two."

Tomara waited until Mandy had left her alone and then slid out of her clothes. She ran her hands over her waist, easing away the faint lines left by her jeans. Naked, she stepped over to the window and looked down on the back side of Copper's business district. Despite the lack of streetlights, she was able to make out the silhouettes of cars, dumpsters, a graveled parking lot. Beyond that waited the moon.

The moon. With her fingers still touching her waist, Tomara lost herself. The moon had always been there, as much of a constant as the Montana wind. True, the moon played out its endless cycle in Idaho Falls, as well, but somehow she'd lost touch with it there. Here the moon had the power to take her beyond dumpsters and tarred roofs. She was being transported back to the prairie, hearing again the sounds of land that man hadn't been able to chain, feeling the beating of her heart.

Good things had happened here along with the bad. She'd known freedom and had had time to think. She'd been restless; oh, God, yes she'd been restless. But there had always been places to run to, endless places. She knew the land beyond the town as intimately as most people knew their own backyards. And she knew the moon.

Tomara was crying when she slipped into bed. She didn't try to give her tears meaning, nor did she try to stop them.

It probably would have taken a thunderstorm to rouse Mandy. Tomara was able to walk into the bathroom off her friend's bedroom and shower without disturbing her. She padded back into her room to dress in a clean pair of jeans and then braided her hair. Although it was only a few minutes after eight, Tomara took a chance on calling Leonard. He was in and would be able to see her in about a half hour. Tomara shoved on her tennis shoes and then poured herself a bowl of cereal. Before she left, she wrote Mandy a note telling her where she'd be.

Copper was quiet. There were a few farmers around the feed store, and someone was parked in front of the nurse practitioner's office, but the other businesses hadn't opened. Tomara made it to Leonard's office without asking herself what she was going to say. As soon as the lawyer acknowledged her, her mind turned briefly to this afternoon's promise. No matter what else the day brought, she would lose herself in a baseball game.

"Good timing, Tomara," Leonard said as she sat down. "You'd think in a town this size there wouldn't be enough to keep a lawyer busy, but there's a lot more to my practice than what exists in Copper. Every farmer in this part of the state— You didn't come here to hear that, did you?"

Tomara didn't bother to shake her head. She'd been in such a hurry to get here, and yet now she was loath to begin.

"I'm going to be representing them."

"You've—I mean, you've discussed that with them?"

Leonard laughed, the sound as spare as his frame. "Your father's going to take a little convincing. I think Hoagy has a better grasp of the trouble they're in. He's trying to convince your dad that they need me. He'll get there."

There were four, maybe five plants bunched around the window in Leonard's office. His desk was of flawless mahogany, the white walls contrasting with the dark wood. The outside of the building might be no different from any other in town, but obviously Leonard Barth believed in making his working conditions as comfortable and appealing as possible. "Defending them won't sit too well with some of the people in town," Tomara made herself say. "Why are you doing it?"

"Why? Let me tell you something, Tomara. Then maybe you'll understand. Most of the work I do could be handled by a secretary. Taking on land disputes, settling wills. A few negligence or personal injury cases. I worked on a fraud case once—took months to pull together and gave me more of a sense of satisfaction than I'd had in years. Now I get to defend at a murder trial. I'm sorry it has to come at the expense of your relatives."

Tomara studied her hands. The cut was almost healed now. Her fingers were long and strong, her nails short. She'd never make a penny as a model with those hands, but they served her well, and she was proud of them. "What do you have to do? I mean, you'll have to prepare a defense."

Leonard settled back in his leather chair, his weight barely enough to disturb the swivel base. As if he were discussing nothing more emotional than a trip to small-claims court, Leonard explained that he was still in the planning stages of his defense. Al and Hoagy maintained that they had stumbled across both the antelope carcass and Bart Renfree's body. Leonard was willing to go along with that, but he needed more. He needed someone to step forward and say they'd seen Al and Hoagy at the time the murder was determined to have taken place. Barring that, he had to try to find out who had actually fired the shots.

"Like I said," Leonard wound up. "I've got my work cut out for me. You're going to try to see them today? The best thing you can do is convince those two hardheads to work with me. Right now I feel like I'm pulling teeth, especially with your dad."

The phone had rung twice while she was talking to Leonard. She didn't want to take up any more of his time. "I'll do what I can. I'm not sure how much they'll say to me."

Leonard got to his feet. "I know you and your dad didn't always see eye to eye, Tomara, but I've never heard him bad-mouth you. You've made something of yourself, and he knows that. If you walk into that jail and take charge, I think he'll listen."

Tomara stuck out her hand for a shake. Concentrating on that simple act was easier than trying to deal with what Leonard had just told her. "I'll get back to you," she said around the lump she could neither deny nor explain.

Seeing Jay was harder than talking to Leonard had been. She could have stalled the moment by going back to see if Mandy was up yet, but Tomara knew better than to give herself an excuse for backing down.

Jay had been a year ahead of her in school. Tomara remembered watching the powerful Sioux, who might have had a shot at a football career if he'd been focused, and wishing she had the courage to talk to him. There'd been perhaps a half dozen Indians at the school, and they'd run together. Jay had stood out because, like her, he spent much of his free time on the prairie. Tomara had seen Jay out on his horse more afternoons than she could count. Sometimes they'd acknowledge each other's presence. Other times Tomara would see no more than a boy's outline on a distant horse and know it was Jay.

The boy had grown up to become Copper's law enforcement.

Jay's office was maybe half the size of Leonard's, rough and unfinished, carrying the stamp of the man who'd shoved himself into it. This morning he was standing beside his chunky desk. The phone at his elbow was black and solid, standing in contrast to the compact computer waiting to be brought to life. There was a photograph. The picture was that of a woman and two small, smiling boys.

Jay's head came up.

"Tomara."

"Jay."

There was a molded plastic chair Tomara could have sat in, but she felt more comfortable on her feet. For too long she could think of no way to begin the conversation. "Will you talk to me?" she wound up saying, knowing it was all wrong. "I mean, can you?"

"I don't know what I can tell you."

As she had last night, Tomara felt herself close to tears. She hadn't seen Jay for at least six years. If this were any other time, they would be trying to bridge that gap, looking to recapture their relationship. But a murder charge had erased a great deal; there was only today.

Do you think they did it? No. She wasn't going to say that. "Do you mean you aren't allowed to?"

"No. Tomara, sit down. Please." Jay waited until she'd forced herself into the uncomfortable chair and then leaned against his desk, overpowering it. "You look good."

"Thank you."

"You should run by the school. They put on a new roof. There's a new principal. He used to teach eighth grade. Damn it, you don't care about the school, do you?"

Tomara shook her head. "Ah…if I go to Sidney—if I go to the jail—will they let me in?"

"Tell me when you'll be there. I'll make sure there won't be any problems." Jay folded his arms across his chest. "They didn't resist arrest. I don't know if anyone told you that."

"I heard. Hayden told me." It was still awkward, but at least Tomara was able to get the words out. "Did they say anything?"

"Nothing you want to hear."

"I've heard it all before, Jay," Tomara told him honestly. "When you arrested them, what did they say?"

"Not much. Hoagy hardly said a word. He looked like he was in shock. Al, well, you know your old man. He started cussing and wound up threatening to sue me for everything except libel. He would have done that too if he'd had time to think about it." With his arms now hanging at his sides, Jay walked to the dusty window and looked out. He spoke with his back to Tomara. "I read them their rights, and then I told them what they were suspected of doing. And so you don't have to ask, I didn't ask if they'd done it. That's up to the detectives in Sidney."

"Have you seen them since you took them to jail?"

"Yeah. They'd like to get out. But the judge took one look at their records and turned down the request for bail. You've talked to Leonard?"

Tomara nodded. "Things are up in the air. I guess my dad's not sure he wants Leonard representing them. Leonard says he'll do it. I'm going to try to work that out with them today."

Jay turned back around. For a long time he was silent, and Tomara could think of no way to break the silence. "I always wondered if you'd come back. I never thought it would be like this."

Tomara shifted her weight. How could Jay stand to stay in this miniscule office? "Neither did I."

"I don't suppose you did. I'd like to give you my opinion, but I don't think I should. Go talk to them. See Leonard again. See if someone from the D.A.'s office will talk to you. You deserve more than gossip.''

"If—" Tomara stopped. She should be weighing this question carefully, but the need to ask it overrode her caution. "If I ask you things, will you give me straight answers?''

"What kind of things?''

"I'm not sure. If my dad and Hoagy tell me that man was already dead, will you tell me if that's possible?''

"That's not up to me to say. The autopsy—"

Tomara didn't need to hear the rest. They were talking about a murdered human being, not a nightmare to slip away like mist as the day came to life. Still, she had to come away with more than she had now. "You don't know how long he'd been dead when Mr. Conover found him?''

"Not long. You talked to Hayden, didn't you?''

"Not about that. I didn't know if I should,'' Tomara said, once again shifting her weight in the impossible chair. "Jay? What kind of man is he?''

"What do you mean?''

Until she'd heard the words, Tomara hadn't been aware she was going to say them. Now it was too late to backtrack. "I'm not sure,'' she began. "I guess I mean does he judge people? He told me he used to be a cop. I got the impression he was pretty cynical about some of the things he's seen.''

"It's an occupational hazard.'' Jay had come away from the window and was once again leaning against his desk. He looked older, and yet the aging process had served him well, Tomara thought. "Hayden's been on his own for a lot of years,'' Jay was saying. "Taking his lumps and learning from them. As to whether he's come to any conclusions about Al and Hoagy, I guess you'll have to ask him that.''

"I guess.''

"Tomara, I was going to get in touch with you. I've got a search warrant. I need to go through the house. I'd like you to be there when I do that. You don't have to if you don't want to, but—"

"Oh." Could one word bring on a headache? Or maybe what she was feeling had been created by Jay's words.

"Renfree was killed by a bullet. When I arrested Al and Hoagy, I didn't see any guns or rifles. There wasn't time to do much looking then."

"They have them," Tomara said in a small voice.

"I know they do. I just need to find them."

"When?"

"You say."

She'd been here long enough, Tomara decided. "I can come here again? I mean, if after I've talked to them I have questions, you'll talk to me?"

"You know I will, Tomara. As long as it isn't privileged information."

Tomara had no idea what Jay might mean by privileged information, but she was too eager to get outside to find out. She had only one thought, to get in her father's Jeep and drive to Sidney.

She was reaching for the keys in her back pocket when Hayden Conover pulled up behind the Jeep. As had happened in the Metcalf house last night, there was a moment of panic, an instant of wanting nothing except to run from him.

But she was a civilized woman, and civilized women faced their problems.

Hayden's eyes were on her. She felt . . . she wasn't sure what she felt. Something between fear and wanting, hesitancy and a desire to strip away everything that had happened since the man spotted something that didn't belong on the prairie. What she wanted was to be looking at him for the first time with nothing between them.

Hayden spoke first. "You've seen Jay?"

A nod was all Tomara could give him. She'd just spent time with Jay Eagle. Jay, who'd arrested her family. He should have been the one to unnerve her, but he hadn't, not like this game cop with the top two buttons of his shirt open and his jeans hugging well-muscled legs. Because there were things she wanted to prove and things she wasn't ready to face, she stood her ground and gave him a more complete answer. "There wasn't much Jay could tell me. The system has taken over. Now it's in the hands of the lawyers and investigators."

"Nothing's going to happen for a while, Tomara. You're going to have to be patient."

Tomara had spent the first nineteen years of her life being patient. She hadn't forgotten the lessons. "I know that," she told the man with shoulders broader than she could ignore. And eyes that wouldn't leave her alone. "But there are so many holes, so many gaps. I have so many questions."

"What do you want to know?"

She hadn't expected that. "I don't have any right asking you."

"I'd think it's better if you hear it from me instead of listening to rumors. I was out there, Tomara."

"I know." Copper had come to life since she went to see Leonard. A woman with a pickup full of preschoolers was pulling into the grocery store parking lot. Employees at the feed store were unloading a delivery truck, and someone was walking out of Leonard's office. The wind killed the voices of Tomara and Hayden before they carried twenty feet, but that didn't stop others from turning to look at them. Tomara knew there would be gossip passed on at the post office and Mandy's. "Maybe later." She sidestepped the confrontation. "After I've talked to Al and Hoagy."

Hayden grunted. Spreading his legs slightly, he hooked his hands in his back pockets. "They're putting you through hell."

Tomara wanted to draw away both emotionally and physically. She'd felt off balance around Jay, but that was nothing compared to the way she felt now. She knew Jay; Hayden was an unknown. A disturbing unknown. "If they are, it isn't the first time," she said, and was sorry she'd said anything. "I'm sorry. I don't want to delay you."

"You aren't." Hayden hadn't moved. She could step around him and get into the Jeep, but somehow his presence held her.

"I thought you had to go flying," she said when he continued to study her with his cop's eyes.

"At dawn. I got back an hour ago."

"Oh. Flying a helicopter." She grabbed at the straw of a conversation he'd given her. "Did you know how to do that before you came here?"

"No. But I learned." A car bearing out-of-state license plates eased past. Hayden wasn't distracted. "It's a different world when I'm in the air. Flatter. Even more isolated because I see miles and miles of nothing. There's Copper and the reservation, but that's all."

"That must be quite a change after Los Angeles." Tomara didn't care about this. And yet, maybe she needed to learn everything she could about this big man.

"Better. A hell of a lot better. Tomara? Do something for me, will you? Call me after you get back from Sidney."

There was so much to him. Muscle and bone, a voice capable of carrying and yet wrapping itself around her. And layers. Mostly layers. "Why?"

"Because I think you're going to need to talk to someone."

"There's—" This wasn't right. They should be talking about helicopters or antelope. "There's Mandy."

"Someone who'll do more than try to insulate you from what's happening."

"Mandy isn't like that," Tomara tried to say. Hayden Conover shouldn't care what she was going through, and she shouldn't want him to care. "She never tried to insulate me from anything."

"Still." Hayden left the rest unsaid.

"Still what?" Tomara wanted to ask, but she didn't. If he said anything more, it would only delay the end to the conversation and maybe force her to give away more of herself than she already had. Somehow she found words to say goodbye and forced herself to go to the Jeep without turning around to look at him. When she was finally able to see the entrance to Jay's office through the rearview mirror, he wasn't there.

She was glad.

Wasn't she?

* * *

The law enforcement center in Sidney was about twenty years old, tan brick, single story in front but expanding at the rear to encompass the jail. Every step Tomara took was in slow motion. The dark interior smelled of not enough air. She had to wait to talk to the thin desk sergeant.

Yeah, she was told. Al and Hoagy Metcalf could have visitors. In fact, he'd gotten word that she was coming here and should have precedence over any other visitors the two might have. At that the man laughed. "Not running over with friends, those two. You can't take your purse in there, miss, but I'm not going to frisk you. Sheriff in Copper, he said to treat you decent."

Tomara nodded her thanks. The walk back to the interviewing room took forever and left her feeling as if she was on a journey into the bowels of the building. She hadn't known what to expect, glass walls and talking through telephones maybe, but she was led into a small, spare room without windows and directed to sit at an institutional desk. A few minutes later Al and Hoagy filed into the room. A guard stationed himself just inside the room, a silent and yet constant observer.

Her father's belly had expanded. Broken blood vessels splayed across his cheeks and nose. There was an opaque quality to his eyes that made her wonder if he was developing cataracts. His hands were still those of a man who'd once kept food on the table by dint of the strength in his back. He was going bald.

Hoagy looked better than Tomara expected. The past six years had stripped him of his youth. Where before he'd had a tendency toward flab, that had been replaced by a fair amount of muscle. Tomara looked for hardness in his eyes. Instead she found a trapped and confused man. He was trying to smile for her.

"Leonard said he'd gotten in touch with you," Tomara's father said by way of greeting. He pulled out a scarred, wooden chair and molded his body to it. "You been out to the place?"

"Yes." Tomara had seen her father twice in the past six years, both times when he and Hoagy had come to Idaho Falls for no better reason than they had a full tank of gas. She should have known from those meetings that there would be no attempt to bridge the past, and yet Tomara was hurt. Hurt and hurting. Al had been as good a father as he knew how. True, he'd never had anyone to teach him parenting skills, and keeping alive and within reach of a bottle had taken a great deal out of him, but in his own way he had loved her. At least he'd never made Tomara feel unwanted.

Today she could do nothing less for him.

"No one's broken into it," she told him. Then she went on to explain that she was driving the Jeep and staying with Mandy. While Hoagy sat staring at his fingers gripping his knees, Tomara told them that she'd talked to their lawyer and the man who'd arrested them. Finally, and for some reason this was harder than the other things she had to say, she told her father and brother that she had met the man who saw them running from a body.

"Conover," Al spat. "We wouldn't be here if it wasn't for him."

Tomara hadn't come here to argue her father's concept of right and wrong. Still, she didn't try to sidestep the quiet outburst. "You shouldn't have run, Dad."

"Tell me about it." Hoagy spoke for the first time. "That's what I tried to tell him, but he wouldn't listen." Hoagy jabbed a quick finger at his father. "We gotta get the hell out of here, he yells at me. He's running for the rig, and like a fool I'm running with him."

"Why didn't you stay?" The guard had to be able to hear everything they were saying, but Tomara was fast learning that the Metcalfs had gone past the point of being able to keep anything private.

"Beats the hell out of me." There was nothing funny in Hoagy's laugh. "Think about it, Tomara. If you'd come across a body, a man's body, and suddenly someone in a helicopter shines a light on you, what would you do?"

I wouldn't run, not if I was innocent. But there weren't many things her father and brother were innocent of; they didn't understand innocent behavior. She chose her words carefully. "You said you came across the body?"

"What'd you think? You think we did it?"

Tomara accepted her father's hard, honest question. As difficult as answering him was, she was grateful that they weren't playing games. "You tell me."

"If I tell you, no matter what I tell you, you gonna believe me?"

"Yes."

Tomara heard her father's breath coming out in a kind of sigh. It was all she could do to keep her hands quiet on her side of the table. "We didn't do it, girl. I know what you're thinking. There've been times when, well, let's just say your old man and the law haven't always seen eye to eye."

That was an understatement. Tomara let it go. "You didn't do it."

"Leonard," Hoagy broke in. "We told him the same thing. He didn't say nuthin'. He just kept looking at us for the longest time and then he said, if we didn't kill that man then who did?"

Was it possible to be frozen and still go on functioning? Tomara had never felt the emotion before, but she felt it now. No matter how repulsive the subject, she would deal with it. "What did you tell him?"

Al snorted. "What do you think we told him? If we knew who did it, don't you think we'd be telling everyone we could get to listen? Look, girl, Hoagy and I, well, we had business out there that night. Business that's no one's concern except ours. We came across that man all right, but he was already dead. We heard a rifle being fired. That's how we found him. Now all we gotta do is get someone to believe us."

Tomara didn't waste her breath trying to tell her father how hard that was going to be. He had to know. And she knew better than to question him about what they were doing out on the prairie; he'd made it clear he wasn't going to tell her. "You're going to have to start working on your defense," she said in that voice that belonged to a woman stronger than she thought she would ever have to be. "When are you going to see Leonard again?"

"Leonard." Al half rose, looked over at the guard, and sat back down. "We don't have the money for no lawyer. You get us one of those public defenders, girl."

Hoagy was shaking his head at his father, but when he said nothing, Tomara took up the slack. "It isn't going to work, Dad. A public defender's all right for the scrapes you've been in. But this is no scrape. You're not going to get away with a fine this time."

"You think I don't know that?"

"Then talk to Leonard," she pressed. "He's willing to defend you. He's probably the only lawyer in the state who is." Tomara stopped a moment, absorbing the reality of what she'd just said. "He knows what he's getting into, and he knows you."

"That's not all he knows."

"What are you talking about?"

Ignoring the guard, Al leaned over and whispered into his daughter's ear. "You think he doesn't know about the river land? Your grandfather gave me those twenty acres. Worth thousands, that land is."

It isn't worth anything if you're in prison, Tomara thought. Instead she said, "That's always been something for you to fall back on, Dad. I know how you feel about it."

"Damn right. I'm not going to let that lawyer get his hands on it."

"Even if it means we go to prison?"

At the question, Tomara turned from her father to her brother. There was both anger and an unsettling resignation in Hoagy's eyes. "He's right," she made herself say. "That land isn't going to mean anything to you if you don't ever get out."

"You think that's going to happen, don't you? Maybe you think we did it."

She was being tested, but that didn't surprise Tomara. Too many hard years stood between her and her father. "I already gave you my answer. Besides, Dad, I'm not sure how much that land is worth. Maybe something to a farmer, but there aren't that many of them around. When I talked to Leonard, money wasn't on his mind. Do what he tells you to, help him plan your defense. Worry about money later.''

"You ordering me?"

There was more to the aging process than Tomara had first noticed. Despite the layer of fat, she saw lines that weren't there before. Her father's hands might still be roughened, but she doubted they could do what they once had. Her father was an old man, an old man asking his daughter for direction. "Yes. I'm ordering you."

Al's grunt let her know she would be held accountable for whatever happened. She would have liked to be able to end with that, to tell her father and brother she would be back in a couple of days—after she'd come to grips with today's reality—but she wasn't finished.

"I saw David Kemper," Tomara told her brother. "He said he was going to try to see you."

"David." Hoagy looked over to where a window should have been. "He said that?"

"I like him," was the only thing Tomara could say.

"He won't stay in Copper." Hoagy was still looking out the windowless window. "He's too smart for that."

"You could have left, Hoagy."

"Too bad I didn't. Now it's too late."

Tomara had experienced an incredible array of emotions since being called down from a telephone pole. Until now she'd been able to delay fear. Maybe Hoagy was right; maybe it was too late for him. She said something inane about how they shouldn't focus on that and instead try to develop a defense and work with their lawyer, but she was only half listening to the words. She wasn't sure Hoagy was doing any better.

Finally there was no putting it off. "Jay has a search warrant. He's waiting for me to go through the house with him."

"What's he looking for?" Al asked.

"Weapons. A rifle."

"'Cause that man was killed with a rifle?"

Tomara nodded.

"And you're going to help him."

"What do you want me to do?" Tomara didn't mind anger. The emotion was easier to handle than fear. "Let him go into the house when no one's there?"

"You could tell him that's my place and for him to keep the hell out of it."

A look passed between brother and sister, one that said something about accepting their father for what he was. Tomara didn't bother telling her father that was impossible. Instead, fighting off the fear that threatened once again to consume her, she got to her feet. "You going back to Copper?" Hoagy asked.

Tomara explained that Mandy was expecting her. She wanted to tell her brother about going to watch David play baseball, but if she did that he would be reminded of the freedom she took for granted.

"You keep your mouth shut, girl," Al told her. "People are going to be pumping you for all kinds of information."

"I don't think so. I'm not talking to anyone."

"Just Mandy and Eagle and that Conover character."

"I trust Mandy," Tomara told her father. "And I'm not going to tell Jay any more than I have to."

"What about Conover? He's a good-looking stud."

"Dad." Tomara sighed. If her father didn't now understand where her loyalties lay, he never would. "You don't like him, do you?"

"Damn right." Al grunted his way to his feet. "That man tried to put me in prison once."

Tomara stopped. "Tell me about it," she said between lips that barely moved.

"Said I tried to murder old man Blake's cattle. It wasn't like that at all."

"I heard, at least a little," Tomara told him. "You poisoned a watering hole."

"It was just a warning. That's all it was, a warning. Blake was spreading stories about me. Saying I was poaching his cattle. I've never done that. Never. I figured I'd throw a little poison in that hole he's got in the west pasture. Wasn't nothing in it 'cept a couple of old mules too old for anything. I was doing him a favor getting rid of those hay burners. How was I to know he was going to run those beef cattle of his in there? That's what I told Conover. Told him this was between me and Blake and for him to keep his nose out of it. But no. He comes and arrests me, and Hoagy's gotta sell that engine I was going to drop in the Ford so he can come up with the bail money. Then Conover keeps after things till I get slapped with that damn fine. I called him every name I could think of, in front of the judge, too." A took a deep breath against one of the longest speeches he'e ever given. "Conover's had it in for me ever since. He was so damn sure I was going to get jail time. But I fooled him The judge allowed that I hadn't meant to kill any cattle."

The anger behind her father's outburst surprised To mara. He believed Hayden was out to get him.

She didn't know how to handle that.

Chapter Five

Mandy was right. David Kemper was a gifted athlete. Watching him kicking the mound or bearing down on a batter reminded Tomara of the sense of peace, no matter how fleeting, that had come from being able to run until her legs trembled. She hadn't gone for a run since coming to Copper but made a vow to do so tonight.

"I wish he could stay here," Mandy said between innings. They were perched on the faded and splintered bleachers along with a goodly percentage of the town's population. "I know his folks will be sorry to see him leave. But David's been offered a scholarship. I guess he'd be a fool to stay here and dry up."

"Not everyone who stays here dries up," Tomara said, thinking of Mandy.

"I know that. But for youngsters—well, I think they're doing themselves a disservice if they don't go take a look at the rest of the world. I didn't even hear you leave this morning. You accomplish everything you needed to?"

"I'm not sure." Tomara kept her voice low, aware that she was drawing more than her share of attention. "I feel as if there are so many loose ends, so many unanswered questions.''

"I'm sure you do. We'll discuss those questions later, when we can talk. Leonard came by just as I was getting ready to leave. I guess I'm giving in. We'll be taking off as soon as he gets off work Friday."

"It sounds like fun," Tomara said in a distracted tone.

"I don't know. I don't like leaving you alone for a couple of days."

Tomara would argue that with Mandy later. Right now the only thing she wanted to think about was who was going to win a baseball game on a windswept diamond on the edge of a small town. The pace of the game lulled her. She concentrated on balls and strikes, coaches' signals, good-natured taunts from the opposing players. What she was watching had been going on long before she was born and would continue after her death.

Somehow, for a few minutes, that put things into perspective.

And then Jay and Hayden pulled up in the police car, and reality intruded. "Those two." Mandy shook her head. "Thicker than thieves. You'd think the two of them were brothers the way they hang out together. I'm sorry, honey. I had no idea they'd show up."

Tomara didn't bother saying anything. The two men, alike in the way they handled their bodies, were moving among the small crowd, shaking hands, exchanging greetings, occasionally stopping for a more serious conversation. Jay had lived here all his life, and yet Tomara was aware that Hayden conducted himself like a man who belonged as much as Jay did.

He'd told her he'd come from a city. She hadn't understood. Maybe he needed to get away from organized crime and people who'd been conditioned to accept violence, but until now she hadn't been able to see him putting down roots in Copper.

That changed with a laugh, a few whispered words to a rancher, the thumbs-up sign flashed to the player on deck. The wind ruffled his hair. Hayden's boots were dust caked.

is flesh tempered by the weather. He was half game warden, half next-door neighbor.

And he belonged.

She wouldn't think about that. Not while she needed to find out if there was anything to what her father had said about Hayden having a grudge against him.

Tomara was aware when Hayden spotted her. He could have dismissed her presence, done no more than dip his head to acknowledge her and then gone on with his visiting. Instead he stood with one foot on the bleacher bench above the one he was standing on, his jeans straining against bunched thigh muscle. His eyes were brown, brown bordering on jet black. Reaching out, testing her. His wasn't a look simply to let her know he was aware that she was there.

We aren't done with each other, she read in his look.

I know, she answered.

"Good game," Jay said as he made his way around Hayden and sat down next to Mandy. "They ought to start charging for these things. Collect enough to reseed the infield."

"They aren't going to draw crowds once David's gone," Mandy pointed out.

Hayden sat on the seat below Tomara. He was turned halfway around as if listening to what Mandy and Jay were saying to each other. Having him below her should have helped Tomara regain her sense of equilibrium, but it didn't. He was too big; there was too much to him. And in the five years since he'd come to Copper he'd made his impact in a way she'd never been able to. Hayden Conover was part of the town. There might be times when he came in conflict with some of the town's residents, but he'd earned their respect.

How? she needed to know. Why? she wanted to ask.

Jay leaned across Mandy and spoke to Tomara. "After the game? Can you meet me at your dad's place then?"

Tomara didn't care who might have heard the question. Hayden was watching her, silent, and his was the only reaction that mattered. She nodded and went back to watching David Kemper.

Although Jay moved on to talk to others, Hayden stayed where he was. He spoke occasionally to Mandy. He watched the game. He said nothing to Tomara.

The truth was, Hayden wouldn't have accepted Jay's suggestion that they'd been working too hard and needed to take an hour off if he'd known Tomara was going to be there. It had been easier to talk to her before she'd gone to see her family in jail. Thinking about her trapped in that building, asking Al and Hoagy impossible but necessary questions, listening to and absorbing whatever they might have told her changed things.

In part because Al Metcalf hated him.

In part because he wanted to insulate her from this.

Hayden wondered what Tomara would say or think if she knew he'd spent the day with her on his mind. But until he better understood what was happening to him, he would remain silent. Silent and questioning and wary.

Still, he wished there was a way he could ask if there was any possibility Tomara wanted him along when she went out to her father's house and looked for a weapon that might wind up being the nail in the coffins of Al and Hoagy.

The game ended with the Copper team winning 8-0 thanks to David's one-hit pitching performance. Tomara, eager to get away from Hayden's silent, unnerving presence, had reached the bottom of the bleachers and was waiting for Mandy to join her when David left the dugout and motioned for her to come to him. Whispering, he told her that his dad was going to be out of town on Friday and after he'd gotten his chores done, he was thinking about going over to Sidney. "I don't know. Do you think they'll let me in?"

"I didn't have any trouble," Tomara told him. Then because she was afraid David might change his mind, she told him that Hoagy had appreciated hearing that David had asked about him. "It would mean a lot to him."

"I thought it might. We aren't all that close because, well, just because. But we both love hunting. We've always been able to talk about that. Are you going to see him before I do?''

Tomara wasn't sure. By then Mandy had joined her. Jay stood a few feet away, distracting Tomara from David's question.

She could have stalled Jay, but if she did, he might decide to drive out to the house by himself. Tomara couldn't let him do that. If the policeman walked unescorted into the house, it would feel too much like a conspiracy against her father and brother.

"You going out there now?" Hayden asked the question.

"It's up to Tomara," Jay supplied, looking at her for his answer. She could do nothing except nod.

"Do you want me along?"

Why? Tomara wondered, but maybe, just maybe she knew the answer. If it hadn't been for Hayden, Al and Hoagy wouldn't be in jail. He'd once been a police officer; in many ways he still was. This was an investigation, one Hayden would want to be in on.

Everything in her screamed "No," but she didn't say the word. If she did, Hayden might believe she was trying to keep something from him—some piece of evidence, some emotion. Somehow it was very important that Hayden, more than Jay, understood that she believed her father and brother innocent of murder.

"It's up to you," she said without looking at Hayden.

"Then I'll be there."

She should have come out here to clean up instead of going to a ball game, Tomara thought as she let the two men in the back way. The house had been closed up too long. It smelled as if it were dying.

Silent, she pointed toward her father's bedroom and followed Hayden into it. A rifle stood propped against a wall. Then Hayden retrieved it and faced her. He said nothing, letting his burden speak for him.

She should never have let him come into her father's room. The room spoke of a man who cared almost nothing about what happened within these four walls; if he'd ever cared, that had been stripped from him. Hayden handled himself like a man who believed in himself, who cared, who felt. She didn't know him well enough to understand what had meaning in his life, but she did understand that, whatever else he might or might not value, he valued his life and intellect. He would look at the bare walls, a tangled blanket on a naked mattress, cracked and faded boots thrown in a corner on top of a pile of jeans and grayed T-shirts. He would look at those things and learn a great deal about her roots.

And, with the afternoon giving over to evening, and her father sitting in a jail, she couldn't tell him how far she'd come from those roots.

"Is that the only rifle?"

Tomara responded to Jay's question. "I don't know. Jay, I don't know what they have anymore."

"They'd have more than one rifle."

Jay was hard enough for her to deal with. Hayden? Hayden was impossible. "Probably. They always did."

"Where else might they be?"

As much as she hated the question, at least it gave Tomara something to focus on. With the men watching, she opened what stood for a closet. The sliding door wouldn't slide, but she managed to pry it open. A half dozen flannel shirts hung on rusty hangers. More boots were strewn on the floor next to a collage of socks. A shotgun was propped against the back wall. Tomara stepped back. If Jay and Hayden wanted that, too, they would have to get it themselves.

"That's not it," Jay said even as he brought the weapon out of the closet. "That's not what killed him."

Relief warred with fear at the word *killed*. "Dad always kept the guns in his room," Tomara said almost defiantly. "That was one thing he was adamant about—never leaving guns in the living room."

"What about Hoagy's room?"

Hayden still carried the rifle he'd picked up. The weapon made him appear unapproachable. Intimidating. "Maybe," she said before turning and leading the way. This time the blankets stretched down the middle of the room mocked her. Maybe this was all that stood and had ever stood between her and her father and brother. If it wasn't for that faded, sagging fabric, maybe she would still be living here.

Hoagy's room was a twin of his father's except that Hoagy had more clothes heaped on the floor and had put a sheet between him and his mattress. While Hayden peered into her brother's closet, Tomara stood silent, sad and resigned. She wanted more for her father and brother. She wanted to believe that they wanted more for themselves.

She also remembered what her father had said after he'd wrestled Hoagy and her from their mother's arms. "I'll take care of the two of you. Me. No one else."

His idea of care probably should have landed them in foster homes, but only because social workers wouldn't have understood. Al might not have been much of a father, at least not when it came to providing for and supporting his children. But he'd kept a roof over their heads. And never once begrudged doing that. And in his own limited way he'd loved his children.

"Tomara." It was Hayden speaking. "I thought you said they didn't own handguns."

He was holding up a revolver, not one of those small, sleek models carried by city dwellers as interested in making a fashion statement as they were in protection. The gun weighing heavily in Hayden's hand tugged at the muscles of his forearm and forced him to stretch his fingers over its bulk. Tomara had never seen it before.

"I didn't think they did," she said around a tongue suddenly gone dry. The barrel of the gun was pointed in her direction. Although Hayden didn't have his finger against the trigger, she could sense the potential. The boundaries.

His eyes, trained on her for longer than she could comfortably handle, were now sweeping the room. He said nothing as Jay dropped to his knees and looked under

Hoagy's bed. Jay straightened; the two men exchanged a look. Tomara could think of nothing to say.

The only thing she wanted was out. Out of this room. Out of the house. Out of Copper and this damnable nightmare.

But that wasn't to be, and the need to run grew.

Jay wanted to look around the garage. Tomara was almost grateful for the distraction. Her relief lasted only momentarily; Hayden wasn't going with Jay.

"This isn't all of them."

"What?" Tomara jerked her head around.

"There were always rifles in the racks in Al's pickup. I notice that kind of thing, Tomara."

He had to stop saying her name. Hearing it roll out of his chest confused her when she needed to know exactly where she stood with the game warden, when she wanted their relationship to be uncomplicated. When she wanted—to feel nothing.

"I don't know," she said ineffectively. "I told you, I don't know what they have anymore, or where it's kept."

Hayden, still holding the weapons he'd confiscated, walked into the living room. He went to the window so he could stare out at some of Hoagy's accumulation of car and truck parts. His back was somehow fitting; it made it easier for her to understand the rules. They'd talked that first night in the cafe. Maybe they'd been slammed up against the reality of what was happening. The man she'd talked to and shared a meal with had turned his back to her, and she was alone.

What would it feel like to have him touch her? She killed the question.

"How did you do it?"

"How did I do what?"

"Survive." Hayden turned back around. Tomara guessed that he'd shaved this morning, but the effort looked wasted now. There was nothing polished about him, nothing she could dismiss. There was only masculinity and a question that wouldn't die after all.

"What business is it of yours?" Tomara said, hating the defensiveness in her voice.

"Maybe none," Hayden answered in a lazy tone that covered what he was really feeling. He needed to insulate himself from her impact, but she was standing, small and alone, in the suffocating room, and he understood what was happening to her because she wasn't the only one with unmet emotional needs. "There must have been some reason why you turned out the way you did and not like your brother."

"You don't know my brother. And you don't know how I turned out."

She was a tigress protecting both her brother and herself. He would be wise not to forget that. He would also be wise to remember that she didn't want to share anything with him. "Let's go outside."

Hayden wasn't sure whether she'd follow him, but she did, and he was grateful. He hated the dying smells of the house; they brought him too close to his own past. He made a show of sitting on the front porch and making room for her next to him. For a long time she stood, her eyes quick and intense on her surroundings, but when Jay didn't emerge from the barn, she slid spinelessly and yet gracefully to the splintered step. She leaned forward and wrapped her arms around her knees.

Hayden said something inane about Hoagy's interest in automobiles, but she barely responded. Next he asked her what her father had done to earn a living. This time she pulled her eyes from her study of nothing and everything and fastened them on him.

He loved the black of her eyes. He didn't know what to do with what lay below the surface. And for this moment he hated his parents for keeping so much of themselves from him. If things had been different, he might understand a great deal more about Tomara Metcalf.

"Don't push it, Conover," she told him in a voice too old for the rest of her. "I'm not going to say any more than I already have."

"We were able to talk earlier."

"That was before you came here to look for what might bury them."

"You don't pull your punches, do you?"

"I can't." Her voice sounded even older. "Look. I don't know what's going to happen, how this is going to turn out. The only thing I know is that it's my family we're talking about."

"Your family. What about your mother, Tomara? Where is she?"

"Dead."

Until Mandy brought it up the other night, Hayden couldn't remember anyone talking about Mrs. Metcalf. He'd simply accepted that Al and Hoagy lived together. Given their life-style, it hadn't surprised him that there was no woman in evidence. And until he'd learned that Al also had a daughter, he hadn't given thought to the fact that there had to have once been a woman in Al Metcalf's life. Now, with her single word slapping him, he wished he'd asked Mandy more.

He could ask some stupid questions such as how long ago did she die and did Tomara remember her, but he wasn't sure she would answer, and if she didn't, that would carve an even greater distance between them

He didn't ask himself why the distance bothered him.

It didn't matter, Tomara thought. If she didn't tell him, someone else surely would. Let them. There were enough people dying to pass on the story of the Metcalfs. But if she left that up to that nebulous someone else, the story would be twisted. She didn't want that to happen.

"My mother drank herself to death," Tomara began with her eyes on the darkening sky and her heart in the past. "At least she drank enough that by the time she stopped it was too late."

"Oh."

Tomara barely noted Hayden's comment, and yet it gave her the energy to go on. "Cancer of the pancreas. Fast. At least I hope it was fast for her. I didn't see my mother again after—"

"After she tried to take you and Hoagy away from here and Al came after you."

She was wrong. He'd already heard the stories. "Who told you that?"

"Mandy."

Mandy would have told him the truth. "I was eight," she said. "I don't believe in replaying the past, but I remember arguments between my parents. Mother saying she wasn't going to stay here any longer, and Dad saying there wasn't anywhere else for him to go. She drank. I already said that, didn't I?"

"Yeah. You did."

Something in Hayden's tone stopped her. That wasn't the voice of a man who knew a great deal about the necessity of keeping emotions in locked boxes. "I don't know if she drank before she got married. But I think she went a lot of years without being sober, really sober. I don't think her jumping in a truck with Hoagy and me and taking off was something she'd planned ahead of time. It just happened."

"Where did you go?"

Jay's flashlight was still bouncing around inside the outbuilding. If she concentrated on what she was saying, maybe she could get it all said before he returned. "I don't remember. I do remember driving for hours, maybe days. I was so tired of being in the truck. And then..." Tomara closed her eyes to bring herself closer to the past. "We came to a city. I'd never seen so many lights. There was an energy to the place. I was excited, and Hoagy, he was bouncing off the walls talking nonstop. Mom found a place for us to stay." Tomara tried to hold back the bitter laugh, but it escaped. "It wasn't much better than what we'd left."

"How long were you there, Tomara?"

There he was again, turning her name around into something she didn't understand. Something she told herself she didn't want. "Not long. Maybe a week. Mom got a job as a waitress in the bar she went into the night we found a place to stay. I think she stayed sober. I think maybe she knew she had to."

She had to stop talking, Tomara thought. She was telling this near stranger things he had no right knowing, things she had no business sharing. But the house she'd grown up in was behind her, and stars were coming to life in the endless sky and—Tomara wasn't sure how to finish the thought. The rest had something to do with who she was talking to. "I never asked Dad how he found out where we were staying. Maybe Mom wanted to be found—I don't know. Hoagy and I were alone in the motel room and Mom was working when he showed up. He hung around until she got off work. There was a fight."

Tomara waited, wondering if Hayden was going to ask for more of an explanation. If he had, she probably would have told him to go to hell, but because he was silent, she went on. "Mom got drunk and Dad packed Hoagy and me up and brought us home."

"Did you ever see your mother again?"

"Twice." Tomara got to her feet with no idea of where she was going other than away from Hayden Conover who'd pulled too much out of her without her knowing how that was possible. "That's how I knew what happened to her. She was sick. She wouldn't come back to Copper. And she was broke. She simply—she wasn't much of a parent."

"And your father was?"

"I didn't say that." If he came any closer she'd slap him. "Look, I don't know why Dad did the things he did. I just know he never turned us out."

"That doesn't necessarily mean he was capable of giving you the emotional support a child needs."

"And you're an expert on that? You know what rules parents and children are supposed to abide by?"

"No. I don't know that."

He was letting her get too close. She'd said what she did because she didn't want him to hear the story from someone else. He had no business, no right, making her want to know more about him. "What is he doing in there?"

"Looking. It takes time."

"It shouldn't take that long."

Hayden watched Tomara stride through the dark until he had nothing except the memory of her long legs, her curving hips, her too-tiny waist. The guns weighed heavily on his lap, but he couldn't concentrate on them long enough to do anything about that.

Was that what happened to people in a crisis situation? he wondered. Take them out of their routines and they spilled their guts? As a cop he'd witnessed profanity, silence as thick as a stone wall, tears, hysteria. He couldn't remember anyone pulling out their secrets and sharing them with him. He couldn't remember admitting his own inadequacies.

Tomara and Jay were standing a few feet apart, staring at what was left of a tractor when Hayden joined them. Jay was talking. "It has to be the Blake tractor, Tomara. Neil reported it stolen several years ago. He wanted me to come out here then, but I didn't have enough evidence to do that."

"Blake." Tomara sighed. "Dad really knows how to hold a grudge, doesn't he?"

"It looks like it. I'll call Neil, tell him he can come after it if he wants."

Tomara took another look at the tractor. It had once been a piece of machinery a man could take pride in, but now all four tires were flattened and most of the wiring in the engine had been yanked out. Someone had taken a sledgehammer to the body. The tractor looked like the victim of someone's wrath.

If they were capable of this, what more might they have been capable of?

Hayden whistled. The sound distracted her. "They really did a number on it, didn't they?"

"Don't they deserve a trial? You've already condemned them." She stopped. She was talking crazily, and Hayden and Jay had to know that. Of course Al and Hoagy were responsible for this. And maybe for more than this.

Jay hadn't found any more rifles in the garage. As the three were walking back to their separate cars, Jay repeated his belief that there had to be more weapons around. Hayden seconded the statement; it didn't hold water that Al and Hoagy had gotten rid of their rifles.

Unless they'd hidden them.

"I need you to do me a favor, Tomara. I think you know what it is," Jay said before Tomara could ease herself into the Jeep.

"I know. If I find something—"

"I don't like asking this."

Of course he didn't, Tomara acknowledged. Still, she was unable to give him the smile that would salve his conscience. They weren't discussing the weather, and she wasn't going to pretend they were.

Watching Jay leave should have held her attention. He was the law enforcement officer. But when all was said and done, it was the lights from Hayden's Bronco that followed her down the long, rutted road. She didn't understand him or his impact on her. She didn't think she ever would.

Tomara slept even less that night than she had the night before. She had stayed up late talking to Mandy, not about anything important because Mandy's customers might hear, but asking questions about people she hadn't seen and hadn't thought about for six years. As she perched on the stool closest to where Mandy held court, she'd fought off the pounding in her legs. She couldn't run at night. Even she didn't know the prairie well enough to take off into star-touched ink. In the morning, she promised her spirit and muscles. In the morning she would run.

She did. Without bothering with breakfast, Tomara slipped out of bed as soon as it was dawn. She tugged on jogging pants and a T-shirt and once again left Mandy alone to sleep.

Not even the feed store was open yet. Tomara jaywalked across the main street, through an alley and down a short residential street. She could have taken her Jeep, but she didn't want to risk the sound wakening Mandy. Instead she half walked, half trotted until she'd put the town behind her.

Then, her lungs expanding to accept the job they'd come to love, Tomara lengthened her stride and put the world behind her.

In two directions farmers' fences came right up to the city limits, but Tomara headed west across land owned by but all but forgotten by the government. The earth under her feet was cold. As soon as the sun gained strength it would warm, bringing to life the insects and small animals who found life in seemingly lifeless ground. This time of the morning, however, Tomara was the only one moving.

She didn't have to think about what her legs were supposed to be doing. She had been running so many years that her body instinctively chose a pace that would allow her miles of freedom without putting a strain on her lungs or muscles.

Freedom. Running was freedom. From the minutes and emotions back at her father's place. From what she'd told Hayden Conover.

Hayden. His name, his presence was the first thought she allowed access. He might be out here himself, not tied to the earth as she was but skimming over the surface in his helicopter looking for—what? Antelope? Poachers?

Could he see her? Tomara glanced upward, but she didn't need her eyes to reinforce what her ears had already told her. She was alone.

Tomara ran for over an hour. By the time she returned to town, she was sweating. She was also more at peace than she'd been in days.

The sense of peace lasted most of the day, a day filled with running errands for Mandy and servicing the Jeep. In the afternoon Tomara went out to the house and without thinking, without asking, went about cleaning up. She washed dishes and scoured the sink and bundled up Al's and Hoagy's dirty clothes. She also kept her eye out for anything that might have been missed yesterday. Because she didn't want to have to spend tonight berating herself for being a coward, she walked into the barn and stared at the tractor. It was a mess. Neil Blake would be furious. But, unless her father had done something to the motor that she couldn't see, the tractor could be brought back to service. She wondered if Jay had told Neil yet. She wondered what she would say to the rancher if they came face-to-face.

Tomara spent the late afternoon in town, then went back to Sidney early that evening, after saying goodbye to Mandy, who was leaving for the weekend with Leonard. There was a restlessness to Hoagy that Tomara understood when he mentioned that David had just been by. David had made up his mind which of three athletic scholarship offers he was going to accept. Although they could have talked about why Hoagy was in jail, the two young men had filled their time together by speculating about what would happen if David did well enough to be noticed by the pros.

"He's going somewhere, sis." Hoagy was looking at his shoes. "He's trying to get his girlfriend to go to the university with him. Can you believe that? Someone from Copper going to California. Those beaches. Hollywood. All that money."

Tomara hurt for her brother, but she didn't know how to change his mood. Instead, hating herself a little for having to say it, she told them about going out to the house with Jay and Hayden and finding a rifle, shotgun and pistol. "They think there's more weapons," she said with her attention riveted on her father. "Hayden says you always have rifles in the pickup."

"He does, does he?"

"You've hidden them, haven't you?"

Al jerked his head up. Dry, graying hair flew. "Maybe. Maybe not. What'd you want to know for? So you can turn them over to the cops?"

Tomara didn't know the answer to that. "Jay found Neil Blake's tractor."

"Did he now," Al said with a rasp that might have been a laugh. "Bet old Blake's going to have a cow."

"Why did you do it?"

Al shrugged. "I told you, girl. I got problems with someone, I handle those problems myself."

"By destroying someone's property?"

"By whatever it takes."

The meeting, Tomara admitted, had gone as badly as she'd thought it would. Her father was defensive. There was no way she could reach him when he was like that. And

Hoagy was so depressed that his depression had become hers. She wasn't going to see them again, she told herself as she was driving back to Copper.

By the time she parked behind Mandy's she knew she couldn't desert them. She was all Al and Hoagy had.

And they were the only family she had.

When the phone rang, Jay was out talking to a business-man holding a bad check compliments of someone he'd never see again. Hayden was the one who picked it up. The call was from the jail in Sidney. They thought Jay should know. Al and Hoagy Metcalf had broken out an hour ago.

"How?" Hayden's free hand was already becoming a fist. "How'd you let that happen?"

"We didn't 'let it' happen. They had a gun. A Saturday night special."

"Was anyone hurt?" Hayden asked. He barely heard the "no." His mind was already on the question of how he was going to tell Tomara that.

The question died before it was full born to be replaced by another. What if Tomara already knew?

Chapter Six

Jay could have told Tomara. In fact his argument that it was his job and not Hayden's made a lot of sense. But so did Hayden's that Jay would do well to get over to Sidney to find out everything he could about the breakout. "If she's hiding something, I think I can sense it as well as you can," Hayden said by way of argument. "Maybe better. She might not be on her guard as much around me."

"You really think she's capable of—"

"I don't know what she's capable of." Hayden hated having to admit that. "But if she dropped everything to come back here, who are we to say what's going through her mind?"

Jay shrugged his shoulders. "I don't think I want to know what she was thinking of if she slipped them a gun." His groan was loud and unexpected. "Damn! I told them to do right by her, to let her spend all the time she needed with Al and Hoagy. If she got in without being checked out because of what I said—"

"You get on the road," Hayden encouraged. "That's a hell of a lot more important than standing around here asking questions neither of us can answer."

Five minutes later Jay had locked up his office and was heading out of town. Hayden waited until he could no longer see the police car before crossing the street. Mandy's Saloon wasn't yet open for the day. Tomara's Jeep was parked behind the place. Most likely Tomara was still up in Mandy's apartment.

The idea of catching Tomara before she'd readied herself for the day gave Hayden pause. There was something vulnerable about a person in their nightclothes. If Tomara looked vulnerable enough, if she transmitted that emotion, he was going to have a hard time concentrating on reading between the lines.

Nonetheless, Hayden climbed the stairs and knocked on the door he suspected Mandy never bothered to lock. It opened; he was looking at a woman dressed in a T-shirt that had plastered itself to her damp body. He should have been grateful that she was wearing a bra, but too much was still exposed.

Tomara stepped back. She wrapped her arms around her middle, whether because she knew what was exposed or because she was protecting herself against his presence, Hayden didn't know. About the only thing he did know was that a feeling he thought he'd forgotten slammed itself into him. A feeling that brought back the months of sleeping alone.

"What is it?"

So she'd cut through the pleasantries, had she? It didn't surprise him that she'd guessed he wasn't here to pass the time of day, and yet a part of him wished that could be possible. Below the hapless T-shirt she was wearing a pair of running shorts no more up to doing their job than the shirt was. That job, Hayden decided in less than a second, should have been to keep him from looking at too much flesh.

"Jay just got a call. From the jail."

Tomara backed up and sat. Her legs splayed out in front of her on the couch. Hayden would have to be dead not to notice that they were a runner's legs. An athlete's legs. A woman's legs. He should have been concentrating on her reaction to his words, but he wasn't. With a shake, Hayden fought to remind himself why he was here. "Where's Mandy?"

"Gone. She and Leonard won't be back until late Sunday. What was the call about, Hayden?"

Had she ever spoken his name before? Of course she had. What he didn't understand was why it was so damn hard for him to dismiss the way she made it sound. He was a trained professional here to get some information. Her chest was going in and out quickly and deeply, giving reinforcement to his belief that she'd just come back from a run. She wasn't big breasted; neither was she the kind of woman who could exercise without wearing a bra. Once again Hayden fought to shake himself free. He wasn't succeeding.

"They've escaped."

Tomara took another breath, deeper than any she'd taken since heading out onto the prairie. It didn't help. Hayden Conover was telling her something she didn't want to hear. Maybe if she concentrated on breathing she could make him and his words go away.

"When?"

"Earlier this morning. We don't have all the details yet."

"Where's Jay?"

"On his way to Sidney."

"Why are you here?"

"Someone had to tell you."

This was insane. Their conversation sounded like something out of a cop movie, when the last thing Tomara wanted to think about was cops. Or jails. Or murder charges. Think, Tomara warned herself. She wanted to ask questions, a thousand of them. More than that she wanted to tell Hayden that he was wrong. But she knew it wasn't so.

He was watching her closely. Too closely. It might simply be that he hadn't expected to find her dressed the way she was, but Tomara dismissed that. He had been a cop. She didn't dare forget that. And she was related to two men who'd escaped from jail.

That was all he was thinking about.

Tomara straightened. She couldn't help the way she was dressed, but she could dictate what she was going to say. "Maybe you're thinking I already know. Is that why you're here? To see if I give anything away?"

She'd hit a nerve. Although he didn't say anything, she could read it in the narrowing of his eyes. "You tell me," Hayden said after a silence that stretched and tightened.

"I don't have to tell you anything." Tomara got to her feet. It wasn't until she felt the weight of her body that she asked herself what she was going to do now. She could order him out of Mandy's place, but if she did that she would be sealing herself off from the only person who could tell her what had happened. "What did the people at the jail say?" she asked.

"I'm not sure how much I should be telling you."

She'd asked for that. Still, maybe because he'd stood in her childhood bedroom and asked hard and gentle questions, Tomara did what she had to to keep the lines of communication open. "You didn't just come here to tell me they escaped," she said softly. "What else?"

"To ask if you know anything about how they managed to get their hands on a Saturday night special."

A gun. Al and Hoagy had used a gun. "Was anyone hurt?"

"No. The trustee—apparently he's just a kid—knew better than to argue with a loaded gun and a man who ordered him to drop his own weapon."

Weapons.

He was watching her. No matter where she turned in the too little room, his eyes followed her, trapping her, touching her. "How did they get—"

"How did they get their hands on a gun? That's what Jay is going to try to find out. The last anyone saw of them, they were hightailing it down the street just after dawn. The trustee had been shoved into Hoagy's cell. His keys stripped from him."

"He didn't yell for help?"

"It's a little hard to do when a man's taken a knee where it'll do the most harm. Yeah. He yelled. But it was too late by then."

"Running?" Tomara repeated because she didn't want to think about what had happened to the young man. "They were on foot?"

"That's the story we got. There wasn't anyone waiting for them once they were out."

And Hayden had come here and found proof that she'd been in Copper or more precisely on the prairie surrounding the town. At least he had an answer to one of the questions he must have been asking himself. She hadn't been in Sidney driving a getaway car.

She felt hot. Sticky. Her sweat had dried, but that didn't prevent the thin nylon of her outfit from staying with her contours. She should have stuck with the sweats she'd worn the other day, but she'd gotten so hot running with fabric around her legs. Now Tomara would give a great deal to be less exposed.

But the exposure she felt came from a great deal more than what she was or wasn't wearing. This man didn't trust her. Knew better than to believe her. The feeling the other day that they'd had something in common—what a lie that was!

"When will Jay be back?"

"I don't know. Why?"

"Because I need to talk to him. I'm going to change. First I'm going to get a shower. Then I'll go to Jay's office and wait for him."

"I'll be there."

"Why?"

"Because, Tomara. Just because."

An hour after she watched Hayden leave, Tomara was once again facing him. She'd taken as long as she could with her shower and then stalled by straightening Mandy's living room, but finally there was nothing left to do with her energy. She had no idea how long Jay would be in Sidney.

Maybe she would have to sit in the too small office with Hayden for hours. But if she wasn't there when Jay returned, the men might read something into her absence.

Her indecisiveness confused Tomara. She knew how to take control of her life. She'd gone on with her schooling, working nights and evenings so she would have the necessary skills for a job that would satisfy her. Although many of the male linemen had given her suspicious looks when she first went to work, she'd managed, through hard work, to earn their respect. She could diagnose problems and wasn't afraid of tackling them, no matter what the weather or working conditions. What then was so difficult about walking into Jay's office?

The answer was waiting for her.

Hayden was too large for the room. What made it worse was the way he kept looking at her, studying her as if she were under a microscope. An hour ago she hadn't been aware of what he was wearing. His outfit made its impact on her now.

He wasn't in uniform. True, it made sense to be clad in jeans and a cotton shirt, but if he was playing fair he would have chosen something that wasn't so...molded. Tomara had grown up around men who owned nothing except jeans. They were her uniform and that of the men she worked with, but somehow they looked different on Hayden.

His body was built for the fabric designed for men who earned their living with their muscles.

And his eyes. His damned eyes followed her everywhere.

"Jay isn't back yet?" she asked unnecessarily. When he shook his head, she vowed not to say anything that would elicit that response from him. It was impossible for a simple shake of the head to be so unsettling, such a lesson in maleness, but that was exactly what happened. "What are you doing here?" she asked. "Don't you have work to do?"

"I don't punch a time clock. I work whatever hours need working. Right now I'm a hell of a lot more interested in what Jay found out."

"Oh." Tomara turned from him. Pretending to ignore the game warden, she stepped to Jay's desk and began pawing through the stack of Wanted posters. The charges along with the grainy, black-and-white faces blurred, but Tomara refused to turn from her study. If she did, she might have to go back to listening to Hayden's silence.

Ten minutes later Tomara was a breath away from saying something, anything, to break the mood. Hayden had found something to do and was busily writing a note or memo or something. She half believed she could walk out the door and he wouldn't have noticed she was no longer there. But if she walked, she would give away too much of her emotional state.

And if she stayed, she'd wind up saying something that would expose her just as much as a closing door.

Jay's police car. Tomara was never more glad to hear a vehicle in her life. A half second later she felt herself mentally if not physically drawing away from what the Sioux would have to tell her.

"You heard," Jay said as he came inside. He nodded at Hayden. His words were for Tomara.

"Not much," she made herself say. Her palms had grown damp. She didn't want to give herself away by wiping them dry. "Just that a gun was used."

"A gun that no way in hell should have been there. They had help."

Tomara waited. She'd been expecting those words since Hayden told her about the breakout. "Not by me." Her voice was barely audible.

"No one said you had anything to do with it."

Tomara turned toward Hayden. She wondered if she would like him any better if he'd never been a cop, but there was no way she could answer that question. He had been, and the cop in him was saying things she didn't want to hear. "Not in so many words," she challenged. "But what other suspects are there? Who else gives a damn?"

Hayden shrugged that disarming shrug she hadn't wanted to see. "Good question."

Before Tomara could demand more from Hayden, Jay began. The jail staff had been in an uproar. Breakouts weren't unheard of, but the use of a weapon and violence was. An investigation was under way to determine how a gun could have been snuck into where the Metcalfs were being kept, but Jay hadn't been interested in investigations. Only a couple of things concerned him. Who had visited Al and Hoagy? Had anyone seen them since they broke out?

The jail staff had been able to supply the first answer. If the log book was a complete record, in the past three days the Metcalfs had had three visitors: David Kemper, their attorney and Tomara. Before Tomara could think to speak, Jay supplied the answer to his second question. It had been luck pure and simple. News of the breakout had made the radio stations. A trucker had picked up the news and had waved Jay down on the outskirts of Copper. He'd just dropped off a couple of hitchhikers. He wouldn't have given it much thought except they seemed kind of nervous and although the trucker was coming through Copper, they wanted to be dropped off five miles out of town.

"I described Al and Hoagy. He said it was them."

Five miles out of town. Tomara hugged the thought to her, not knowing what to do with it. Five miles out of town and a little over four miles from the road was one of her relatives' favorite "hunkering down" spots. Tomara had been in the roughened foothills a thousand times. Only someone who knew exactly where he was going would be able to find the small cave bored into the rock.

Hayden waited. He saw it in her, the drawing within herself, the preoccupation with her thoughts. If he pushed, she would only draw away farther, but if he could be patient...

"I'm going after them."

Jay's statement only partly distracted Hayden. "Not by yourself."

"Who else? If I wait for the state police, it's going to be hours before we get something going."

His eyes still on Tomara, still on hair so thick and rich it challenged any man to look at her and not think of it, Hayden touched the gun strapped to his waist. "You're not going by yourself."

"You're not a cop."

"You're not going up against two armed men by yourself."

The sound coming from Tomara Metcalf wasn't one Hayden had ever heard before. It was not quite human, not quite civilized. He doubted that she was aware of what she'd produced, but the sound told him a great deal more about her than she would ever want known. Despite the point he was trying to make with Jay, Hayden turned so he could watch Tomara's every move, her every emotion.

He couldn't say that she'd paled, but there was a change, as if something essential had been sucked out of her and she'd been left to fill up the spaces. Hayden had known a number of people who wouldn't have been able to pull together what was left of themselves after a crisis and go on. Tomara wasn't one of them. She was spreading her legs to accept her weight and lifting her chin and unclenching her fingers.

In the move, in the acceptance of what life had thrown her, Hayden's admiration grew. He'd been intrigued by her from the day she walked into Mandy's Saloon. Now, like it or not, he wanted to extend his hand to her. To tell her that, maybe, they had a great deal in common.

But he didn't. There was a line, invisible and yet impenetrable between the two of them. She was being claimed by loyalty, he by responsibility.

Hayden wondered if she understood that line, if it was even on her mind. Probably not; he wasn't that important to her. He watched, absorbing impressions he hadn't begun to try to sort out as she took the step that placed her closer to Jay and him. "I'm going with you."

Jay's head snapped around. "No, you're not."

"Yes, I am." The simple words were clipped and left no room for argument. "You're going out there, armed, looking for my family."

"They're armed, too, Tomara."

Tomara turned from Jay to Hayden. Why was it, she wondered on the heels of a thousand other emotions demanding attention, that she was capable of dealing head-on with Jay while simply being around Hayden affected her in ways she had very little understanding of? It didn't matter; nothing did except keeping her brother and father alive. "They'll listen to me," she made herself say. "If they see me with you two, they won't fire."

"And maybe you'll be able to keep us from firing. That's what you're thinking, isn't it?"

Suddenly Tomara understood. Facing Hayden was difficult because he asked impossible questions and demanded impossible answers. What was it she'd heard? That the eyes were the window to the soul. She couldn't see that deeply into Hayden. She wondered if anyone ever had. "I don't give a damn what you think. I didn't help them escape. That's not how I believe in dealing with life."

"You might not still be saying that by the time this is over, Tomara."

"Maybe." She made herself look at him. "Maybe."

Hayden's words haunted Tomara as the three bent over an aerial map of the area. Her fingers jabbed at the route she was certain her relatives would take, the very spot where the small cave existed. She didn't want to be doing this. She was driving a wedge between her family and herself. They'd once trusted her to support them, and now she was bringing the police to them. But if she didn't do this, her father and brother might be killed.

Despite the turmoil, Tomara's thoughts, her consciousness even, remained on Hayden. It wouldn't be like that if he weren't standing so close, if she weren't aware of his heat. If what he thought and felt and experienced didn't matter to her.

Less than ten minutes later, the three were sitting inside Jay's pickup, Tomara in the middle. No one spoke. Tomara tried to concentrate on Jay's driving, on how long it would take them to reach the spot where the trucker had let her father and brother off, on how far the four-wheel drive would be able to travel before they'd have to continue on foot.

Those tactics didn't work. Her right leg was pressed against Hayden's. Had they touched before? She couldn't remember. If they had, maybe she would be immune. And then maybe that would never be possible.

Because of the gearbox between her and Jay, there was no way she could put an end to the contact with the game warden. Through two layers of denim she felt strength and challenge. The truck bounced and bucked, every rut pressing flesh against flesh. Now his hip ground into hers. She could have tried to scoot away on the plastic seat, but the next bump would only throw them back together, and, no matter what the cost to her nervous system, Tomara wasn't going to let Hayden guess that he unnerved her.

Let him stare, unaffected, out the window. Good! She would do the same thing. Or at least she would make him believe he'd been dismissed. Tonight, if they all came back from the prairie in one piece, she would run again. In the dark she would run until she'd left him behind.

"I haven't been out to that cave for years," Jay said as he eased the truck off the road and found his way onto the trail that consisted of two tire tracks scarred into the earth. "I'd forgotten it was out here."

"I was there. Once," Hayden said. "Unless someone knows what they're looking for, it looks like another shadow."

Once again silence reigned. She could see for miles in all directions. Her eyes were trained on the low, barren, rugged hills they were heading toward. A few clouds hugged the hills like lovers reluctant to say goodbye to the night. The cave was the most prominent feature of the hills, but a man or men flushed out of its cool darkness could hide almost anywhere in the roughened spires and caverns that served as contrast to the prairie that surrounded them. Most of the hills ended in flat tablerock formations and would serve as yet other hiding places. Maybe that's where her father and brother were. Maybe they were staring down at the slowly moving pickup, waiting, making plans.

Tomara tossed the thought away. It was unthinkable that they would have any plans other than escape. What was it her brother had said when she visited them yesterday? That he was afraid he'd never get out, that what David Kemper took for granted would never again be his.

That's what she wanted to tell Hayden—and Jay. Al and Hoagy were scared. Unwise and impulsive but only scared, not dangerous.

But if she said that would Hayden counter with words that would make her question what she was trying to believe?

The tracks carved by some long-forgotten vehicle and retained by years of antelope hunters and ranchers looking for stray cattle ran up to the base of the hills and then died. Jay cut the engine and got out. Hayden did the same, releasing Tomara from his physical presence, but she was slow to move. Her side was heated, pressed upon and heated. She should be relieved to have the wind touch her, erasing Hayden's imprint from her body if not her mind. She was, she told herself. Still, for a moment she sat, her hand aching with the need to touch him.

"I was thinking." Hayden was speaking loudly, his eyes relentlessly on Tomara. "You and Al and Hoagy have pretty much decided that this is their place. Is it possible this is where they keep the rest of their rifles?"

No! Tomara jerked her body out of the pickup, her thoughts of a second ago forgotten. She glared back at Hayden, hating everything about him. Al and Hoagy weren't armed desperadoes.

Or were they? What did she really know of the two men she hadn't seen except briefly for six years? Her father, and maybe now her brother, had always looked at rules and laws with eyes different from most. She wanted to believe it was inconceivable that they'd squirreled away weapons with the thought of holding off law enforcement officers. But then she still couldn't make herself believe that David Kemper had brought in the means to their escape. She didn't want to believe that of the young man. She wouldn't, except that nothing else made sense.

Hayden, and then Jay, slung their rifles over their shoulders. Tomara watched in horrified fascination. This wasn't really happening. Jay and Hayden looked like a couple of antelope hunters, not cops in pursuit of two-legged game.

"Don't kill them. Please don't kill them."

Damn! Why had they brought her up here? His flesh was still trying to fight off her impact. Even with the wind in his nostrils, Hayden could still smell what was feminine about Tomara. She should be back at Mandy's, safe, waiting. No, he amended. She wouldn't be safe from her thoughts, her fears, and that was why she was here. Why she'd made the impossibly hard decision to help them. Why she'd just said what she had.

"We can't make any promises, Tomara," he said, his voice rich with feeling. If he dared, he would take her in his arms and try to kiss away her fears. He would make both of them believe that they would survive the day. If he was wise, he would remind himself that they probably wouldn't be here if it wasn't for her.

"I know. I'm sorry I said that."

"Tomara?" It was Jay. "I want you to stay here."

Tomara jerked. "No. Jay, I came this far. I'm not going to stop now. Besides, you need me."

"Do we?"

He didn't want to look. To admit that he knew, really knew what she was going through. He didn't want to see her body stiffen. Most of all Hayden didn't want to hear what Tomara was saying.

"Yes, you do," she was saying. "I don't care whether you belive me. Whether either of you do. I didn't have anything to do with their getting their hands on a gun. I wanted them out of jail, but not this way. They have to get back. Face what has to be faced."

"Tell them that."

"That's why I'm going with you," Tomara made herself say in response to Jay's clipped words. "They won't shoot if I'm with you."

Thank God Jay didn't say anything, Tomara thought as the silent trio started upward. If he'd tried to argue with her, she wasn't sure what she would have done. If he'd once again told her to wait, she would have fallen apart.

They were walking side by side, two long, powerful sets of legs pitted against her slimmer and yet strong ones. Tomara tried to think of something, anything, to keep her mind off their reason for being here. Unfortunately the only thing her mind fastened on was the presence to her right. Hayden. She knew Jay belonged here. His roots and his great-grandfather's roots were in this land. His people had been living on the reservation on the other side of the hills for generations.

What she didn't understand was why she was coming to the same conclusion about Hayden.

He was city-born and raised. He should be there, not trudging through land beyond the reach of telephone poles and electricity. But he was. He knew how to dress, how to fit his muscles to the demands of the rugged hill. He understood what silence truly meant and that messages brought by the wind could mean the difference between life and death.

They had things in common. Tomara was only beginning to understand.

The better part of an hour later the trio made a discovery. Someone had been in the small, stale-smelling cave.

Clutching the remnants of a box of granola bars, Hayden freed his body from the confining space. "It wasn't that long ago," he said as he shook crumbs from the discarded wrappers. "Maybe earlier today even. Rodents haven't been in here to cart off what was left. Tell me something, Tomara. Is this the kind of thing Al and Hoagy like to eat?"

Tomara wanted to say no. She still wanted to deny that any of this was happening. "I don't know." She wouldn't look at Hayden. "Maybe."

"Maybe." Hayden was waiting for her to come out of the dark enclosure. "You can give us better than maybe, Tomara."

"No, I can't." The cave was safe. She felt insulated from him in it. But because she didn't want Hayden to know she needed to feel that way, Tomara backed out and rocked to her feet. The air out here was at least twenty degrees warmer than in the cave. "You want me to say it was Al and Hoagy who were in there. It might have been kids. Maybe someone else—"

"There's no one out here, Tomara."

Tomara wanted to argue the point. She could have pointed out that there was more than one approach to the hills. A vehicle could have come around the other way on the spur road leading from the reservation. Even now there might be any number of vehicles hidden on the far side of the hills. For years hunters had gravitated to the higher ground where they could keep an eye on the prairie below. All right, maybe it wasn't yet hunting season, but it wasn't inconceivable that—

Tomara discarded that thought. Another surfaced. For as long as she knew, there'd been rumors of petroleum deposits in this part of the state. Maybe some geologist had been through recently. He could have come across the cave and stopped for a meal.

No. If there were officials in the area, they would surely have checked in with both Jay and Hayden before taking off into the wilderness.

"All right." She felt defeated. "It's them."

"That's right, Tomara. It's them."

Why was he taunting her? Was Hayden getting some perverse pleasure out of forcing her to face what her family had become? If that was what he was trying, Tomara was equally determined not to allow him his pleasure. "If it is," she said through lips that refused to move, "then we all know what has to be done."

"Yeah. Damn. I wish we'd used the chopper. The hills go on forever. They could be anywhere."

"What do you want to do?"

Hayden seemed surprised by her subdued question. "I think we're going to have to spread out."

"That's what I was thinking," said Jay.

"But no so far apart that we can't hear a shout. A rifle shot."

A rifle shot. "Don't you have walkie-talkies?" that cold, accepting woman she'd become asked.

"Not on us," Jay supplied. "But I do have the binoculars. As long as we can see each other we should be able to cover a lot of territory."

Tomara let the men make their plans. It was only when they turned toward her that she fully understood what was being silently suggested. She was to go with one of them. Instead Tomara shook her head. "We have three people," she said through lips that once again failed to do her bidding. "Three can cover more territory than two."

"No." It was Hayden. "You're not going off by yourself."

"Why not? Never mind. I know the answer. You're thinking maybe I know where they are. That I'll sneak away and find them and maybe you'll never see any of us again."

Hayden didn't speak.

"It's not true," she went on when her own silence pressed against her. "I don't care whether you believe me or not, but it's not true. Look. You have the binoculars. You can keep an eye on me."

Widespread legs and eyes that didn't waver told Tomara she hadn't made her point.

"If they're here, they came all the way on foot. They won't be able to outrun your bullets."

"If you do your job, they won't try to."

Damn him. "That's right," Tomara made herself agree. "If I'm able to talk them into surrendering, there won't be any problems."

"And if you can't?"

"It isn't going to be that way, Hayden." No matter how deeply his eyes dug, she wasn't going to back down. "I wouldn't be out here if I didn't believe there was a peaceful way to end this. Let me be part of this, and I promise they'll come back with you. In one piece."

"I don't think we have a choice, Hayden."

Tomara acknowledged what Jay was saying, but she still didn't turn from Hayden. They were discussing something he'd never in her life thought she would have to and yet somehow, some way, she had the courage to say and do what was necessary. Either Hayden acknowledged that, and maybe even admired her for it, or he didn't. In the end that wasn't really the important thing.

Getting her father and brother out of this alive was.

When Hayden didn't say anything, Tomara shouldered her canteen and headed north. She was aware of a lonely hawk spiraling down and then up with the whim of the wind. A lizard slithered out of her way. Untrained eyes would never have noted the spider's nest trapped against a summer-baked bush, but Tomara saw that, as well. She divided her attention between keeping her footing on the ungiving rocks and scanning her surroundings for signs of humans.

Her thoughts were on the man who was probably even now watching her.

She didn't want it to be like that. Tomara wanted to be able to deal with Hayden in the same way she dealt with Jay. They were all engaged in an emotionally charged situation, but something else was operating where Hayden was concerned. Tomara couldn't give that something a name any more than she could pretend it didn't exist.

It was nearing noon. With the sun almost directly overhead, Tomara was able to take in a great deal of her surroundings. Occasionally her route took her into the small valleys connecting the hills, but she tried to stay along the ridges where she could see. And be seen. She thought about calling out her father's name, but she didn't want to arouse the suspicions of Hayden and Jay. If her father and brother were out here, they would spot her. They would probably see the two men, as well, but maybe it was better that way. Al and Hoagy had to understand something. What they'd done was serious. In a lifetime filled with scrapes and skirmishes, they were finally in over their heads.

And their daughter and sister had taken a stand on the side of law and order.

Usually Tomara was able to dismiss the summer heat. When she was walking or running she usually didn't give her footing a second thought. Today she was aware of everything.

Lifeless. At the same time filled with life. That was how Tomara saw the prairie below. It had a sound, a rhythm. The smell changed with the seasons but was always there, always a part of her.

Why did it feel as if Hayden belonged here? Tomara's thoughts went back to her earlier question. Was it simply because he wore the uniform of someone who was expected to fit? Or did it have to do with a body molded and shaped for a physical existence? He seemed to understand that the prairie could be both unforgiving and a lifetime mistress. Had he heard the siren's cry in the wind, tasted the seasons, watched an antelope race with power and grace over land that had been his since the beginning of time and understood that certain things had a right to be?

Would she ever be able to ask him?

She shouldn't be thinking about Hayden Conover. She was here to find her father and brother and convince them to give themselves up.

Although she didn't wear a watch, Tomara guessed that she'd been out on her own for the better part of an hour. She'd taken a drink and was mentally pacing herself for another once she was over the next ridge. She'd been able to see Hayden and Jay for the first fifteen minutes or so but no longer had any idea where they were. If Hayden was trying to keep an eye on her, he wouldn't be able to cover much territory.

That was his problem. If he couldn't trust her—if there was too much cop in him—

The sound very nearly stopped Tomara's heart. It rang out, echoed, echoed again. Instinctively Tomara dropped to her knees, thinking of nothing except that someone was shooting and she wasn't going to present herself as a target.

The sound wasn't repeated. In the silence Tomara understood a great deal. No matter what she might find, she had to follow the sound to its source.

Chapter Seven

At the sound of the rifle shot, the hawk who'd been float
ing above Tomara disappeared. Even with the hard crack
still echoing, she felt utterly alone. Her feet ought to keep
up with her emotions as she sprinted along one ridge, dipped
into a small valley and then hauled herself onto the next
crest. She could see a kneeling figure in the distance, but it
was another couple of minutes before she was close enough
to make out Hayden's dull green shirt. She hurried closer
but asked no questions.

Hayden was crouched over Jay. Jay wasn't moving.

Powerful eyes bored into Tomara's.

Hayden felt nothing. No. The truth was, he was feeling
too much. And hating every emotion. "They shot him," he
said. "And now they're gone. Running like the cowards they
are."

No! For some reason she didn't fully understand, To
mara refused to give the word life. Instead she hugged the
horror to her and dropped to her knees beside Hayden. She
was aware of nothing except the bright, wet stain spreading
over Jay Eagle's shoulder. Hayden had cupped his hand

under Jay's head and had gone back to his silent study of his friend. With her hand both numb and shaking, Tomara went to work. Carefully, so carefully, she pulled the buttons free and lifted the cotton away from Jay's flesh. In a distracted way she was aware that his lids were beginning to open. In a minute she would prepare herself to respond to whatever might be in them. Right now she had to know whether he would live or die.

Tomara had seen what a bullet could do to flesh. The open, bleeding hole didn't repulse her. She could only pray that he hadn't been hit by a bullet designed to explode on contact. She placed her hands on the outside of Jay's shoulder and lifted his inert arm off the ground. There was no exit wound.

"The bullet's still in him." Her voice hummed with barely suppressed emotion.

"And I've got to get him down out of here. Damn. Damn it to hell."

If he was damning her, Tomara couldn't do anything about that. "Not until we've done something about the bleeding."

"You've done enough. You keep your hands the hell off him."

"I didn't do this, Hayden. Think about that. I didn't do this."

"You know damn well who did."

Jay was staring up at her, his eyes reminding her of a small child unable to comprehend a hand lifted against him. "It's all right, Jay," Tomara whispered. "We're here. Think about that. We're here." Her father, her brother, couldn't have done this thing to him. They couldn't!

But who else?

There wasn't time to search for answers. Jay needed help. That damnable bullet had to be dug out of him and the bleeding stopped, and then she and Hayden would come back for answers.

She and Hayden. The combination was foreign, alien even. And yet she knew he wouldn't stop without answers. And she wouldn't let him search for them without her.

Hayden was talking to Jay, or at least trying to get the Sioux to listen. Hayden was telling him that they were going to have to somehow get down off the hills and into the pickup. It wasn't going to be easy for Jay. In fact it was going to hurt like hell. But because Hayden wasn't about to leave Jay up here, there wasn't any way out of it.

"You gotta shot of whiskey?"

Tomara ached with the need to touch, to hold, to speak to her old classmate, but with Hayden's eyes warning her to keep her distance, she could only lean over Jay and give him what smile she could drag out of herself.

"No whiskey, my friend," Hayden told Jay. "But once we've got you patched up, the two of us are going to tie one on."

"A promise?"

"A promise." Hayden still hadn't taken his eyes off Tomara. He didn't care if he scared her with what he knew was in his dark, accusing cop's eyes. Just before the shot rang out, he'd been thinking of Tomara, finding it in him to believe that she wanted to find her family and return them to justice as much as he did. They would put the escape behind them. Somehow he and Tomara would find the words that needed to be said. Somehow he would start to deal with what he felt for her and find out if she felt the same way. They would bridge the gap that stretched between them, and he would tell her he understood a great deal because she wasn't the only one to come from a family that didn't know what love and commitment was all about.

Hell. It wasn't going to happen. Ever.

"And then we're going to get our hands on who did this," he said to Jay.

"I didn't see anything," Jay was saying through clamped teeth. "I heard something. Can't say what it was. One minute I was standing. The next—"

"Tell me about it later," Hayden said. "Let's think about getting you fixed up so that lady friend of yours doesn't give you your walking papers." As he spoke, he reached into his front pocket and brought out a small pocketknife. One-handed, he flipped it open and began sawing at Jay's shirt

"What the hell..." Jay murmured. Anything else he might have said was lost under the weight of what he was feeling.

Tomara understood. She met Hayden's cold look with one of her own, then slid the ruined shirt off Jay's shoulder. He was still bleeding but not as profusely. Still, if they were going to get back to town, Jay would have to be moved and that might increase the blood loss. Hayden pulled the shirt out from under Jay. Tomara took the fabric out of his hands, and with Hayden gently positioning Jay, she went about tying a tourniquet. As she knotted the fabric, Jay moaned, but she didn't dare let his pain stop her.

Hayden was explaining to Jay that he was going to help him to his feet and then, if Jay had the strength, Hayden would piggyback him out. Jay's eyes took on a trapped look, but he nodded. "No bullets to bite. No whiskey. Hell of a mess."

"A mess that didn't have to happen," Hayden said with his eyes on Tomara.

It took both Hayden and Tomara's effort to ease Jay to his feet. The Sioux's face went white, and he bit into his lip, but he managed to stand while Hayden positioned himself to accept the burden of a man who weighed as much as he did.

Tomara placed her hands on either side of Jay's waist and called on a strength she didn't know she had, because Jay didn't have it in him to clamp his legs over Hayden's hips. She kept a hand pressed against Jay's back until she was sure he would stay in place. Hayden turned, facing her. His eyes asked questions, questions that had to do with why she was helping, but he didn't say anything. Then he settled his body for the labor ahead of him, and Tomara was privy to one man's bonding with another.

"The rifles," she said.

Once again the silent questions. "It has to be me, Hayden," she told him, wanting him to believe and trust her. "The rifles and the binoculars and the canteens." If it wasn't within Hayden to understand, to trust, then she wasn't going to waste energy trying to explain. Hayden didn't move. Instead he stood, trapped by his burden while Tomara wound the binoculars and canteens around her neck. Then she lifted the two loaded rifles and cradled them in her arms.

Tomara lost track of how much time was spent in the effort to get Jay back to the truck. She sweated. Hayden sweated and breathed deeply. Jay sweated and ground his teeth into his lips. They stopped occasionally to rest Hayden's back and sip at the now precious water. Almost nothing was said. No energy was wasted on something that could wait.

Tomara understood that before today was over she and Hayden, and Jay if he was able, would have to face the ramifications of the bullet lodged in the young police chief's shoulder. Hayden would slam her up against reality. He would more forcefully accuse her father and brother of trying to kill his best friend.

And what would she answer? That they'd been frightened, unthinking? That they couldn't possibly have meant to kill Jay Eagle?

But someone had. And the only someones Tomara could think of bore the same last name as hers.

Jay's wound was bleeding enough that the strip of fabric over it was crimson by the time they finally reached the truck. Hayden lowered himself until Jay was able to stand and then with an arm that shook, he yanked down the tailgate. "You're better off back here," he told Jay. He tore off his shirt with an angered movement, exposing glistening flesh. "This'll do as a pillow."

"I'll stay back there with him," Tomara offered. Her arms and neck ached with the weight of her own burden, but she wasn't about to expose her weariness. Hayden had carted a two-hundred-pound man.

"I don't trust you."

"Fine." Tomara's jaw ached. Her head pounded with backed-up emotion. "Then I'll drive, or don't you trust me to do that, either?"

His eyes, his damnable eyes were still tearing at her. "I have to, don't I? I don't have any choice."

Jay almost passed out from the effort of easing his body into the back of the pickup. Tomara searched the cab for something to cushion his body but was unable to come up with anything except the floor mats. With Hayden's help, she was able to position those under Jay, and then Hayden slid in next to his friend and lifted his head while Tomara slipped Hayden's wadded-up shirt under Jay.

Tomara didn't want to get close to Hayden, but there was no way that could be avoided in the cramped quarters. Her movement brought her close enough that she inhaled his sweat, the man scent of him. For a moment she was caught, a willing listener to an unspoken message. Then, the effort taking a great deal from her, she jumped out of the truck's bed and climbed into the cab, still carrying the primitive smell deep inside her.

Hayden talked to Jay. He was only half aware of what he said; what he wanted to do was give Jay something to think about. His mind felt as if it were going in a thousand directions at once. He wasn't sure he was looking for answers; he wasn't sure he'd want to acknowledge them if he came up with any. Tomara had put herself out. She didn't have to. There was no one to force her. But she'd sweated almost as much as he had, and she hadn't been able to hide her reaction to what had happened to Jay. Whether or not she had anything to do with the breakout, she certainly hadn't anticipated anything like this happening.

Was she going through hell?

He didn't want that for her. He didn't want any of them to have gone through this. Not Jay, because his friend was in pain and would be flat on his back for too long. Not him, because his legs were killing him and for a few seconds he'd been scared that Jay was dead and he'd had to ask himself if a rifle was pointed at him, as well.

But mostly not for Tomara, because he needed to believe that she was as good as she was beautiful. That what he felt for her went deeper than the usual male reaction. That he was capable of that kind of compassion and she worthy of it.

Every bump registered in Tomara's arms, forcing her to concentrate on making the trip as smooth as possible for Jay. Occasionally she glanced at the rearview mirror, but all she could see was Hayden's bulk crouched over his friend. It would have been easier on her nerves if she'd done nothing except drive and think about the goal. But Hayden was back there. And she had an insane need to be touched by him. Simply touched. It wasn't something she could shake off, any more than she could dismiss the simple fact that six years away from the prairie hadn't taken her far enough from its brand on her soul.

She understood she had to leave, soon, if she was going to remember how essential leaving had been.

She also knew that was impossible.

Driving commanded less of her attention once Tomara was on the main road. She garnered a few curious glances from people who recognized Copper's law enforcement vehicle but not the driver. Once again Tomara looked in the rearview mirror. This time Hayden was looking back, making contact.

She didn't understand what was in his eyes.

Tomara pulled around to the back of Waylin Saul's office and hurried in to tell the nurse practitioner that he had an emergency. Somehow she warded off his questions, leaving that up to Hayden and Jay.

Jay was conscious. Conscious and in pain. "I don't care what those old cowboy movies make you think. This hurts like hell."

"I'm sure it does," Waylin muttered as he skinned into the pickup. He tossed the ruined bandage aside but didn't touch Jay's bleeding shoulder. "It's still in there. What'd you do? Scare some poachers?"

"Something like that," Hayden supplied. He hadn't left Jay's side. "Can we get him out of here?"

"I thought we might," Waylin said before ordering Tomara to go in for a stretcher. A few minutes later the two men were lifting Jay out of the pickup and Tomara was trailing behind, not sure her presence was wanted, but unwilling to leave before she knew whether Jay was going to be all right.

Jay was going to need surgery, the nurse practitioner announced once he was finished his examination. Nothing major, he assured Jay, but he didn't figure Jay wanted to go through life with a bullet lodged in his collarbone. Jay had his choice. He could either sleep through the operation or stick around for the fun. Jay opted to remain awake. He wanted his fiancée told but not until the surgery was over.

"The two of you are going to have to get out of here," Waylin told Tomara and Hayden. "There simply isn't going to be room for all of us in there."

Hayden nodded. "Keep the bullet," was all he said.

"Evidence? Yeah. I guess so." Waylin shook his head, disturbing the long strands he never seemed to find time to have cut. From the way his eyes traveled from Jay to Hayden to Tomara, Tomara guessed he was beside himself with curiosity but trying to maintain his professionalism. He would get the whole story soon enough. And once he did, it wouldn't be long before the whole town knew.

"Where are you going?"

Startled, Tomara turned to look at Hayden. They were standing outside the operating room in a dimly lit, empty hall. He was at least ten feet away, and yet Tomara felt no sense of freedom. She remembered her need to be touched. By him. "You tell me," she returned. "Where can I go?"

"Nowhere. Least of all back out where we were."

"Of course not. You wouldn't want me to tell *them* that they didn't finish the job. That they'll have to come back and gun Jay down."

Hayden blinked. He hated her courage. He hated the wall between them. Irrationally he wanted to hurt her, to see if she could hurt as much as he did. He despised himself for doing what he was doing, but he wasn't going to apologize. His emotions, the emotions he always believed himself capable of keeping under control, were getting away from him. He didn't know what to do with them. Except to let them out and face the consequences later.

He took a step closer; Tomara willed herself not to move. She was losing her self-control. If she didn't plan every move, every word, he would discover everything the day had done to her.

"Do you really think I'd do that?" she went on. "Hayden, I've known Jay all my life. Do you really think I wanted this to happen to him?"

"I don't know. Right now I don't know anything. I want to make sure he gets through this all right."

"He will," Tomara said because she needed to hear the words as much as she believed Hayden did. He still wasn't wearing his shirt. She wondered if he was aware of that. She wondered if she would ever forget how he looked standing spread-legged not enough feet away with what they'd gone through deep in his eyes and his body too strong to be ignored. "He's going to be all right."

"Does that matter?"

"Stop that!" Self-control was dust in the wind. Another second and it might be gone. "I didn't have anything to do with that. And neither did they."

"You expect me to believe that?"

Of course she didn't. The truth was, she wasn't sure she believed it herself. If she gave herself the space and time necessary for thinking, she might not survive her conclusions. The only thing Tomara knew was that she couldn't answer Hayden's question.

"I'm going back to Mandy's," she said. "You'll tell me when he's done with Jay?"

"You aren't going to stay here?"

"I can't." Somehow she had to find the strength needed to give power to her voice. Somehow. "You don't want me here."

He was coming closer, eating away at the space, taking away the air she needed to breathe. "I hope to hell I never again have to do what I did today. Jay means a lot to me, Tomara. A hell of a lot."

"He means a lot to me, too." No. He was only inches away. He hadn't touched her, and yet she felt his imprint. His anger. His pain. It wasn't supposed to be like this.

"Does he?"

Too much. Hayden was asking too much of her. There was no way she could keep what had happened out there from crawling out of her. Tomara blinked. It didn't help. She blinked again, feeling something hot and dry and dangerous. She saw Jay sprawled on the rocks, blood ruining his shirt, his body stiller than a body should be. She remembered the endless echo of a rifle shot—a trigger pulled by her father or brother?

She wasn't going to be able to go on standing. The wall. Yes. She could lean against the wall and breathe in stale air and the scent of the man who was standing too close and try to right her world. Despite what she knew she was giving away, Tomara closed her eyes and tried to concentrate on putting order back into her world.

Instead she saw Jay. And Hayden crouched over him.

"They might not be much of a family, Hayden. I know that better than anyone else. Breaking out of jail was stupid. But trying to kill—killing."

"Don't make excuses for them. And don't delude yourself."

Anger slashed through Tomara. "That's not what I'm doing. I don't know why I'm talking to you. I don't know why I'm wasting my breath. But there's something I'm going to say. And like it or not, you're going to hear it." She waited a fraction of a second, daring Hayden to deny her this. He didn't. "They aren't violent men. They wouldn't do this. I don't have proof, now. But I can't believe they'd do this." She jerked her head in the direction of the operating room.

"I said it once, Tomara," Hayden said in a voice that tried to mask his emotion. "Don't delude yourself. *Family?* It's a word. Only a word."

"And you're an expert on that? You know everything anyone needs to know about blood ties? About what goes on inside the heart and mind of someone else?"

No. He wasn't an expert on blood ties. The truth was, until he'd come to Copper, he'd known nothing about what held people together. A few days ago he'd wanted to tell her how it was for him, but he didn't anymore. "Get out of here, Tomara. Now."

Hayden was giving her an order. Another time she would lash out at him, tell him he had no right. But everything Tomara was and had ever been was locked up in the impossible task of trying to ward off the nightmare that today had become. What had been hot and dry turned wet.

She was crying. Hated, resented tears that pushed past her defenses and exposed her to the man who'd shared the nightmare with her. In an effort to distance herself from the helpless feeling, Tomara opened her eyes.

She hadn't been able to read what was in his eyes when they were on the road coming into Copper.

Now— No. That couldn't be confusion. Or pain.

Mandy's house was too silent. The thought of having to stay here until her friend returned was more than Tomara could handle. She tried to busy herself by doing a little housework, but Mandy could resent someone else—even her—taking over. TV didn't interest her. She would have gone back to the medical office if it hadn't been for the thought of having to face Hayden. Somehow she would have to kill at least an hour until she was sure Jay was out of surgery.

Home.

It wasn't really home, Tomara reminded herself, but it was a place she could go and be herself. Tomara locked the door behind her and climbed into the Jeep.

As she drove, her thoughts shifted to what the day had brought. She still wanted to scream her denial that her relatives had used a gun to get themselves out of jail, but denial had never been her way.

Tomara faced facts. Al and Hoagy had leveled a gun at a young, scared trustee and buffaloed their way to freedom. They'd convinced some trucker to give them a ride, not back home where someone would be sure to look for them, but to a desolate spot where a couple of desperate men might find a hiding place while they tried to plan their future.

Jay had been shot with a rifle.

Tomara worked the thought around in her mind, trying to make it hold water. If—oh, God!—if Al or Hoagy were responsible for the bullet in Jay, then they would have had to get their hands on a hunting rifle. They hadn't come home. The only place the rifle could possibly have been was in the cave.

That didn't make sense. The town's youngsters knew about the cave. They might not go to it often, but there was always the possibility that someone would hike up there. Her father wouldn't risk anyone coming across one of his prized possessions. He simply wouldn't have left a rifle up there.

But no one else had been in the hills. At least, as far as Tomara knew, no one had.

She pulled into the yard and cut the engine. Maybe if she had someone to share her thoughts with—someone to help her put the pieces together. But there was no one. Two people had been in the hills with her. One was in no shape to talk. The other would rather go through hell than have anything to do with her.

Neil Blake hadn't come after his tractor. Tomara wondered if she would be able to force herself to call the rancher and offer to help him get it out of the garage.

Cleaning up the kitchen had helped. At least some of the stale odor had dissipated. Tomara glanced around, eager, desperate for something to do. Her short laugh was mirthless. She could spend weeks here and not accomplish everything that needed to be done, and to what end? Al and Hoagy Metcalf were probably never going to live here again. And she couldn't imagine herself staying out here alone.

Without facing what she was doing, Tomara once again went through the house inch by inch. She didn't give a name to what she was doing, but she was looking in places large enough to hide a rifle. When that search proved fruitless, as she knew it would, Tomara wandered out to the garage and did the same thing.

She'd given up and was coming back into the sunshine when she heard the sound.

Someone was going into the house through the back door.

No vehicles had pulled up while she was in the garage, which led to only one conclusion. Whoever had come was on foot.

And that could be only Al and Hoagy.

They were in the kitchen. Al was eating cereal dry out of the box while Hoagy was attacking a can of beans with a rusted can opener. When she walked in, Hoagy started but her father didn't even blink. "I figured you were around here somewhere," he said by way of greeting. "Using the Jeep all the time, are you?"

Anger was such a ready emotion today. It was going to be next to impossible to keep it in check. "What are you doing here?"

Al crushed corn flakes in his palm. "Eating. You've been working on the place."

Tomara felt like knocking the cereal box from her father's hand. Instead she reached into a drawer for a clean spoon and handed it to Hoagy so he would have something to eat with. "You broke out."

With his mouth full, Hoagy responded to his sister's comment. "We were scared, sis. Leonard, he's been telling us we're in deep trouble. That man doesn't pull his punches. We're going to hang."

"They don't hang people anymore," Tomara pointed out, wondering why making that distinction was necessary. "Hoagy, Leonard's going to give you the best defense possible. I can't believe he'd tell you that you don't have a chance. And now you've screwed everything up by breaking out."

Al crunched down on another handful. "What would you have done? Sit there and wait for them to come and fry you?"

"I would not have grabbed a gun and forced my way out of jail." Tomara spoke every word as if she were trying to make a small child understand a fundamental fact.

"Says you. The gun's there. Someone's giving us a key to the front door. I'd be a fool not to take it."

Someone had given them the gun. Tomara already knew that and yet hearing it made the situation even more impossible to understand. "Who?" was the only question that needed to be asked.

"Who? How the hell do we know? Maybe it was you. All I know is, it showed up in the cell."

"I wasn't in your cell." This was insane. Why was she arguing with her father about this when she wasn't ready to believe anything he told her anyway?

"Neither was anyone 'cept the guards. You figure it out."

Tomara couldn't. "What are you going to do now?" she asked, sounding like a small child seeking her father's wisdom. Unfortunately she wasn't a child. The adult she was knew that whatever she heard, it wouldn't be filled with wisdom.

Hoagy belched. "We don't know, sis. We ain't got any money. I've been trying to tell him—" Hoagy jabbed a finger at his father "—we ain't got anywhere to go."

The impulse to shake her brother, and her father, was so strong that for a moment Tomara could do nothing except ride the wave. But the deed had been done. Al and Hoagy had broken out of jail.

And maybe that wasn't all they'd done.

Tomara chose her words carefully. "You hitched a ride with a trucker. He dropped you off out of town. Why'd you have him do that?"

Al laughed, a grating sound. "What do you think we should have done? Prance through town and invite everyone out here for a party? I figured if someone tracked us, they'd get as far as where we were dropped off. We'd skirt Copper and come here when no one was looking. We'd get a few things and be out of here before anyone knew anything."

"What kind of things were you after?" Tomara asked because she wasn't ready to ask the one question that had to be asked.

"Food. A little protection."

At the word, Tomara cooled. "What kind of protection?"

Again Al laughed his hard laugh. This time Tomara caught a small echo of fear behind the sound. "What do you think? We're going to have to live off the land for a while, at least until we can figure where we're going. We're going to need to hunt."

Tomara took a necessary breath. She didn't want to think about her father's being afraid. She didn't want to think about two desperate men searching for solutions that simply weren't there. "Jay and Hayden were out here. I told you, they confiscated the weapons that were in the house."

"Yeah."

"Then what are you going to hunt with?"

Hoagy had finished off his can of beans. With his head in the cupboard, he answered his sister's question. "There's a place. A secret place where we keep things."

The cold she'd acknowledged a second ago rushed back. "The cave?"

"Cave? You gotta see this, sis. No one'd ever think to look behind the garage. Someone goes out there, all they see is a little pile of lumber. But under that pile—"

Al interrupted his son with a warning look. "We can't stay around. Hoagy, you throw together some food. I'll get the rifles."

"No, you won't." Although she couldn't feel her legs, Tomara planted herself between her father and the door. "Not until you answer some questions."

"We don't have time."

"You'll make time. Dad, Hoagy, Jay was shot today."

Tomara had thought she'd have to say more to spell out the point she was trying to make, but the look on her father's face allowed her to remain silent. He blinked. The muscles in his jaw seemed to ooze out of him. "He gonna be okay?"

"I think so." *Maybe, no thanks to you.* "You know why I'm telling you this, don't you?"

"We didn't do it."

Tomara didn't reach deep enough to ask whether she believed her father. She would deal with that later. "Where's the gun? The one you used to break out with?"

"You haven't said it yet, girl," Al pressed. "I said we didn't shoot Jay. Do you believe me?"

"Answer my question. Where's the gun you had?"

Hoagy's laugh slid across the room. "It was empty. Not worth a plugged nickel. If that was someone's idea of a joke—"

Tomara pressed a palm against her forehead. She had no idea how long the headache had been building, only that it was now fully grown. She felt as if she were staring down at a thousand-piece puzzle with no idea how to begin putting it together. "You have to give yourselves up." Once again she was a teacher speaking to a slow pupil. "Come with me now. We'll go to Hayden—"

"Not Hayden. He's not the law in Copper."

"He is while Jay's hurt." A week ago Tomara's world consisted of work, fixing up her place, quiet evenings with a few friends. Now she was discussing murders and shootings and people on the run from the law. That those on the run were her family made the situation even more impossible. "You'll have to go back to jail. Tell Leonard everything about that gun. Make people believe that you didn't have a rifle, and you didn't shoot Jay."

Hoagy was weakening. Tomara could see it in his eyes. But because he turned to his father, Tomara concentrated on the older man. "Dad," she began, thinking back to the years when it had been easy to call him that. "This isn't some game you're playing. It isn't a matter of trying to outrun the law, providing you can hide from them. If you don't face up to this—if you—"

The low, steady cough of a large engine cut through what Tomara was trying to say. Feeling too much like a hunted animal, she sprinted into the living room and looked out the window. Hayden's Bronco was easing to a stop next to the Jeep. A thousand half thoughts chased through her mind, but only one held.

Hayden was here. Hayden with his condemnation of everything she stood for.

If it hadn't been for the sound of the back door slamming, Tomara might have stood there forever watching the big man unfold himself from the Bronco. With a cry propelling her, Tomara raced back into the kitchen. It was empty. She jerked at the door and ran outside. The two figures were little more than blurs heading for the prairie.

Something was cutting into her hand. When she could no longer see her father and brother, Tomara turned her attention to what was unimportant. Somehow she'd grazed her hand along the door and picked up a sliver now embedded in her palm.

Tomara was trying to clamp her fingernails around the sliver when Hayden joined her a minute later. He stepped close enough that he could see what she was doing, but said nothing. Did nothing. Finally, grimacing a little, Tomara managed to yank it out. She flicked her tongue over the wound to catch the small bubble of blood and thought of a man with a bullet in his shoulder.

"You followed me out here."

"I put two and two together and figured that was where you'd be. Maybe you don't care, but Jay's all right."

How could Hayden say she might not care? Tomara wanted to slap away his words, but there'd already been too much violence today. Too much unearthing of emotions. "When can I see him?"

"Tomorrow. Waylin says he's going to spend the next few hours sleeping. What are you doing out here?"

Tomara wondered if Hayden had seen her father and brother fleeing. No, she answered her own question. Otherwise he wouldn't be standing here talking to her. She could, some primitive part of her told her, keep that to herself. She and Hayden could talk about Jay and stalk around each other like wary warriors, and she wouldn't have to complicate an already incredibly complicated relationship.

"I couldn't stay at Mandy's. I had to do something."

"That's all there was to it?"

How could she possibly tell him about emotions so tangled that if she didn't do something her head might explode? "No." Tomara didn't say anything else. Instead she turned around and walked back into the house. She was going to run water over her palm. She didn't care whether Hayden followed her or not.

The moment she was inside the kitchen, Tomara knew treating her small wound wasn't why she was here. On the kitchen counter stood a spilled box of cereal and an empty can of beans.

"They were here."

Tomara turned around. Somehow the day had turned to late afternoon. The colors in the kitchen were richer, and the man in the tiny room with her was absorbing too much of that richness. She should hate him; life would be much simpler if she could do that. But he was strength and competence, and beneath that, compassion for his friend, and Tomara couldn't dismiss that. He was also the only man she'd ever met who challenged her in this frightening and yet somehow exciting way.

"Yes. They were here. I talked to them."

"Did you? Why am I not surprised? After all, that's what you came out here for."

Hayden's words were to be expected. All he'd done for days now was attack her. Still, she wasn't going to go on thinking that way. "No." Without being aware of what she was doing, Tomara scooped up the loose cereal and put it back in the box. "I didn't think about their being out here. I told you. I was restless. Upset. I couldn't stay where I was."

"And you expect me to believe that? Come on, Tomara. I'm not a fool." Hayden placed his hand over the empty can and leaned, flattening it in a telling motion. "This isn't a damn game we're playing. It's about time you stopped lying."

Damn him! If only she could dismiss him. If only she'd never met this potent game warden.

There was something she could do. Silent, Tomara turned her back on Hayden and stalked from the house. She was right; he was following her. Good, she thought as she made her way to the far side of the garage. It was just as Hoagy had said, a short pile of lumber propped against the garage's outside wall.

Ignoring her injured palm, Tomara started throwing the lumber aside. Slowly, with no idea of what she would find, she lifted the last one. It wasn't exactly a trap door, but there was a piece of wood tamped into the earth. A rope handle made removing the wood easy. Underneath Tomara found a small, long hole lined with gunny sacks. The hole housed three rifles.

Tomara straightened. He was close. Too close. In another world she would have reached out and touched him. "I haven't lied about anything, Hayden. Maybe now you'll believe me."

Chapter Eight

Hayden accepted the rifles Tomara handed to him. His mind was a million miles from what his arms were doing. Although the woman beside him hadn't said a word, Hayden heard the silent message.

Tomara was giving him a great deal more than three weapons. For a reason he either couldn't or didn't dare understand, at this moment she was being utterly honest with him. The guns represented what the police needed to seal her family's fate. Surely one of these would produce a bullet scarred identically to the one that had put an end to Bart Renfree.

He'd never seen eyes that large and hurting on a human being. Tomara looked utterly vulnerable and alone, and although Hayden had spent too long struggling to distance himself from people who were hurting, the lessons he'd learned during those years as a cop failed him now. With her eyes, Tomara was asking to be trusted. With her defiant chin, she was asking to be believed.

And with her woman's body, she was challenging him to ignore a message as old as time. Hayden couldn't make himself believe that Tomara knew what she was doing. Her world had become a nightmare. Surely she wouldn't be aware of her body right now. He might want to believe her a sorcerer, a cold, calculating witch using her knowledge of men and their reaction to her to twist him to her will.

But he couldn't.

"What else did they tell you, Tomara?" he asked, surprising himself with his ability to be gentle. "Is this all of them?"

"I think so." She hadn't dropped her eyes. Her courage made an impact he wouldn't forget.

"Then I think we better get out of here."

"You're not going to go after them?"

For answer Hayden let his eyes sweep over the horizon. "Even if I knew which way they headed, I'll never be able to catch them now."

Tomara pointed. "That's where they were going."

She'd begun the day with her hair braided into submission, but several strands around her face had wrestled their way to freedom. They slid along her throat and cupped around her ears, giving Tomara a femininity Hayden would have to be unconscious not to be aware of. A quick look at her slender waist and he wasn't sure even being unconscious would be enough of an insulation.

Coming out here hadn't been wise after all. He'd come because he might catch her at something—at least that's what he'd told himself. Now he wasn't sure that had been it at all. "Tell me something, Tomara. If I jumped in the Bronco now and took off after them, what would you do?"

"The Bronco would never make it."

"That's not the point. You didn't have to tell me where they went, and you sure as hell didn't have to tell me about these." Hayden indicated the rifles.

"No. I didn't."

"Then why?"

After a look that went on long enough to make Hayden uncomfortable, Tomara turned on her heels and started back toward the house. Hayden followed, trying to keep his eyes off the easy sway of her hips and not succeeding. Beyond all reason he wanted to go back in time . . . and rewrite history. Tomara would walk into Mandy's Saloon and he would be there. Waiting. Her father and brother would be at home waiting for her to come visit, but first she was stopping by to say hello to Mandy. She would walk into the dusky saloon, and the radio would be pounding out a love song, and Hayden would get to his feet and hold out his hands and she would melt into him.

In that new beginning things would be right between them.

"Come back with me, Tomara."

"Why? So you can arrest me?"

The challenge hurt. Enough that Hayden was determined to change things between them. Or at least to try. "No. I'm not going to arrest you. What I'd like, what I think we need, is for the two of us to sit down and talk."

"I've told you everything I know, Hayden. I don't know where they're going." She'd stopped walking. She planted her hands in her back pockets and turned around. "I was wrong," she said softly. "I haven't told you everything. When I told them about Jay, they were shocked. You don't have to believe that. I don't expect you to, but they were."

It wasn't going to be as easy as he'd tried to make it sound. No matter how much he wanted to turn things around with Tomara, too much stood between them. For a moment Hayden almost convinced himself that he didn't need that after all. Tomara Metcalf was cooperating with the law. That was all she was required to do.

The argument would have held water except for one distracting factor. She was the most compelling woman he'd ever known.

"I need to get these rifles back to town. And I want you to come with me."

"It's the last thing I want to do."

"I don't think so." Without saying anything more, Hayden carried the rifles to the Bronco and slipped them inside. His hands free, he turned around. She hadn't moved. Good. It was easier to think with her that far away. "I think you want to talk to me as much as I want to talk to you."

"Why would I want to do that? You don't believe anything I say."

This wasn't the time to speak. Words only swirled around them, clouding the air. Without knowing enough about why he was doing it, Hayden left the Bronco and came to stand no more than two feet away. He wanted to take her hand. He wanted to touch and hold her. The hell of it was, he had no right to do either. He could do nothing except wait. And care.

Jay. She should be thinking about Jay. The policeman might not want to see her, but he couldn't very well turn her away. She would stand beside his bed and convince herself that he really was going to live, and she would tell him how terribly sorry she was that this had happened, and then—

Tomara had no idea what she would do with her life after that single act was completed.

"Are you waiting for me? You aren't going to leave until I do?"

"That's right. But not because I don't trust you. Because I don't think you should be out here alone."

That was why it was so hard to think about Jay. Hayden had her so off balance that Tomara had no idea what to do with her ricocheting emotions. "I don't believe *you*."

"Believe, Tomara."

"Why don't you just walk out of here, Hayden? Take your rifles and do whatever you're going to do to them so you can tie a noose around my father's and brother's necks. Do your damn job and leave me."

"Is that what you really want?"

No. "I don't know what I want." For a heartbeat the words made no impact. And then Tomara was left with no choice but to accept the consequences of what she'd just said. She touched the words and the meaning, or lack of meaning behind them. It was so desolate out here. So lonely. The few minutes she'd been able to spend with her family had nearly torn her apart. She wanted to be able to tell herself that she had her emotions back under control, but with Hayden Conover here that was impossible.

He was touching her. Not with his hands, his fingers, but in a way that went deeper. How was that possible? Tomara asked as Hayden waited, strong and silent, for her. He was a man. Only a man. Words and eye contact and an emotion-charged day spent together shouldn't make that much of an impact.

But it was happening.

Tomara didn't try to speak. If she said anything, it would reveal too much. He would know she had no strength around him and that right now all she wanted out of life was his trust. His respect. Maybe even his love. Silently she took refuge behind the wheel of the Jeep. If Hayden wanted to follow her back into town, that was his right. She wasn't going to ask permission, and she wasn't going to explain her actions. Most of all she wasn't going to question what she was feeling.

Jay was numbed from pain pills but alert enough that he was able to acknowledge Tomara's presence. She hadn't expected him to smile or welcome her with open arms, but at least he thanked her for her role in bringing him back to town. "It's a hell of a mess, isn't it?" he said. "Even when I knew you were coming back here, I never figured it would turn out this way."

Tomara had just taken Jay's hand when Hayden walked into the room. Hard as it was to face Jay, it would be even more difficult to pick up where she and Hayden had left off. Fighting off the fear that today was a long way from over, Tomara concentrated on telling Jay what had happened at the house. She thought about repeating what she'd told Hayden about her father's reaction to hearing Jay had been hurt, but because she was afraid it would only lead to another argument, she left that up to Hayden.

Instead, Hayden explained that he'd been in contact with the state police. "They're throwing a lot of manpower our way. They don't take too kindly to the wounding of a fellow officer."

"Waylin's been in and out of there a couple of times," Jay said around his thick tongue. "I don't know if he's gotten the gossip mill running yet."

"It doesn't matter." Hayden had come closer than was necessary. Tomara wondered if it was in an effort to protect his friend, or because he had no intention of anything being said that he wasn't privy to. "It's going to happen. And soon." He turned toward Tomara. "How are you going to handle it?"

Tomara wasn't ready for the question. She especially wasn't ready for her reaction to what she sensed was compassion on Hayden's part. "No one's going to talk to me," she whispered. "They'll talk behind my back."

"They won't if you confront them."

"Why should I do that?" Hayden had her so off balance. If only she could count on what she was going to think and feel around him.

"Why shouldn't you? You aren't the one who's going to be on trial."

"There won't be a trial if you don't catch them."

"We will, Tomara. Don't you doubt that. We will."

This conversation, like the one at the house, was going nowhere. It might not have been wise, but Tomara leaned forward and touched a gentle kiss to Jay's forehead. "Did Waylin say how long you'll be in bed?"

"I'll be out of here in the morning," Jay said, his slow speech making Tomara wonder whether he'd be able to make good on his statement. "I figured I'd get some sleep tonight. Make Waylin happy. But first thing in the morning Lisa is going to take me to her place. She's taking the boys over to her mom's right now. I don't know how she's taking this. I want her to see I'm doing all right."

"Don't push it, Jay," Tomara said. Then she told him goodbye and left without saying anything to Hayden. She closed the door with fingers that were reluctant to do her bidding and started down the hall leading to sunlight, her shoes silent on the floor.

Hayden waited for the presence of Tomara to stop. When that didn't happen, he pushed aside thoughts of a young woman with hollowed-out eyes and told Jay about the rifles and Tomara's admission that her father and brother had been at the house when he pulled up. The two men talked briefly about who Hayden needed to get in touch with at the state crime lab. Then, because it made no sense to go back over everything that had happened since morning, Hayden stepped to the window and looked out at what was left of the day.

He had no idea how long he'd been silent when Jay spoke. "It's been hell for her."

"Yes. It has."

"I thought you might give me an argument about that."

Hayden turned back around. "Yesterday I might have. But—out at the house—she looked pretty raw. She's hurting."

"Did she tell you that?"

"What do you think?" Hayden's voice was soft. "No. She's keeping everything locked up inside her."

"And we're not making it easy on her."

"Us?" Hayden laughed, but there was nothing light about the sound. "That's nothing compared to what her relatives are putting her through."

"Maybe." Jay drew out the word, and Hayden thought he might be falling asleep. "But I've been thinking. Except for Mandy and maybe Leonard, she's isolated from everyone in Copper. You and I have spent more time with her than Mandy has and what happens? She's forced to go around feeling like a suspect herself."

"You don't think she is?" Hayden asked.

Jay closed his eyes. He breathed deeply several times before speaking. "I can't believe that. I just can't. Hayden, I grew up with that girl. All right, maybe we weren't close. But there's one thing I knew about her. She had a code. That code would never allow for something like that."

Damn it, there was no way Hayden could get Tomara off his mind. He stayed with Jay a few more minutes, but it was obvious that his friend was nodding off. After assuring herself that Waylin was around to keep an eye on Jay, Hayden walked over to the police station. Not long after, two state patrol cars pulled up and Hayden spent the next half hour with them. Once they'd split up, one car heading back to the spot where the trucker had dropped off his hitchhikers, the other on its way to the Metcalf house, Hayden put in the necessary call to the state crime lab. They weren't able to send anyone out right away, but if Hayden could get the evidence over to Sidney tonight or in the morning . . . Hayden told them he'd be by early in the morning.

Then there wasn't anything left to do. Sure, he could have jumped into the helicopter and headed out to look for Tomara's relatives. But it was almost dark. His guess was that Al and Hoagy were still on foot and had little more than the clothes on their backs. Even if they tried to get out of the county, they weren't going to be able to accomplish that overnight.

Tomorrow, after he'd finished his business with the crime lab, he'd connect with the state police and see about coordinating a land-and-air search.

Tonight he'd find Tomara.

So this was what it felt like to be trapped. If she left Mandy's house, she would have to face stares and whispers. But staying here meant no respite from her emotions. Only half aware of what she was doing, Tomara went in search of something to drink, but Mandy didn't keep her cupboards stocked with liquor. She picked up a magazine, thumbed through it and put it down without any recollection of what she'd read. The TV held no distraction, and although she was hungry, she couldn't put her mind to the complexities of fixing a meal.

If only she'd had more time to talk to Al and Hoagy. If only Hayden hadn't interrupted them.

Hayden.

No. She wasn't going to think about him. Somehow she would have to find a way to get in touch with her father and brother and convince them to give themselves up before there were more injuries. Or another death.

That was what tonight's restlessness was about. Lives were in danger, the lives of two people who might be undeserving but nonetheless were incredibly important to her. They were in danger because Hayden was after them.

Hayden.

Angry, Tomara paced. No matter where she went in the room, and in her thoughts, she kept colliding with Hayden Conover.

But maybe it was better to face him straight on instead of trying to pretend he didn't exist. She could ask him what kind of danger her father and brother were in. Somehow she would keep desperation and emotion out of her voice and ask logical questions and demand impartial answers. She wouldn't stand for this condemnation, and she certainly wouldn't let herself react to whatever it was that lurked below the surface of the man.

That was it. She would call him up and—

But maybe he was looking for Al and Hoagy right now.

Mandy. Was that Mandy home early? No. Mandy wouldn't have knocked.

Hayden.

"I wasn't sure you'd be here. Do you mind if I come in?"

Don't talk like that. Tomara could handle anger and distance from the man. What she couldn't handle was this politeness. "Do I have any choice?"

"You always have a choice, Tomara." He was inside; Tomara couldn't remember whether she'd given him any indication that he could do that. "But I thought maybe you'd like to know what's happening."

"Happening? Jay's all right, isn't he?"

"Jay's fine. Sleeping. I've been talking to the state police and on the phone to Sidney."

"And?"

Hayden told her about what tomorrow would entail for him. She managed to concentrate on his words, but too soon he was finished. She should be reacting to the reality of more police out at the place—her place. "I didn't think about that," she said softly. "About the state police getting involved."

"That bothers you?"

What about this nightmare didn't bother her? "They don't know Dad and Hoagy. They won't understand how confused they are."

"The state police's concern will be with protecting themselves and others against two men they consider dangerous."

Tomara sat. What she wanted to do was wrap her arms around her body and begin rocking, somehow finding her way back to a more innocent time. She needed to cry, and yet it was terribly important that she didn't let Hayden see her weakness.

He was sitting beside her; she had no idea how that had happened. "Do you want to talk about it?" he asked. His tone was different this time, gentler, softer. With all her heart, Tomara wanted to believe what she was hearing.

"I don't think so." He shouldn't be this close. He had no right to challenge her. She was finding it difficult to focus on anything except him. "I think I'm talked out."

"Maybe. Maybe not. I wasn't going to come here tonight. But—"

"But you did. Why?"

It was a moment before Tomara realized she wasn't going to get an answer to her question. Hayden was staring at the window across the room. For the first time since they'd met, she wondered if he was as aware of her as she was of him.

The awareness grew. She pushed to her feet and walked over to the window. It was dusk; the sky around Copper had turned rose. The sunset did something beautiful to the quiet town. Tomara didn't want to be aware of the romantic painting. She didn't need this.

But it was happening. She thought of the man watching her, of the slow settling of what might be the worst day of her life, of the promise of night's peace.

She began speaking for herself, not caring whether Hayden heard or believed. "I wanted to hate Copper. Long before I left, all I could think about was getting away. I told myself I'd never come back, that there would never be anything here for me. I was wrong. I'm back."

"And right now you're thinking you're trapped."

"Yes." The admission was given grudgingly.

Hayden joined her. Tomara didn't want him that close, and yet she did. She'd been wrong. There would be no peace for her tonight. There would only be loneliness, but as long as he was here, she could put off the sense of being utterly alone. Even if he was a reminder of everything that had gone wrong, he had someone to focus on.

The only someone.

"You didn't have to come back," he said. "When Leonard called, you could have told him you didn't want anything to do with this."

"Maybe," Tomara said, although she knew that was impossible. "I can't explain it. Not to you. Maybe not even to myself. I don't hate them. I love them. Does that sound insane? I love them."

"Why?"

Continuing to look at the slowly darkening world beyond Mandy's window might be easier, but for reasons she didn't pretend to understand, Tomara needed to give Hayden an answer. And she had to know why he would ask such a question.

"You don't need a reason to love people. Maybe there simply isn't a reason." Someone had turned the radio on full blast down in the saloon. Although muted, the tune was strong enough that it reached Tomara. Below her were people with nothing more on their minds than putting the day's work behind them, meeting friends and maybe dreaming dreams better left locked inside.

Tomara had such a dream. Most of the time she kept it at bay by reminding herself how far she'd come since her beginnings. But sometimes, when the music and mood were right, she dreamed of not going through life alone.

"I don't think anyone can explain love," Tomara went on because her dream had surfaced and now held her in its grip. "It happens. It's strong. It has to do with sharing and commitment."

"What did you share with Al and Hoagy?" The question was hard-bitten. "What in the hell have they ever done for you?"

Tomara turned. Night had come too quickly; there wasn't enough light left in the room. If she wasn't wary, she might forget what tomorrow would bring. "Without them I wouldn't have had anyone in my life."

"And that's important? Having someone in your life?"

He was watching her closely. Even in the dim light she knew that. "Isn't it to you?" she asked instead of giving him an answer.

"I don't know."

I don't know. How incredibly sad it was that anyone should have to say that. "I don't understand," Tomara whispered, aware that for the first time since meeting Hayden she was the one doing the probing. "Are you saying you don't know whether having people to care about is important? What about Jay? You care about him, don't you?"

"You know the answer to that."

Something was happening here. Layers were being stripped away, not hers, but those of the strong professional next to her. Was it possible that there was more to him than she'd guessed? Yes, she'd sensed his compassion as she watched him care for Jay. But until now, she hadn't asked what made up the warp and weave of his life.

Now she wanted to know. Everything. The why didn't matter.

"Who else, Hayden? Who besides Jay do you care about?"

He was drawing into himself. Tomara understood what was happening because it had happened to her many times in the past few years. She knew why she had to protect herself, but what reasons would he have? What wounds was she probing?

"That isn't what I came here for," Hayden said with his eyes back on what waited beyond the window. "My personal life isn't the issue."

"Maybe. Maybe not. Hayden, you've been asking me questions that haven't been asked before. I've never had to deal with someone the way I'm having to deal with you. I'd like to know more than I do."

"That isn't how it works." Hayden rested his hands on the windowsill and let it accept some of his weight. "I'm the investigator. I ask the questions."

"And I don't have to give you any answers, but I'm trying to. Whether you believe me or not, I don't want them running from this. I want to be able to trust you to get them back where they belong. I want—" Somehow she would find her way to what was happening inside Hayden. "I want you to tell me they're still alive. And when you tell me that, I want to be able to believe you. I can't do that if I don't know what kind of man you are."

It was cooler outside than in the small room he was sharing with Tomara Metcalf. Hayden could feel the cool coming through the window. He sensed rather than heard the disquieting sound from the radio below them. He wished there were more lights on in the room. Maybe then he could have stuck with what he'd come here for and already be on his way.

But it wasn't going to be like that, and the truth was, at the moment Hayden couldn't imagine himself ever leaving. The day weighed on him, leaving his nerves jagged. He'd been on a fast track since early morning and still hadn't found his way off.

But maybe he had. Maybe the answer lay in the woman standing beside him. She was peace. Despite everything, she was peace. She was also asking him the hardest question he'd ever been asked.

He wondered if she knew how right she'd been when she asked if there was anyone he truly cared for besides the friend he'd carried out of the hills. He could have told her about his relationships with the people who made up Copper's population; she might understand how he'd felt about his partner when he was a cop. But if he did that, she would see the holes in that explanation.

She had a brother. A father. She'd known what love her mother had been capable of giving. He'd had none of those things.

And he hadn't told anyone, not even Jay, about that.

"It's that important that you know what kind of person I am?"

"Hayden?" She was looking at him. Looking. Probing. "Dad's and Hoagy's lives might be in your hands."

The responsibility was an awesome one. Hayden wanted to tell her he understood that, that despite what had happened to Jay, he wouldn't take those other two lives lightly, but suddenly, it simply no longer mattered.

She had released her hair. Hayden couldn't believe he hadn't noticed that until now. The long chestnut mane framed and softened her features until he was no longer aware of her practical jeans, the wrinkled socks she hadn't kicked off along with her shoes, the blouse in need of a washing.

Feminine. The sense of the word swirled and eddied around her. Those straight, strong shoulders? They only framed the soft body and emphasized her breasts. The legs capable of carrying her over miles of prairie? Those legs were capable of wrapping themselves around a man and imprisoning him both body and soul.

Hayden asked himself who she might have left behind her in Idaho Falls, but before the thought had finished itself, he stopped it. He didn't want to know who or what she was beyond this place. He could dream a lonely man's dream and pretend she had come to Copper for no other reason than that he was waiting for her.

The thought was insane. Tonight Hayden was an insane man.

"I won't ask you any more," he heard himself say. "Maybe you're right. Maybe you don't need a reason to love someone."

"It isn't easy. It can be so incredibly complicated."

"I wouldn't know."

"Hayden?" She'd taken his hands. God! She had willingly touched him. The emotion might not last—given what was ahead of them, he knew it wouldn't. But for now, tonight, he would take the touch and turn it into something.

"I didn't mean to say that," he told her. If he wanted, he could pull away, let her know he wasn't going to turn anything of himself over to her. He didn't do that.

Hayden's hands were rough. Rough and warm. How she'd come to touch him, Tomara had no idea, but he was letting it happen. Taking his hands might be the most foolish move of her life, but it was too late to pull back.

And she didn't want to.

The sound of the distant song was an aching throb in her. She both feared and embraced the darkness. Hayden smelled of his day, and yet it was more than that. He was masculinity. Strength. A primitive sensuality. She shouldn't feel like that about him. If she'd learned anything in her life, it was that reality was to be dealt with. Always.

Tonight there was no reality.

"Will you tell me? About your family."

"My family?"

"I think—Hayden, I think that if you had people to love, you wouldn't have to ask me why I feel the way I do about Dad and Hoagy."

"There isn't much to tell. They live in Chicago."

"When did you last see them?"

"Years. Tomara—"

"Years? Why?"

"They have their careers."

"You're their son."

"Their son. Do you have any idea what that meant to them? Having to find baby-sitters. Having to take time from their lives for teacher conferences, buying me clothes, making sure I learned how to drive. The job of raising me is finally over with, Tomara. They don't need to be bothered anymore."

He didn't have to say anything else. Finally. Finally Tomara understood. She hurt for him, more than she'd ever hurt for herself because, if nothing else, she'd known her parents loved her. She wanted to go on holding his hands, maybe giving him something he needed, but she was afraid of the consequences if they didn't take back their separate space. Her hands felt empty without his strength to draw on, but it was better that way.

"Families come in all sizes and shapes, Tomara. Some are close—others aren't."

"I'm sorry."

"Don't be. It's history."

"Is it?"

Hayden shrugged. And then he touched her.

Fingers in her hair. A breaking down of barriers better kept up. He shouldn't be touching her; she shouldn't allow herself to be touched. Tomorrow they would be at odds again. Even the vibration of a song and the night-dusted room couldn't convince her that they weren't who and what they were. But he had taken a strand between thumb and forefinger and was slowly running his hand down over her shoulder to the trailing ends, and Tomara could think of nothing except how much she needed to be touched. Not just in understanding. Not just in compassion. But in ways that gave her a taste of what it meant to be a woman.

He was doing that to her. Yes, he might know exactly what he was doing. He might be touching her only to get through her defenses. It might be calculation on his part. But Tomara didn't believe that.

It was in his eyes. She could see little except the glow, the light, but in that she read something that couldn't be faked.

Whatever had affected her since the moment they met had affected him, as well.

"I wanted to know what it felt like," Hayden whispered when he was finished. "I looked at that thick braid and asked myself why you kept it tied back like that."

"Loose hair could be dangerous in my line of work."

"You could cut it."

Tomara had been told that before. Her explanation had always been that it was quicker and easier to lash long hair into a braid than put up with beauty parlors, but that wasn't the whole story.

"I could."

"Then why don't you?"

"I don't tell many people this."

"Tell me."

Was that an order? No matter. She was too raw for anything except the truth. "I remember my mother's hair. It was the same color as mine. And so long she could almost sit on it."

"It's something of her that you can keep with you."

Tomara nodded. They were close, so dangerously close. She was looking up at him, all too aware of the test she was being given. Knowing she would fail.

She didn't know which of them moved first; it didn't matter. The end to standing alone came slowly, a sweet unfolding of emotions, a giving up of a great deal, a reaching out into the unknown.

Danger.

Tomara accepted the warning, accepted and then cast it off. No one who knew who and what they were would understand what was happening, but because those other people weren't there, there would not have to be an explanation.

She'd been wrong. Hayden possessed some softness after all. She touched his forearms to steady herself, and felt muscle and sinew. Still, there was more. Warm lips pressed against hers, questioning and giving at the same time.

What was and could be gentle about him undid Tomara. She didn't ask herself whether she wanted him to be like that, or whether it would be safer if he were cold and distant again. It was too late for that, and in one kiss Tomara understood only that things had changed between them.

Chapter Nine

Why didn't you get in touch with me? Oh, no! I didn't leave you a phone number, did I? How are you managing?''

If it had been anyone else, Tomara would have side-stepped the question, but she needed to talk, and Mandy was the only one she could be open with. Sunday had been incredibly long and stressful, both because Hayden was in the air and because three state police cars had been assigned to the area around Copper. The reason for all this activity had been obvious to everyone in town. Al and Hoagy Metcalf were on the run.

Tomara had tried to get through the long hours by seeing what she could of Jay, but it had been almost impossible to find time alone with him. Finally she'd fled the clinic and gone out to Hayden's place hoping he would tell her what was happening.

Unfortunately, Hayden was gone all day. When the state police tried to grill her about her father's and brother's habits, Tomara had almost lost what little self-control she had. In the end she'd once again taken refuge in Mandy's house, pulling herself out of her isolation only when Hayden called.

"I feel so helpless," Tomara admitted. "I want to be doing something, anything. Even riding around with the state police. But they don't want me."

Mandy dismissed the police with a snort. "You don't want to be with them. Believe me, you don't want to be asking yourself every minute what's going to happen if they suddenly come across Al or Hoagy."

"But that's what I spent the day asking myself. I can't help it. Where's Leonard? I thought he would come in with you."

Mandy shrugged. "I told him you'd probably be here. He said he wanted to drop by his office and then he'd give me a call. There's going to be hell to pay when he finds out."

Tomara had followed Mandy into her bedroom while the other woman unpacked her small suitcase. She was aware, in a distracted way, that Mandy's nightgown, what there was of it, looked new. "I didn't think about that," she admitted. "Mandy? What if he refuses to defend them after what they did?"

"I think we'd better think about getting those two fools rounded up before we start talking about trials. Lord, this is a mess, isn't it?"

Tomara agreed. She allowed herself to be distracted as Mandy told her about her weekend, which consisted of going out to eat and spending hours in bed. "I keep telling myself I'm an old warhorse. That I can go it alone. I can. I sure have enough times. But . . ." Her voice trailed off. "Having someone care what I eat, whether I'm having a good time . . ."

"If I wasn't here, the two of you could spend tonight together," Tomara pointed out.

"Don't you get in a fuss over that," Mandy admonished. "We're not a couple of honeymooners, you know. In fact, what we're going to do right now is skinny over to Leonard's office and give him the straight scoop. Unless he's deaf, I'm sure he's already heard the gossip."

Leonard had heard some but told Tomara that he hadn't formed any opinions. He let the two women in and then, after getting Tomara's permission, switched on a tape recorder. Tomara began unemotionally, but by the time she'd gotten to the part about having to haul a wounded Jay out of the hills, her voice was pregnant with feeling.

Until now Mandy had remained silent. "He's been hard on you, honey, hasn't he? Not Jay. I know he wouldn't blame you. But Hayden—"

Tomara decided to be honest. Yes, she agreed, it had been hard. But she'd been able to manage because, despite the raw emotions, she believed that she and Hayden had been honest with each other. "I don't know whether he thinks I had anything to do with the breakout. He didn't say, and I didn't ask. But I told him how hard this has been for me. He understood."

"I hope he did," Mandy muttered with her eyes steady on Tomara. "That man can be kinda hard to figure out sometimes. Doesn't let people get close to him, if you know what I mean. I've never been sure what he's thinking."

"That could become important," Leonard broke in. "When and if Al and Hoagy are arrested again, Hayden's testimony is going to be damning."

Tomara shuddered. Certainly she knew what Hayden's official responsibilities were. But they'd shared a kiss. "Leonard?" Tomara paused. "Do you really think they're going to be caught?"

Leonard flipped off the recorder. "Not if they have anything to do with it. Tomara, your relatives are resourceful. If there's one thing they understand, it's self-preservation."

"But they don't have any money. They're on foot," Mandy offered.

"And they're running for their lives."

Tomara couldn't think of a thing to say. It took several proddings from Leonard before she could concentrate long enough to get back to the rest of her story. Leonard was particularly interested in the conclusions the jail staff had come to regarding the breakout and the possibility of an accomplice. When Tomara mentioned that the only visitors of record had been her, Leonard and young David Kemper, Leonard laughed. "You take that list with a grain of salt, Tomara. Not every name gets written down."

"There might have been someone else?"

"I'm saying it's possible. Quite possible. They must have some friends. Other good old boys more interested in drinking than working."

Tomara didn't know. "I'm the one they're going to be looking at," she pointed out. "I think if Jay hadn't been hurt I would have been questioned already."

"Jay's not going to like having to do that. I bet he's beside himself having to be cooped up like that," Mandy said.

Talking about Jay and speculating when he would sign himself out of the clinic was easier than rehashing yesterday's events. Tomara told Leonard that she'd tried to see Jay but had fled when others had come by to check up on Copper's law enforcement officer.

Although it was late, Leonard announced his intention to talk to Jay, and Hayden, too, if he was anywhere around. Tomara couldn't supply the answer to that question.

"There's nothing you can do now," Leonard said as he was letting the two women out. "Unless they know a lot more than I think they do, the jail staff isn't going to have enough to charge you with anything."

"Would you listen to that man," Mandy snorted once the two women were alone. "One minute he tells you not to worry. The next he drops that little bomb about maybe you're being charged with whatever they'd charge you with. He might be a smart man, but sometimes I think he doesn't know the first thing about what goes on inside people." Mandy shrugged. "I don't know. Maybe that's what it takes to be a good lawyer, but I happen to think what's going on inside someone is a hell of a lot more important than anything else."

Mandy was still expounding on her personal philosophy as they passed in front of her saloon. "I'll tell you what. I'm going to buy you a drink."

Tomara held back. "I don't know. Someone might be in there—"

"You're damn right someone's going to be there. A whole room full of busybodies. What we're going to do is march in there with our heads held high and shut up everyone who probably has you behind bars by now. Face it straight on, honey. That's what I've always done."

Mandy was right. Still, there was something Tomara had to ask her. "Do you think I could have done it? Smuggled in a gun, I mean."

"I'll tell you what I think. Whether you did or not is none of my damn business, but if I was a betting woman, I'd say no. A man carting a gun, even an unloaded one—which of course that poor trustee didn't know—is liable to get himself shot. You aren't going to risk that happening."

"You're right." Tomara sighed. "I guess I can see those two breaking out, especially if they were handed something that was as good as a key. Even what they did to that young man—at least he's going to be all right. But not shooting Jay."

Mandy didn't say anything until she'd poured them each a beer and elbowed her way to the one free table in the bar. Keeping her voice low so that none of the curious could overhear, Mandy said what Tomara needed to hear. Al and Hoagy Metcalf might have done a lot of stupid things in their lives. But not murder. Not even attempted murder.

"Jay's always been fair with them. Maybe they haven't always seen eye to eye, but I think Al and Hoagy have always respected Jay. He—honey, someone's coming in."

Tomara turned. Despite the dim surroundings, she quickly picked Hayden out from the others. She let her breath out in a shaky sigh. "You want to leave?" Mandy asked.

She *wanted* to leave, but if she got to her feet, everyone, most of all Hayden, would notice. Instead Tomara sat with her fingers wrapped around her beer and waited.

The wait wasn't long. Strength surrounded her, and Tomara looked up into dark eyes. Hayden looked tired. Something simmered inside him, something Tomara recognized as frustration and controlled anger.

Without waiting for an invitation, Hayden sat down. "Not a sign. Hours of air and land search and not a sign. I wanted you to know."

"I'm sorry."

"Are you?"

Were they back to being antagonists? Did it have to be as if their kiss had never happened? "This is only making it worse. It isn't solving a thing."

"Tell them that."

"I would if I could."

"You had the chance, Tomara. Out at your place."

Tomara didn't attempt to battle his argument. She understood his frustration. He couldn't vent it on her father and brother. She would do. "What are you going to do tomorrow? Look some more?"

"I guess. That's what the state cops want to do. I tried to tell them I've got my own job to do, but until Jay's ready to take over again, I don't see as I have any choice."

A thin line of moisture was running down the outside of her mug. Tomara stopped its course with her nail, becoming absorbed in the act. "Have you been back to the hills?" she asked.

"When would I have time? What are you thinking?"

Tomara looked up. His eyes hadn't changed. The exhaustion and anger was still there. Then she looked at his mouth and remembered when things had been gentle between them. She didn't want to have to answer his question. She wanted back the time they'd spent in Mandy's living room.

"I want to go there. Back to the cave. Back to where Jay was shot."

"What for?"

"I don't know," Tomara said in frustration. "Maybe nothing. But I keep thinking someone was up there with us. Whoever it was might have left something behind."

"Al and Hoagy were up there."

No, they weren't. Because she had no proof other than her father's word, Tomara didn't try to argue. "I have a right," she went on doggedly. "Unless you lock me up, I can go anywhere I want."

"Not alone."

Someone switched on the radio. As had happened a thousand other nights, country and western music cut its way into the conversations. Tomara listened, trying to recapture the beat that had become so much a part of her the night she and Hayden discovered what else existed between them. The beat was there again, stronger this time, almost strong enough to chase away the rest of the world. Across the table Hayden's eyes met hers, and she knew he was thinking the same thing.

"I'll go as soon as it gets light," she said softly. "The Jeep should be able to get a little closer than Jay's pickup could."

"I'll come here, and we'll go out together."

Hayden stood. For a moment he leaned forward and rested his large hands on the table. He said nothing, but Tomara didn't need to hear words. She was aware that she was nodding her head. She was much more aware of the need to touch his arms and the desire to rest her head against his chest and listen to his heart beat.

"Something's happening between you two," Mandy whispered after Hayden had gone.

"I don't know." Tomara hadn't thought to pull her eyes away from the spot where Hayden had last stood.

"Well, believe me, something's happening. Lord, girl, I could cut it with a knife. You and Hayden, the two of you talk about it?"

"We don't talk." Tomara went back to her study of the ways moisture could transform a mug. "Only about Al and Hoagy."

"I think the two of you better start talking about other things. Otherwise it might be gone before you've figured out what you're losing."

"Mandy." Tomara paused, debating. No. It was too late to keep anything from her friend. "I don't know what's happening. I shouldn't want anything to do with him. I wouldn't blame him if he hated me."

"That's what makes it all the more complicated. Other than sending out electricity every time you're around each other, has anything happened?"

In a strange way Tomara was glad for Mandy's direct questions. Still, it wasn't easy to expose herself. "We kissed. Once. Briefly."

"And then?"

"And then nothing. I didn't say anything. I couldn't think of a thing to say."

"And Hayden?"

"He didn't say anything, either. He walked out the door."

Mandy whistled. "Let me tell you something. I don't envy what you're going to be going through. Unless a hell of a lot changes, and in a hurry, you're going to be hurt."

Tomara wasn't sure she believed Mandy's dire predictions. It had only been a kiss, an insane, unplanned kiss. She couldn't explain why it happened, what emotions had been in operation. But she did know enough to put the moment behind her and think ahead to tomorrow, when she and Hayden would be together for more hours than was wise.

Morning came after a night of not enough sleep. Mandy was snoring gently in her room when Tomara woke before the alarm went off. Quietly she slipped out of bed. She showered and dressed in her uniform of jeans and a cotton shirt. Just before she pulled on her jeans, she caught her reflection in the dresser mirror and asked herself if she'd ever be anything except denim and cotton.

Hayden was waiting beside the Jeep. He nodded but said nothing. Tomara climbed in behind the wheel and coaxed the Jeep to life. With Hayden sitting silently next to her, she put the town behind her and headed toward the spot where things had fallen apart for Jay. It wasn't until she was pulling off the main road that Hayden spoke.

"Jay went home with Lisa last night. It's killing him, but he promised not to do anything until tomorrow."

"Does he know what you're doing this morning?"

"He knows. You should know, I haven't heard anything from the crime lab. They don't work weekends. Besides, until we have Al and Hoagy locked up again, what rifle those bullets came from is a moot point, isn't it?"

"I don't think it is." Tomara tried to concentrate on driving, but there wasn't enough to distract her. "I need to know whether the bullet that wounded Jay and killed that man came from a rifle Dad or Hoagy own."

Hayden gripped his side of the Jeep and leaned out the open expanse of what should have been a door, concentrating on the way the Jeep handled the ruts. He wanted to ask Tomara if she had slept last night or if she'd been as restless as he'd been. No, he amended. To hell with last night. What had she thought about after that too brief moment in Mandy's house when there hadn't been any barriers?

He'd kissed her. And he'd told her things about his past that no one here had ever heard. Most of all he'd kissed her.

Was she thinking about that this morning, or had she convinced herself that it had been nothing more than a mistake?

That's what it was, all right; Hayden had spent hours telling himself. A mistake that wasn't going to be repeated.

"What does Leonard say?"

If Tomara was bothered by the turn the conversation took, she didn't show it. She told him, in detail, about the conversation with the lawyer. But after asking the questions, Hayden didn't seem to be listening to her answer all that closely.

The truth was, it was almost beyond him to think of anything except what she was physically. Her hair was back in its damnable practical braid, but that didn't make it any easier for him. The braid was like knowing a woman wore lace under stiff jeans.

Was it no more complicated than that? Hayden asked himself as his mind caught on the erotic thought. Had he been sleeping alone so long that any woman would look good?

No, the answer came immediately. Tomara Metcalf would touch the senses of any man. She was like a colt, a quick-moving colt with its eyes on the horizon and lightning in its hooves.

Hayden wondered what Tomara would say if she knew he was comparing her to a horse. Most women would probably tell him to take a flying leap, but Hayden couldn't quite believe that would be Tomara's reaction. She might not know a great deal about horses, but she'd grown up watching and being affected by the swift wild creatures who called the prairie home. If she felt anything for the antelope, which he believed she did, she would understand that certain comparisons could be made.

Tomara was speaking. It was a long time before Hayden realized that she was responding to the question he'd asked. She was saying something about Leonard reaffirming that he was still willing to defend Al and Hoagy. Leonard, however, wasn't sure that would ever become necessary.

"He doesn't think we're going to find them?"

"That's the way it sounded. He also said it's possible someone came to visit them whose name didn't appear on the list."

"He did, did he?" Hayden neither confirmed nor denied that possibility.

"Yes." Tomara looked at him. "Have you talked to David?"

"I have. And he's going to see Jay today." It would be much easier on both of them if he didn't say anything else, but he wanted to hear the sound of her voice. Although he didn't give a damn, he asked about Mandy's weekend and voiced his opinion that Mandy and Leonard made an unlikely pair. Listening to himself, he admitted that he sounded like a damn gossip.

Thank heavens they'd now come as far as the Jeep could travel. They didn't speak while they got out of the Jeep and shouldered the canteens and binoculars they would need. Because they were at the base of the sharp, barren hills, it was possible for them to walk side by side. In spite of the physical closeness, Hayden and Tomara still said nothing.

She could hear him breathing. The sound was deep and even, something no one should be aware of. Tomara was aware of her own body, as well. It felt alive this morning, more sensitive somehow. Although Hayden was enough inches away that there was no danger of them accidentally touching, she was consumed by thoughts of what she would feel if his hip happened to brush against hers.

The hill tugged at Tomara's calves, but her only response to the terrain was to thrust her body silently forward at the hips. Her breathing, conditioned by years of running, remained as steady as Hayden's.

They could walk like this for the rest of the day. And maybe by dark she would no longer react to him.

No. This awareness wasn't why she was here; she had to remember that. She'd wanted and needed to come back to the hills because the hills might hold some answers, some way of making her believe that her father or brother hadn't shot Jay.

When their footing became less sure, Hayden took the lead, which left Tomara with the responsibility of having to watch her step despite the distraction of his muscled legs and lean hips. She was pleased to see that he'd accommodated his body as well as his life-style to the country around Copper. Not that he probably hadn't been in good physical shape when he was a policeman, but the prairie, if one was to be at home in it, demanded certain things. Foremost was the physique necessary to survive.

But Hayden had done more than that. Tomara noticed each time he paused with his head tilted to catch any sounds brought in by the wind. He knew to keep his attention both on what was near and in the distance. His movements were slow and deliberate; an untaught man might move quickly, thus disturbing the wildlife and more easily giving himself away.

He was tanned. Deeply. The back of his neck looked as if it had never known anything except heat and cold and wind. His arms swung easily by his sides in a rhythm designed to conserve energy.

Who had taught him these things? Jay? Or had he somehow instinctively known how to make himself one with his environment?

Hayden stopped. Aware of the necessity of keeping space between them, Tomara managed to halt before she bumped into him. "Jay and I talked last night," Hayden was saying. "He thinks the shot came from a ridge above and slightly ahead of him. I have a pretty good idea which one that is."

"Hayden? Why didn't whoever it was stay to see whether they'd killed Jay? If they knew we were out here with him, why didn't they kill all of us?"

"I don't know, Tomara. Maybe we'll never know the answer to that."

At least he hadn't tried to make her say that her relatives were the ones responsible. Being here and having to go back over the events of that horrible day had affected Tomara's nervous system. She was still aware of Hayden, more aware than she wanted to be, but that emotion was warring with another one.

An attempted murder had taken place here. And there was no guarantee that the owner of that rifle wasn't still in the hills.

Hayden lifted his binoculars and slowly scanned his surroundings. The perusal took so long that Tomara knew the same thing was on his mind. Then, without breaking the silence, Hayden struck off toward the spot where Jay had been shot.

Gullies and hills. Boulders and pebbles. A few tufts of tenuous grass and acre after acre of nothing except stone. That was Tomara's world. Occasionally they stood on a spot high enough to allow her to see down to the plains below them. Tomara felt exposed, and yet, somehow, with Hayden Conover ahead of her, she felt safe.

When he reached the spot where Jay had been wounded, Hayden spread his legs in defense against the uneven footing, opened his canteen and lifted it to his lips. Tomara watched the simple and yet sensuous act. She wondered what his water-moistened lips would feel like against hers.

"I dreamed about this last night," Hayden told her. "It wasn't a pleasant dream."

Tomara decided to be honest. In truth, with his impact surrounding her, she had no choice. "I've had nightmares. I hear the shot. I start running. And running. Only I can never get to Jay."

"It changes things."

"What does?"

"Something like what happened to Jay. It changes our lives. No matter what happens in the weeks and months to come, that will always be a part of us."

"Like our upbringing," Tomara said, with her eyes not on the bluff where the rifleman had probably waited, but on Hayden.

"Yeah. Like our upbringing. What I said about mine—"

"Please don't say you're sorry you said what you did." It was a clear, cloudless day. Summer felt as if it would last forever. And yet Tomara sensed the reality of winter. Winter with its storms. But maybe the storm was inside her.

"No. I'm not going to say that. My family consisted of people who lived under the same roof, but that was as far as it went. My father would be gone sometimes for months at a time, and we wouldn't know where he was. My mother had her own career. And when she wasn't working, she did what she wanted to."

Tomara wasn't going to tell Hayden she was sorry for him. The words wouldn't change what had been. "Do you have any brothers or sisters?"

"No. They were wise enough to know they'd made a mistake with one."

Because he was watching her, Tomara nodded, but the storm was increasing, and she needed all her energy to brave it. The little he'd told her about his family had told her a great deal. She knew why he couldn't understand her coming back to Copper. His childhood, maybe, answered the question of why he wasn't married.

He'd shaved before coming to see her. If she reached out and touched his cheeks and chin, his flesh would feel smooth. She wanted to touch. Yet she knew she shouldn't.

With fingers that had to be told what to do, Tomara took a drink from her canteen before scanning her surroundings through the binoculars. Rocks surrounded them, so she was unable to see as far as she would have liked, but at least the effort gave her something to do.

"I feel as if we're being watched."

Hayden grunted. "I feel the same way. Maybe it's nothing more than a reaction to what happened."

"Maybe." Tomara wasn't sure she believed that, but with Hayden demanding so much from her, she couldn't count on any of her reactions. She dropped her eyes, now looking at the faded stain that was Jay's blood. "We aren't going to find anything here."

Hayden pointed. "Up there. That's where Jay thinks they were."

They. They could mean her father and brother. With her eyes still on the ground, Tomara nodded. She slung the binoculars over her neck again and stalked away, not caring whether Hayden kept up with her or not. It was impossible. Everything about this morning was impossible. How could she think with his impact assaulting her? How could she stand to be around him if he insisted on reminding her who the prime suspects were?

All she wanted to do was get this over with and take him back to Copper so she could be rid of him.

The climb up the ridge was a steep one. Both of them were breathing deeply by the time they shinnied over the last boulders and stood on a small, flat area disturbed by a few tufts of grass.

Hayden knelt beside the grass. He said nothing, but Tomara didn't have to be told. The grass had been flattened, not by the wind, but by a weight that could have come from a man's boot. Her spine prickling, Tomara shaded her eyes with her hand and swept her eyes over her surroundings. From where they were, she could see much of the far side of the hills, including much of the prairie behind them. This time her binoculars told her a great deal more about the landscape. The prairie at the back side of the hills had been disturbed only by a single dirt road that had been there so long that it had become part of the environment. The road began at the reservation. From here it was impossible to tell whether any vehicles had been over it recently or how much of a climb it would be to get from the road up to where she and Hayden were standing.

Tomara noted the movement. Because she'd seen it a thousand times, she didn't need a second look to know what it was. "Antelope."

Hayden joined her. His elbow touched her as he lifted his binoculars. "Three of them," he said a minute later. "The summer's been good to them."

Although it was hidden by the wave and sway of the ground, Tomara knew there was a watering hole beyond where the antelope were grazing. If it were later in the day, they might be able to see range cattle gathering around the precious resource.

Hayden was speaking. "They're peaceful. They don't act as if they've been disturbed."

"I noticed." Tomara lowered her binoculars. There were a few ridges slightly higher than this one, but because the one they were standing on was close to the middle of the range of hills, it was the perfect spot for keeping an eye on the flat land where the antelope were. Tomara couldn't see her Jeep on the road they'd come in on. That didn't make sense if it had been Al and Hoagy standing here a few days ago. They would want to keep an eye on potential traffic coming from Copper, wouldn't they? From here the view, although spectacular, was that of an isolated area seldom seen by humans outside of hunting season.

Hayden put words to her thoughts.

"There's no way we can track anyone's comings and goings from where we are," he wound up. "How the hell are we going to find out where this footprint came from?"

Tomara squared her shoulders. "You have to ask?"

"What are you thinking? Do you have any idea what time it is?"

Tomara didn't wear a watch, either, but she didn't need one to know it was almost noon. "I can't let it go, Hayden. I have to find some answers."

"By climbing down the back side of these damn rocks and seeing if anyone's been on that spur road?"

"You can wait for me."

No, he couldn't, Hayden admitted as he stepped around Tomara and started to lead the way. She knew as much as he did about the wilderness. Probably more. But this was rugged country, and violence had taken place here once. If anything happened to her, he would spend the rest of his life in regret. As it was, they would be lucky if they didn't spend the rest of the day out here.

Two hours later, they finally jockeyed over the last rock and once again reached level ground. No wonder he seldom had call to come out here. The area was so damn remote that most hunters didn't know it existed. He was hot and tired and hungry. Mostly he was hungry.

When Tomara caught up with him, Hayden revised his priority list. Mostly he was aware.

It simply wasn't possible for a woman to spend hours crawling over rocks and still look more feminine, more desirable than any other woman he'd ever seen. Suddenly figuring out why that was became more important than killing his thirst. Hoping she wouldn't notice, Hayden turned so he could study her. The hair along her temples was plastered to her. Her blouse was dirty. She wore no makeup. She was breathing as deeply as he was and not trying to disguise the fact.

Maybe it was the forbidden. Tomara Metcalf and Hayden Conover were supposed to be adversaries. The dynamics of what had taken place put them at odds with each other. What was it Jay had said last night, that life would be a hell of a lot simpler if Tomara had stayed where she belonged.

That thought sent Hayden's mind off in another direction. He'd been to Idaho Falls. It was a nice enough place. But it wasn't for this woman. All right, so he had no business believing that and would undoubtedly get an argument out of her if she knew what he was thinking. Still, he didn't try to change his mind.

She was looking at him, a strange, almost childlike look of innocence and curiosity in her eyes. She took another deep breath, freeing Hayden from his thoughts and taking him into even more dangerous territory. What in the hell was he doing out here with her?

"I remember the last time I was here," she said in a tone at peace with her surroundings. "It was years ago. The year after I graduated from high school. I was supposed to be scouting some hunting spots for hunters. I'd taken the road from the reservation out here. I'd seen a wolf earlier in the day and was trying to decide whether he was alone or with some others. It was getting close to night when I spotted him again. He was hunting."

Hayden believed he knew what was coming. Because he wanted to see how Tomara handled the inevitability of life and death, he waited for her to continue. "His prey was a young antelope." Tomara's voice hadn't changed. "It had been born late and was small for that time of the year. It had wandered a little distance from its mother and didn't see the wolf."

"It happens," Hayden said when her voice trailed off.

"Not that time." Tomara's eyes had glazed over as she stepped into the past. Now she focused. "I didn't want it to happen. Not while I was watching. I leaned on the horn and scared both of them."

"The wolf had to eat, Tomara. And the odds are that antelope didn't survive the winter."

"I know. But it didn't happen that day."

"And then a little later you brought hunters out here."

"That's something I'll never do again. Saving that little one—I don't know if I can explain it. Those times when I guided, it was as if I put my heart on ice. I did what I thought I had to do if I was ever going to leave here. I knew all about herd management. At least I knew the logic behind it. It was the emotional component that finally caught up with me. I don't ever want to see something die again."

To hell with caution! She wasn't shaking. She probably didn't need human contact, especially from him. But she was going to get it, and if she rejected him, then that was something he would have to deal with.

Only she wasn't rejecting him. He'd put his hand on her shoulder and, good God, she was covering his hand with hers.

It wasn't quite a smile; as much as he wanted to believe she could give him one, he couldn't call it that. But in some deep, unexplainable way, Hayden knew that they'd taken a step neither of them believed could have been taken.

Chapter Ten

They'd come there to look for evidence. If they didn't complete their task and make their way back to the opposite side of the hills, they would have to spend the night there.

At the moment Tomara didn't care if they spent the rest of their lives in this land beyond reach. Hayden had touched her, and somehow she'd had the courage to touch him back.

Now. Now anything could happen.

Her legs ached dully with the day's efforts, and she was hungry, but Tomara could dismiss those feelings. She couldn't, however, ignore the sense, the promise, the possibility that form might finally be given to what she felt whenever she was around Hayden, and finally she would understand. She could almost handle the possibility that when today was over whatever was happening between them would turn out to be nothing.

"They're new."

Although she resented the distraction from her thoughts, Tomara followed the line of his eyes to the ground. He was looking at the tracks cut into the earth. She nodded. Over the past few months, grasses had found a toehold in the ground, but they'd recently been flattened.

"But there's no way to tell how long ago it happened."

"Maybe the day Jay was shot."

"Maybe." Tomara waited for Hayden to bend over for a closer look at the tracks, but he didn't. He still had his hand on her shoulder. Hers was still cupped over his....

And his eyes were meeting hers, and Tomara felt closer than she'd ever been to another human being. That they were together called for a great deal of trust on her part, and maybe his as well. "I don't know why I thought we might find more than this. I hoped—"

"I know."

He could have said anything else, and it wouldn't have meant as much as those two simple words. Unless she dropped her eyes, there would be no keeping her emotions secret. For a moment the old protective instinct flared. Hayden had already seen so much of her. He could, if he wanted, use his knowledge to his advantage and leave her hurting.

But he'd come out here with her. He was touching her. And she believed what was in his eyes. "I feel so tired. So tired of struggling," she admitted.

"But you'll go on fighting, Tomara. Because no matter how hard it is, that's the kind of woman you are."

"Sometimes I wish I wasn't."

"I don't believe you." The pressure from his fingers increased. "You have to say that. You have to get it out of your system. But you aren't going to turn your back on them."

"I know."

He could have told her that her commitment would continue to stand between them, but Hayden didn't want to talk about that. He didn't want to talk at all.

Feeling this protective about another human being was a new emotion for him. In some strange, indefinable way, the admission made him feel vulnerable and exposed, but he neither wanted nor was capable of changing. This woman, this slim, competent woman deserved to be sheltered. She'd stood alone enough years and fought enough battles with no one to stand beside her. She might argue the point. He would be surprised if she didn't.

But she couldn't stop his thoughts.

A kiss. That was all he wanted. All he dared allow himself to think about. They would take one step at a time, and when one of them said "stop," the other would be wise to heed.

She wasn't fighting him. The fact gave Hayden courage. At first he was afraid she wasn't going to respond to the light touch of his lips against hers, and he wondered how he'd come so far in life without knowing it was possible to want something as much as he wanted to have this woman return what he was offering.

And then slowly, she unfolded. He was being given more than acknowledgment. She was with him on this journey.

It couldn't be any other way. On some subconscious level, Tomara had known that the day would end this way, that there would be more to their time together than a search and wary peace. There were barriers. There might always be barriers. But for this moment she could turn her back on them and simply exist.

Simply offer and accept.

A kiss wasn't going to sustain her this time. The other night that had been all either of them had been ready for. But that was history. She knew the touch of his lips. Now she needed to explore the weight and depth of what a kiss could become. She wouldn't think about the consequences.

She fit. Somehow it seemed utterly right that she had been made to fit into him. He surrounded her, his arms pulling her close, his chest and hips molding against her and making her understand the meaning of the word *sharing*. The world stretched on forever around them, the earth under their feet ageless, the sky unbroken by clouds. The prairie silent.

The sound was coming from within her, a sound born of exploration and promise and recklessness. Hayden might never hear the whispers slowly filling her. It was probably better that way. But she could press her body against him and lose a little of herself and sing her silent song.

This was what it could mean to belong.

There was more than a song. It was her body's reaction to his. The touching of flesh on flesh became more. It was a heat, a pressure. A promise and a challenge. Although her body remained rooted in place, seeking and giving, touching and tasting, what was happening within began to slowly, thoroughly claim her.

Hayden's warmth and strength were one and the same. It was impossible for her to tell them apart. She clung to both, recklessly taking what might never be offered again. Needing that warmth, that strength as maybe she'd never needed anything before.

She didn't know who parted their lips first, who took the touch beyond what should exist between two people who knew almost nothing about each other. Tomara couldn't remember bringing her tongue into play, only that once the shy exploration had begun she quickly became bold. He was offering himself to her, giving her a gift she hadn't known she wanted or needed. And in her need she was unable to be anything except honest.

It was no longer a kiss.

He touched her, not on the arms as he'd done when the first contact was made. Tomara sensed his fingers on her throat, a light promise, a precious foreshadowing of what could be. His fingers trailed over, asking and taking her inch by slow inch. She had to concentrate. It was somehow essential that her mind record every moment, every sensation. And yet her feelings were too jumbled for that. Gently he pushed her blouse aside and made contact with her soft flesh. His hips defied her to do anything except return his pressure.

She had to do something. It became a need. Her fingers needed more than fabric. Somehow that new need pushed its way into her consciousness and took over. If he could take possession of her, she would do the same to him. She would learn the feel and heat of his chest, his throat, his shoulders.

Their world became a cocoon. Tomara became less aware of their achingly lonely surroundings or what it would take to bring them back to civilization. She was with Hayden learning her own cravings.

She would give herself to him. She could, without thought of the consequences, forget the rational and allow the physical to take over. He could still be her enemy. She could accept that because with his arms keeping her from the world, she could accept anything as long as they were together.

In another lifetime she would deal with the consequences.

He was pushing her away from him. Before she could think to put an end to the loneliness, she was back against him, back where she belonged, and he'd pushed her blouse upward so he could take the measure of her waist. The touch was somehow comforting, less a challenge to her senses and more a promise. A man who took only after asking with wordless questions was a man she could trust.

Trust. The word was everything to her. Never before had she so deeply needed to trust.

That it was this man who'd tapped that core was all the more incredible.

"I had no idea," Hayden began. "No. That's not the truth. I think maybe this was in the back of my mind since we left this morning."

"I didn't think—I mean, the only thing I dared let myself think about was trying to find out something about my father and brother."

"Instead you learned something about me."

"And about myself."

Another kiss, a little more desperate this time because they'd spoken and thus touched on the real world. Tomara tasted warmth, touched strength, pulled into her the scent of a man who knew no reason to try to be anything but what he was. The play of his body against hers was so incredibly unexpected that Tomara was unable to do anything except react to the newness of him. He was uncharted territory, an adventure perhaps better not begun. And yet, with his mouth touching and reaching and asking, she wanted nothing except to take the steps.

Hot. Tomara understood that her body could respond to a man; it had happened before. But before it had been a conscious effort, an attempt to try to join herself with another human. This time it was happening without her asking, without her will being involved.

This time the heat was a storm, hot and sudden. She had no warning and no control. If the ability to think deserted her, she would pull at him until nothing would satisfy except for them to become one.

She wanted it. Heart and body and soul, that was what Tomara wanted. She would face the consequences later, she told herself. But now she would take and give and in the act learn certain things about herself.

He was touching her breast, a murmur of contact that promised more than it gave. The intimacy was somehow symbolic of trust given and taken. She needed to think ahead to a time when that light touch might become more. And yet, despite herself, Tomara tensed. There was danger in what they were doing; the consequences could become more than either of them dared risk.

"Tomara?"

No. Not yet. "What?"

"I'm sorry. This shouldn't be happening. Nothing's resolved. Nothing has changed. I know better."

She could hate him for those words. If she could somehow convince herself that she'd had nothing to do with what had taken place between them, she would lay the blame on Hayden. But she would have to lie to do that. "Don't," she whispered, knowing she should pull away, and yet not quite strong enough to do that. His hand across her back still held her against him. Because the memory of that final touch might have to sustain her for a long time, she delayed its end. "Don't blame yourself. This took both of us by surprise."

"And it shouldn't have happened."

An end. It didn't matter which of them dropped their hands first. The act had been completed, and Tomara was standing alone. "No." The word tore a great deal from her. "It shouldn't have. We're on opposite sides of—of whatever this nightmare is."

"I know." He almost smiled. "Tomara? I'd like to say it won't happen again. It's safer that way. We both know that." Hayden's hands were knotted by his side. "But I don't make promises I can't keep."

"I can't, either, Hayden," she managed. "I want to be honest. At least about this I want to be honest."

"Then you're feeling the same thing."

"What I feel is as if I'm being torn in two. And I don't want that."

"Don't you?" he challenged.

"No. I don't."

It was easier to turn away than to go on looking at Hayden and being reminded of what might have been. Tomara's body was in chaos. Until she'd once again recovered what she believed herself to be, she would bury herself in physical activity.

When Hayden dropped to his knees beside the tire tracks and began running his hands over the uneven surface Tomara wondered if he was doing the same. She didn't ask. He had been the one with the strength to put an end to what would have blown up in their faces. It was better to leave it at that.

"Al and Hoagy were on foot."

"Yes," Tomara ventured, unsure where Hayden was taking the conversation.

"Then if there's any connection between Jay getting shot and these tracks, maybe it wasn't them."

"Are you saying you don't think they did it?" Tomara pressed her hand to her stomach but was unable to stem the faint hope that Hayden was giving her something to cling to.

"I'm not saying anything, Tomara." Hayden was still looking at the ground. "It isn't my business to. If we were in the city, if there was that kind of manpower in this part of the state, we might be able to get experts out here who could tell us what kind of vehicle made these tracks, and more important, whether they were made weeks or days ago.''

"But there isn't that kind of expertise, is there?'' Tomara dropped to her knees. She wanted to pound away the tracks. They weren't the answers she hoped she'd find. They simply represented more questions. "We don't have a damn thing.''

"I'm afraid not.''

"Then—'' She should be getting to her feet, but that would take more strength than she was able to gather at the moment. "Coming out here didn't solve anything.''

"Maybe. Maybe not.'' Hayden surged to his feet and held out his hand. Although it was safer not to touch him, Tomara placed her hand in his and accepted the pull that brought her up off her knees. They stood for a moment, eyes saying what there were no words for. Then Hayden released her. "Jay's going to be back in operation tomorrow. I'm going to let him be the cop. I'd suggest you do the same thing.''

"I can't.'' A tuft of a cloud had appeared on the horizon. It wasn't enough to distract from the endlessness of blue. "It isn't something I can walk away from.''

Why not? Hayden wanted to ask. He didn't understand Tomara, not nearly as much as he needed to. He didn't understand why she would spend an entire day crawling over rocks simply to wind up staring at tire tracks. If it were him, he would have assessed the situation and made the determination that there was nothing he could do to help his relatives. There might have been a quiet sense of failure at having to come to that conclusion, but he wouldn't have turned his back on his career and uprooted himself to try to do something for people who couldn't possibly appreciate or understand the sacrifice.

But Tomara was making that sacrifice. "What happens now?'' he asked.

"What do you mean?''

"What are you going to do now? Look, I can't be telling you something you haven't thought of yourself, but there's a very real possibility you'll never see Al and Hoagy again.''

"No." Despite the quiet tone, the word came too quickly for Hayden to be fooled. Tomara was unable to comprehend what he'd just said.

"Don't tell me no, Tomara," he pressed on. "They may have found a way out of the county. If you're waiting for them to come back offering excuses and logical explanations, you're going to be waiting for a long time."

"What are you trying to do?" Tomara asked. She'd straightened her shoulders in defiance of what he'd said. Her eyes were dark with pain. "Hayden, the only thing I have is hope. Don't try to take that from me."

"Hope?" He plunged on, not sure where his hard questions were taking him, only that he needed to understand more of Tomara Metcalf than he did. "Hope for what? That someone else is going to step forward and confess? It isn't going to happen."

He was being cruel. A few minutes ago when he pointed out that Al and Hoagy had been on foot the day Jay was shot he'd given her hope. Now that was being yanked away. "That's not what I'm asking for."

"Then what?"

Damn him. Why couldn't he ask questions she was capable of answering? "I don't know what!" She couldn't stay here. If Hayden wanted to go on taking potshots at her, he would have to contend with her back. Tomara took a moment for another drink of water and then without bothering to tell him what she was doing, she turned away and took the first steps back toward the waiting vehicle.

She hadn't covered more than fifty feet when she sensed him behind her. At least he wasn't attacking her with more questions.

Retracing their steps took another two hours. When they once again came to the spot where Jay was shot, Tomara covered the area in painstaking detail. She didn't care if Hayden thought her a fool, and, she told herself, she didn't care whether he waited for her or went on ahead.

Hayden waited. And when she was finished, he suggested that they take another look at the cave. When they were within a few hundred feet of it, Hayden rested his hand on his pistol. Their eyes met in acknowledgment of what Hayden believed he needed to do, but neither broke the strained silence.

The cave was empty. From what Tomara could determine, no one had been in it since they were there the other day. "You can stop thinking like a cop," she couldn't help saying.

"No, I can't, Tomara. I don't think I can ever stop thinking like a cop."

"Then I feel sorry for you."

She wanted him to snap back at her. Somehow his silence was harder to deal with than another argument would have been. But once again Hayden retreated into himself, and Tomara was left with no option but to do the same herself.

More clouds were building on the horizon. They probably didn't mean anything, and yet Tomara saw them as symbolic of how the day had turned out. At least they would be back in Copper before dark.

The only thing that now lay between Tomara and freedom from Hayden's presence was the trip back to town. The trek back to the Jeep was accomplished in silence. It wasn't until they were on the road back to Copper that Hayden spoke.

"I'm sorry."

The unexpected words caught Tomara unawares. She tried to shake them off, but it didn't work. "About what?" she asked, hoping against hope that he would say what she needed to hear.

"That there weren't any answers up there."

Dusk. A time for rest and, for those inclined toward such things, reflection. Tomara stared out at the slowly fading prairie. "They might have been the wrong answers."

"But at least you would have known."

"Maybe..." Tomara allowed the word to tail off. He might go by the title game warden but there was still a great deal of the cop in him. He had been conditioned to balance evidence and come to rational, logical conclusions. Maybe if anyone else were involved, Tomara could do the same thing, but in this case that was impossible. She envied Hayden; he wasn't burdened by emotion.

Or was he? What he'd given her out there today was emotion pure and simple. "I'm so tired of fighting this," she told him because what they'd shared since that first day made anything except the truth impossible. "I took up photography not long ago. I'd like to come out here and take pictures of the prairie at different times of the day. Like now. There's a gentling to the land. It's fading away, and yet it's still out there. I'd like to find out if there's a way of capturing that."

"You wouldn't rather be looking for ways of proving your family's innocence?"

"No," she said, grateful that he was helping her give her thoughts form. "I'm tired of the headache. The questions. Feeling off balance."

"You'd really do that? Spend a whole day out here taking pictures of the prairie?"

"The seasons," Tomara went on with her eyes at half-mast. "I want to try to capture the seasons. To use the most powerful telephoto I can afford, so I can take close-ups of the antelope."

"I think I'd like to try that, too," Hayden said gently. Then, before she could grasp his mood, he went on, "If you captured the seasons, you'd have to stay here for a year."

His voice was a beat, a murmur. There was no way she could ward off its gentle invasion of her senses. "Yes."

"Would you do that? Tomara, if there hadn't been a murder and you were here simply because you were, would you stay?"

He wasn't asking a casual question. The words might not be that complex, but because she'd spent the day with him and known what it was like to be in his arms, Tomara sensed the deeper meaning. Her answer was important, for herself, and maybe for him.

The pull was there. It was reflected in the dying day, the settling of the prairie as it readied itself for night. Somewhere antelope were making their way to drinking holes, birds of prey coasted through the sky as the wind bore them along. The reptiles that had come to life under the sun's caress were once again becoming inert.

Tomara understood the pace. Her greatest joy had come from being a witness to the seasons of birth and life and death.

But, much as she had gained from the prairie, there had to be something else. Some person. She could tell herself that her father and brother should fill that role, but that was a lie. Not only would they resent being thrust into that role, but it wasn't them she wanted.

"I don't know," she said. "No," she amended because she believed she was speaking the truth. "All the time I was gone? I seldom thought about Copper. It was part of the past. That's all it was."

"But just now when you were talking, it was with such nostalgia."

"Nostalgia. That's all it was."

"Idaho Falls? You're happy there?"

For the next fifteen minutes Tomara told Hayden about the life she'd carved out for herself. She focused on her job description, her working conditions, why she'd picked the house she had and what she was doing to fix it up. She told him a little about the friends she'd made there. It was only when she was debating whether to tell him about the man who'd asked her to move in with him that something occurred to her.

She hadn't called any of those people since coming back to Copper.

Hayden had heard almost nothing of what Tomara was saying. He was aware of her voice. Oh, yes, he was aware of that. But he didn't want to know about the neighbor who always had the tools she needed, or the retired army man who'd taught the photography class. He certainly didn't need to hear about some guy who rode a motorcycle.

He'd asked her if she'd ever thought of moving back to Copper and received an answer that left no room for argument. He should be able to accept the word and file it away, just as he'd learned to stop asking why his parents had been incapable of giving or receiving love.

Life didn't always turn out the way people wanted it to. There were disappointments and closed doors and unrealized dreams. It was fact. Reality. So Tomara would be heading out of Copper as soon as she could. Good. She had a right to that life she'd built for herself. She certainly didn't have to put her future on hold because her father and brother were a couple of fools.

There was absolutely no reason for him to feel that his own life wouldn't continue its pace once she was gone.

"Are you hungry?" Hayden asked as Copper absorbed them.

"Hungry? I think I'm beyond that. Do you realize we haven't eaten since morning?"

"Yeah," Hayden said with his hand pressed dramatically against his stomach. "I do realize. I'm taking you back to the cafe."

Hayden had parked the Jeep. But because he hadn't made a move to get out, Tomara put off the moment herself. She was aware that he'd issued an order, but she didn't care. If they ate together, she could put off the time when she would be alone. "This time I pay," she said.

"Whatever." His weathered fingers were on her cheek. "I'm glad we did what we did today."

"It was a waste." The touch was no accident. Despite the dark, Hayden's eyes said he knew exactly what he was doing.

"No, it wasn't," he told her, his voice once again lower and deeper than she could handle dispassionately. "We were together."

"That was important?"

"I think you know the answer to that."

Tomara could think of nothing to say, or at least nothing that wouldn't give away great chunks of herself. He was smiling, an unsure half grin so filled with promise that Tomara was almost undone. She could lean into him and give him what she knew they both wanted and for a few minutes wish away the world.

But their embrace would have to end. And the ending might come close to killing her. Hard as it was, it was easier to stop now.

Every eye in the cafe turned when Tomara and Hayden entered. She leaned into Hayden and took from his warmth what she needed to face the curious looks.

They'd placed their orders and were into their second glasses of welcomed water when young David sat down. "Jay said the two of you went out there today," he whispered. "Where it happened."

"You saw Jay?" Hayden asked.

David nodded. Despite her awareness of her surroundings, Tomara felt a change in David. He seemed less cocky, less in control. He's aged, she thought, but it was important that she listen to what he had to say. She filed the thought away.

When Jay called him this morning, David had gone over to talk to the incapacitated police officer. He hadn't seen any reason to deny that he'd gone to see Hoagy the day before he escaped. David had thought, briefly, about keeping his trip from his father, but when he heard of the breakout, he realized that wouldn't work.

"I told Jay. I saw Hoagy because I felt sorry for him. I figured if it was me I'd be scared to death. I was right. Hoagy was about to lose his mind. We talked some about what the gossip was. Hoagy said he wasn't sure any lawyer was going to be able to do them much good."

"You told Jay this?" Hayden asked.

"Yeah. Look, Jay leveled with me. Unless someone didn't sign in, they only had three visitors that day." David turned his attention toward Tomara. "You, me and Mr. Barth."

"Unless someone didn't sign in," Tomara whispered, not sure whether she believed what she was saying. "Jay? How is he?"

"Mad as a hunting dog on a short leash. He says he's getting back to work if it kills him. Hayden? He wants to talk to you."

After David left, Hayden stared off into space until To-mara broke the uneasy silence. She asked if Hayden was going to try to see Jay tonight, and then when he nodded, she asked him what he was going to tell Jay about his day.

"He needs to know about what we saw."

"What did we see? Nothing."

"I also want to hear what Jay may have heard from the state police."

Tomara hadn't thought about anything or anyone except her and Hayden today. Now, however, his words brought her back to the world. "They might have been captured," she whispered.

Hayden shook his head. "If they had, that would have been the only conversation in here tonight." He nodded at the waitress bringing them their meal. "I want you to go with me."

"To see Jay? Why?"

"Because there might be things he wants to ask you."

"Oh." Tomara picked up her utensils, but she could no longer remember why they'd come in here. Her day wasn't over, after all. She would have to see Jay. Sit in the same room with a man recuperating from a bullet wound. And once again talk about murder and attempted murder.

Jay clumped around Lisa's house in a pair of slippers that should have been discarded two years ago. Other than that and the arm secured in a sling, he looked like a man who'd spent the day at work. He grunted his acknowledgment of Tomara and Hayden, explaining that Lisa was picking up her sons and should be back inside an hour. In the meantime, he was more than a little tired of his own company. "Took your own sweet time getting over here," he grumbled at Hayden. "I know what time you took off this morning. Don't tell me it's taken you all day to climb that damn hill."

Ignoring his friend's foul mood, Hayden filled Jay in on everything he and Tomara had done. Or almost everything, Tomara noted. There was no reason to tell Jay that there'd been a few minutes when both of them had let their guard down.

Jay had questions. What did the tire tracks look like? What made Hayden so sure they were recent? Why had Tomara been so insistent that they get close to the seldom-used road?

"What did you want me to do?" There was a sharp edge to Tomara's question, but she didn't apologize. "Jay, I was looking for something. Anything."

Again Jay grunted. It was his turn. The state police had spent the day futilely canvasing the area looking for Al and Hoagy. Because of manpower limitations, the police would be cutting back on the number of men involved in the actual search. All roads in and out of the county would be monitored, and since both Al and Hoagy had criminal records, it had been easy to supply all troopers with up-to-date pictures.

Leonard had dropped by. He had been curious about the progress, or lack of progress, in the case. "I asked him what he thought of Al's and Hoagy's state of mind the last time he saw them. It was pretty much the same thing David said. Hoagy was nervous as hell. Al was pretty closemouthed. Leonard said he couldn't get him to say a thing."

Tomara nodded. That was the same impression she'd gotten when she saw them. Then she questioned Jay about the possibility that someone could have come in without a guard taking note of it.

"It's a long shot. So long I'm thinking it couldn't have happened."

"Then only three people were in the jail that day."

"That's what I'm thinking."

"And David says you believe him."

"I've never known David to lie."

"Then that leaves me. Unless you think their lawyer smuggled in a gun."

Jay didn't say anything.

Chapter Eleven

That was a hell of a thing to say," Hayden said the moment Tomara slammed the door behind her, "What are you trying to do?"

"Be a cop." Jay paced to the window, watching as Tomara's slim form disappeared down the steps and into the night. "If you'd stop thinking of her as woman and remember—"

"You think I don't remember? I'm the one who spent the day with her. Trying to figure out what was going on inside her head. Second-guessing her."

"And what did you come up with?"

"Nothing." Hayden let the word hang. "Unless she's a lot better actress than I think she is, Al and Hoagy are putting her through hell, and that's what's driving her."

"Maybe enough hell that she decided the only way for her to survive was to get them out of the state."

Hayden snorted. "Do you really believe that?"

"What I do believe is that you've let her get to you."

That stopped Hayden. He could have told Jay to mind his own business, or denied that his friend knew what he was talking about. But if he did, Jay would see through him. "You've been on your feet too long. Get some rest before you lose what you have left of your mind."

"I'm not the one who needs rest. You're the one who spent the day tramping all over God knows where. And if you think you can convince me that you needed that much time—"

"I'm not going to try to convince you of anything," Hayden said with his hand on the door. "David said you were going to get back to work tomorrow."

"I have to." Jay gave Hayden a crooked grin. "This being an invalid is driving me crazy. You want to be there when I talk to the state cops again?"

"I can't. If I don't start doing my own job, I'm not going to have one."

Neither man said goodbye, but it wasn't necessary. It was simply understood that sometime tomorrow one or the other would pick up the phone and the conversation would continue as if there'd been no interruption.

She's gotten to you, hasn't she? Jay was the only one in the world who would have dared ask the question.

I don't know, Hayden answered. *Maybe. Probably.*

Probably became a certainty when Hayden saw that Tomara stood outside the unpainted fence between Lisa's property and the road. She had to have heard the front door closing, but she didn't turn around to acknowledge his presence.

"Are you all right?" Hayden wasn't sure he'd spoken loud enough to be heard.

Tomara started to nod; lying would be easier than having to explain. But then she stopped herself and waited for Hayden to join her.

"Are you all right?" Hayden repeated.

"I never thought it would come to this." Innumerable stars punctuated the sky, making Tomara ache. "Having Jay accuse me—"

"I did the same thing."

"I know." Did he have any idea how close she was to tears? Tomara wondered. She could handle one accusation. But to know that both Jay and Hayden had set up barriers between themselves and her was almost more than she could take.

"He has to. It's his job."

"I know that." Tomara debated saying anything, but she was in no shape to weigh the wisdom of her words. "But it isn't your job."

He was touching her. Once again his fingers found her cheek. And again the gesture said a great deal and yet left a great deal more unsaid. When she'd walked out of Lisa's house, Tomara had believed she didn't ever want to see either man again.

But instead of fleeing to Mandy's, she'd stood there trying to sort through the ruin of her emotions. In the morning, she'd told herself, she would be strong again. Only, this was night, and she wasn't strong. She was lonely.

And Hayden had come to her.

He wasn't saying anything; it was wiser that way. She wouldn't say anything either, because any words might be the wrong ones. Instead Tomara drew Hayden's hand off her cheek and slid it down to her throat. He would feel her pulse and know how close to the edge she was. He would understand that beneath jeans and hiking boots and hair caught in a tight braid was a woman. A lonely, hurting woman.

A touch wasn't enough.

No words existed with which to break through her self-imposed silence. All Tomara could do was offer herself to Hayden and pray he understood what she needed.

He wrapped his arms around her and drew her against him, and a world that had turned itself upside down righted. He sought her mouth; she offered hers to his and no longer felt isolated.

And then, still silent, Tomara pulled free and left, quickly, before it was too late.

At Mandy's suggestion, Tomara made an appointment to see Leonard early the next morning. She let him know how yesterday had gone, but he didn't seem particularly interested. His interest increased when she told him that Jay was skeptical about David's having anything to do with the breakout or that anyone could have paid an unrecorded visit to Al and Hoagy. "Let me give you a piece of advice, Tomara," Leonard said. "Jay's a good cop. He isn't going to tell you any more than what's absolutely necessary. You talked to David, but if Jay's putting pressure on him, do you really think the boy would tell you that?"

Tomara didn't know.

"Put yourself in David's shoes. If you thought you were a suspect, would you tell anyone who didn't have to know?"

Tomara was a suspect. At least that's how she saw herself. And she did know that talking to others about what she was going through was the last thing she would willingly do. "Are you saying you think David might be involved?"

"I'm not saying anything except that Jay's playing it close, and I don't want you to forget that. The same holds true for what he might have learned from the people at the jail. You didn't ask me for this piece of legal advice, but I'm going to give it to you anyway. You don't tell anyone anything you don't have to. Except for your lawyer, that is," Leonard wound up with a smile.

Tomara repeated Leonard's advice as she left his office. Before she'd covered a block, however, she knew she would have to talk to Jay again. Only, he wasn't alone.

Tomara wasn't sure what to expect, but before she could think of a way to gracefully back out of the room, Jay was introducing her to a state policeman. When Jay explained Tomara's involvement in the case, the muscular, middle-aged man gave her and then Jay a long look but said nothing.

Jay filled in the blanks. The state cop was here to coordinate search techniques with Jay and to pass on a vital piece of information. The murder victim had been identified.

"Bart Renfree was an alias," Jay explained. "His real name was Cortin McDonald. And he wasn't just some guy with nothing better to do than wander around the county."

Tomara waited.

"Cortin McDonald worked for the federal government."

"Jay?" Tomara clamped a hand over her mouth. She'd been about to tell Jay that this wasn't a spy movie.

"He was a governmental geologist. And he'd been sent here to research the possibility of petroleum deposits around Copper."

"Petroleum? Jay, those stories have been going around since we were children. Nothing's ever come of them."

"Until now. Now there are much more sophisticated ways of finding out what's under the surface. Tomara, the reason we know this is that Cortin's Washington contacts got worried when he didn't show up. They called the state police. I just got off the phone with his immediate supervisor."

"And?" Tomara asked, unable to wait Jay out.

"And the last time Cortin talked to his boss, he said he'd hired a couple of local men to take him out. Cortin hadn't told the locals what he was doing because the government didn't want to fuel any rumors. Cortin's story was that he was an overanxious antelope hunter who wanted to scout the area before the season began."

"He hired my father and brother, didn't he?" Tomara managed. She vaguely noticed the intense way the state policeman watched her, but she couldn't concentrate on that. If Al and Hoagy had somehow learned Cortin McDonald's real reason for being there— No. That didn't make sense. Neither her father nor brother knew the first thing about how to find, let alone tap a petroleum deposit.

"Why are you telling me this?" she asked.

"Because—" Ignoring the other policeman, Jay came around his small desk and placed himself a few inches away from Tomara. "Because last night you walked out of here thinking maybe I suspected you of something. If I had suspicions, I wouldn't be telling you this, would I?"

"Did he find anything?"

"I don't know. That isn't something Cortin's boss was willing to divulge."

Tomara could understand that, but it left even more un-answered questions. If Cortin's murder was somehow tied in with his job— No. It wasn't her responsibility to try to figure out motives. "Does that change anything?" she asked. "I mean now that you know who he was, and what he was doing, will you be talking to someone else? Investigating—"

"Investigating who, Tomara?"

"I don't know!" she snapped in frustration. "Jay, there have always been people around here who held on to prop-erty because they thought maybe someday it would be valuable because of its mineral wealth. I'm grasping at straws, aren't I?"

"Who knows, Miss Metcalf," the state cop said. "At this point we're grasping at straws ourselves. Your father and brother were seen standing by McDonald's body, but no one saw them pull the trigger."

Tomara's sense of gratitude toward the middle-aged man lasted until she passed this new piece of information on to Mandy. Mandy pointed out, however, that murder was only one of the charges against Al and Hoagy.

"I've been thinking of something," Mandy said as the two women shared a simple meal. "What Leonard said about the police not telling you any more than they have to? It's just possible they have more of an idea where Al and Hoagy are and aren't telling you."

"What are you saying?"

"I'm not sure. Except that all this business with the fed-eral government and geologists and petroleum hasn't changed why you're here."

Hayden put in a long day, but at last he parked the Bronco and wandered over to Jay's office. Jay wasn't there, but the policeman was at home, having moved back into his own place after spending a couple of days recuperating at Lisa's.

"Am I glad to see you," Jay said as he slapped a beer in Hayden's hand. "Everyone's been knocking on my door today. I'm so tired of weighing what I say."

"You want my advice. Don't open your mouth. Otherwise anything's likely to come out."

Jay faked a punch at Hayden but wound up collapsing on the couch. "This damn thing." He indicated his shoulder. "Makes me feel weak as a kid with the flu. I wasn't sure I was going to make it through the day. I didn't say it, but thanks for filling in for me for a couple of days."

"I didn't take the heat for you," Hayden pointed out. "And the only thing I dealt with, or tried to deal with, was the Metcalf business."

"Which is nine tenths of what I'm doing these days. I hope you don't mind, but I'd like to throw a couple of ideas at you. See what you think."

This was exactly why he had come to see Jay. As Hayden savored his first taste of something cold for the day, Jay gave him a blow-by-blow description of his visit with David Kemper. David was smart. Self-confident without running it into the ground. "That boy's going somewhere with his life. He's intelligent. Maybe the most intelligent kid I've ever seen. And he cares about people. It's a combination you don't see a lot of. The only thing is, I keep asking myself why someone who has that much going for him, and as much to do as he does, takes time to run over to Sidney to see someone he has zip in common with."

"Hunting. They have hunting in common."

"David doesn't hunt."

Hayden frowned. Every teenage male in Copper hunted; taking a few days off school every fall to track down an antelope or deer served as a rite of passage. "He has a rifle," Hayden pointed out.

"Which has never bagged anything more serious than a tin can. David told me that today. And he would prefer it if that wasn't passed on. He said, and I tend to believe him, that he went hunting with his dad when he was about eight or nine. David didn't say too much, but something happened then that soured him on hunting. He owns a rifle because that's what's expected, but he's always managed to make himself scarce during hunting season.''

Hayden wasn't quite sure where Jay was going with the conversation, but he was willing to wait. In truth, he'd had a hard time concentrating on anything today, and things hadn't changed tonight.

Jay didn't take long to lay his cards on the table. He believed he'd given David the impression that he had no reason to suspect anything the teenager had told him, but Jay was going to keep a close eye on David's comings and goings. David's concern for Hoagy might be nothing more than a compassionate young man's interest in someone from the wrong side of the tracks. And it might be something more.

Although they were alone, Jay made a show of glancing at the windows before going on. ''There's a little more about our dead geologist. Something only you and I and his supervisor are to know.''

Hayden leaned forward. He was no longer interested in his beer.

''I told Tomara that Cortin McDonald was out here looking for a petroleum deposit. Hayden, he did more than look. He found.''

''Big?''

''Big. As in enough to put this town on the map and maybe make a lot of people rich.''

Hayden whistled. He was silent a moment, his mind working at full speed. ''You say McDonald was killed just after he passed that information on to his supervisor. But—''

Jay was leaning forward, nodding.

''But if McDonald let something slip to someone else and that someone was greedy...''

''Then maybe what McDonald knew was worth killing him for.''

Who? Hayden found the question but answered it himself. ''Al and Hoagy were guiding him.''

''Yeah. Al and Hoagy.''

''And maybe Hoagy said something to David.''

"Maybe."

Hayden was sorry he'd come to see Jay. He'd been willing to accept the possibility that Al and Hoagy had accidentally killed McDonald. Hard as that was to face, Tomara might have learned to live with that. But now there was a new twist, a twist called greed. And if the kid who represented Copper's success story was somehow involved—
"You're sure no one else knows about what McDonald found?"

"That's what his supervisor said. He was adamant that McDonald knew how important it was to keep this sort of thing under wraps. But Hayden, if Al and Hoagy were with him when the discovery was made—"

"You're not going to tell Tomara, are you?"

Jay's look told Hayden that he had no business asking the question.

Tomara sat on a stool in Mandy's Saloon waiting for the older woman to finish waiting on a customer. Although it was after seven, Leonard hadn't come in to see Mandy, and Mandy was looking up every time the door opened.

"Maybe he's working late," Tomara offered by way of explanation when Mandy sat down next to her.

"I don't know. I swear I don't understand the man. The weekend was great. Wonderful, in fact, even if we came back sooner than I wanted to. But since we got back, I haven't seen enough of him to remember what he looks like."

Tomara tried to think of something soothing to say, but stopped herself in time. Mandy wouldn't want to be coddled.

"You know what it is, don't you?" Mandy went on. "It's the nature of the beast. Men, they're put on earth to drive us women crazy."

Tomara laughed. "That sounds like a subject for a research paper."

"What do I need with research? I've spent fifty-two years learning that little lesson. Believe me, I know what I'm talking about. As soon as a woman starts thinking she knows what makes a man tick, he turns around and does something to knock her off balance." Mandy had been whispering. Now she leaned closer and lowered her voice even more. "I gave myself a piece of advice years ago. Every once in a while I need to remind myself of it. And for free I'll pass it on to you. Love a man. Share a bed with him. But keep a little piece of yourself apart from him. That way when things don't go right, you'll still have enough of your heart left that you'll be able to pick up the pieces."

Tomara had heard Mandy say that before. In the past Mandy's philosophy hadn't made that much of an impact, because loving a man hadn't been part of Tomara's life. She was no longer sure of that. "It isn't easy to do," she offered.

"You think I don't know that." Mandy was staring into her glass of iced tea. "But if you want to get through life with your sanity intact, that's the way it has to be. From the way you talk, I'm guessing that's what you did with what's-his-name—the guy who wanted you to move in with him. When the two of you split, you didn't feel like slitting your throat, did you?"

"No."

"See." Mandy managed a smile. "You kept a piece of yourself separate from him."

"And maybe…" Tomara drew out the sentence. "Maybe I didn't love him in the first place."

"If you didn't, then I feel sorry for you."

Mandy was confusing her. One minute she was telling her she had to guard herself against a man's impact on her life. The next she was intimating there must be something wrong with her because she hadn't experienced what it was people call love. "I'm cautious," Tomara offered by way of explanation. "I'm never going to let myself fall in love unless I know exactly what the consequences will be."

To Tomara's consternation, Mandy laughed. "Let? Girl, when love happens there isn't any 'let' to it. Take it from one who's been the route, you'll have precious little control over that particular emotion."

Tomara couldn't agree. Certainly she was intelligent enough and cautious enough that she wouldn't tumble blindly into a personal relationship over which she had no control.

Would she?

Mandy didn't have the time to further expound on her philosophy of matters of the heart. A couple of ranchers came in full of talk about a cattle watering hole that had gone dry and their gratitude to Hayden Conover who'd contacted them earlier today to let them know they had permission to run their cattle on Windswept, which still sported a couple of adequate watering spots. Thanks to Hayden's quick intervention, the red tape with the federal government had been cut. The ranchers had just finished a long day moving their cattle onto the federal rangeland.

So that's what Hayden had done with his day. Tomara tried to shake off her thought. The last thing she needed tonight was Hayden on her mind. She was grateful when Leonard walked in. Between private looks at Mandy, Leonard told Tomara that he'd been in touch with the state police, who were frustrated but pretty sure Al and Hoagy hadn't left the county. "I don't know how much weight to put to what they're saying," Leonard explained. "Of course they don't want to admit that the two got past their roadblocks. The way I see it, either those two are waiting out the police, or they went cross-country and are in the next state by now."

Tomara kept her head close to Leonard so their conversation would remain private. "They don't have any money. And I don't think they have much in the way of supplies. Where would they go? And what would they do even if they were able to get out of the area?"

"I don't know, Tomara. I thought I knew how those two thought, but I'm reversing my thinking on that."

Tomara didn't know whether she wanted to continue the conversation. She was hungry for any information about her father and brother, but all Leonard could give her was speculation. And trying to second-guess the two people she'd grown up around was tearing her apart.

Mandy and Leonard didn't need her around. It was obvious they wanted to talk, which was difficult enough, given the demands of Mandy's clients, and impossible with her underfoot. After giving a weak explanation, Tomara slid off her stool and walked past curious stares to the heavy front door.

The prairie wind was waiting for her.

What was it she'd told Hayden yesterday? That she had a life waiting for her in another state. She did, and yet the prairie wind was in her tonight. Maybe it had always been there, and she simply hadn't known it.

The night wind was a lonely wind.

Tomara accepted it. Life had a cadence. For some people it was music, for others power or greed or an endless search for serenity. For others it went no further than the warmth of family. For her it had always been open spaces.

Strange. She'd gone so far and spent so many years learning that. She'd put those years of wanting more from life than a father and a brother who had little to give behind her now. She understood that what went on inside her mind and heart would be with her as long as she lived. Other people wouldn't change what beat inside her.

She couldn't put burdens on other people. Whether she was or wasn't happy with her life was up to her.

Tomara still wasn't sure where that revelation had come from. She only knew that living for the future was no longer her goal. She was in Copper tonight, and tonight was all she had.

It was too dark to run. But she could walk. And walk.

Five minutes later Tomara was staring out at the darkened baseball diamond where she'd watched David Kemper work his magic against opposing batters. That afternoon she had envied the boy his strength, his grace, his freedom. Most of all she had envied him his future.

She no longer did. She could wish the young man well, but that was all. David had his life, just as Al and Hoagy did. Just as Hayden Conover did.

Hayden. She'd told herself she wasn't going to think about him, but that had been a lie, an uneasy woman's attempt to put off reality.

He'd held her. Kissed her. She'd done the same to him. When her defenses were down and her loneliness had ventured too close, she'd taken refuge in a man's arms.

Only it had been more than that. That first touch had been for exploration. After that their coming together had been because both of them wanted and needed the contact. Yes, she had been trying to deal with something she'd never believed she would have to face, but she hadn't responded to Hayden because she despaired of her father and brother's future.

She'd reached for Hayden because, for reasons she didn't understand, he was the man she wanted in her life.

The one her heart was trying to make room for.

"It doesn't make sense." Tomara was talking to herself, to Mandy, to the night. "Maybe it'll never make sense. All I know is, I want him. I need him."

Too restless to go on leaning against the empty bleachers, Tomara turned around and retraced her steps to the main street. She was too full of her thoughts to try to force herself to remain within four walls. All she could do was walk aimlessly, working off tension and energy.

A light was on in Jay's house. Tomara wanted to talk to him, to retrace their childhood. But tonight wasn't the time. It wouldn't be the right time until she and Jay were no longer participants in this mess that was keeping them apart.

Hayden.

He was coming out of Jay's house, saying something over his shoulder and then closing the door. Tomara hugged the night, waiting. Absorbing his impact on her. He carried himself like a coyote, a powerful, proud wild animal.

He'd seen her. A chill swept through Tomara, but because she was caught in the night's mood, she made no attempt to pretend. He wasn't saying anything. He'd made no move toward her.

Energy. His energy touched her and left her hungry. More than hungry.

It wasn't possible to want a man this much. But she did; she wasn't going to lie away her reaction. She could feel his hands on her, hear words she'd waited a lifetime to hear. They would reach across the storm that separated them, and find the holes in each other and plug up those holes. She would give herself to him, a child exposing her deepest needs. He would know what she needed. Without words being spoken, he would take her, and she would give and he would make her feel whole.

But only in her dreams.

In real life he was only looking at her and she was looking back. And the storm between them continued.

Chapter Twelve

Al and Hoagy had been spotted hitchhiking on the state highway heading north. Speculation was they must be trying to get to Canada. At least that was the rumor as reported by Mandy the next morning. "I'm just passing it on to you for what it's worth," Mandy explained to Tomara when she ran back up to her place an hour after getting to work. "My beer distributor swears it was them, but he didn't stop to ask them their names. He's already told Jay."

"North? There's nothing for them up there."

"There's nothing for them down here, either. Look, my distributor doesn't know Al and Hoagy from Adam, but he's heard the stories. Who hasn't? Anyway, I figure by noon everyone in the country will have passed on the latest, and it'll be so distorted no one is going to know what the truth is. Maybe the two bearded men were Al and Hoagy and maybe they were a couple of drifters. All I know is, Jay took off as soon as he heard the news."

Tomara spent the rest of the day locked in a tension that made concentration difficult. She'd offered to paint Mandy's living room, but she worked without being aware of what she was doing. A dozen times she circled the telephone, trying to work up the courage to call Jay. The first half dozen times she talked herself out of it, and when she finally dialed the number, all she got was Jay's recording machine. She didn't bother to leave a message.

When she'd finally finished her job and cleaned up, Tomara walked over to Jay's office. The front door was locked. She tried to talk herself into walking by Jay's house, but that was even harder than trying to call him had been.

Last night she'd shared something wordless with Hayden outside Jay's house. If she went back there now, the memory might become stronger.

Tomara turned around, her mind sorting through possibilities. She could go into the saloon and listen to rumors, or she could go back to Mandy's house and try to come up with something to eat. She still hadn't made up her mind when a pickup filled with teenage boys drew near. When the driver put on his brakes, Tomara drew away.

"Tomara? We're practicing over at the school. You wanna watch?"

Before she could think of anything to say, the truck took off again. It had been David. At first Tomara told herself she wasn't going to go, but she needed a distraction, and being around young people, even young people who were probably more curious about her than she was about them, sounded wonderful.

The boys were already out on the field warming up when Tomara arrived. A few girls were in the stands. The two coaches were huddled together in the dugout. Tomara found a perch on the bleachers close to the backstop and leaned forward to watch.

A few minutes later David disengaged himself from the others who were rifling balls back and forth. He walked slowly over to the visitors' side of the field and then nodded his head to indicate he wanted Tomara to join him.

"Maybe I should have waited until tonight, but there's something I think you should know."

"What is it?"

"Hoagy." David's rich voice was a low whisper. "He called me this morning."

"David! Have you told—"

"I haven't told anyone. Hoagy begged me not to. He, well, I think Al put him up to it. He wanted to know what I'd heard about what the state cops and Jay were doing."

Tomara kept one eye on the coaches, who didn't seem to have noticed that their star pitcher wasn't with the others. "Did Hoagy say why he called you and not me?"

"He didn't know where you were. He thought you might be with Mandy, but he was afraid Mandy would answer the phone. Tomara? I think he wanted to ask me for money or food or something."

"Where was he? Did he tell you that?"

David shook his head. "He didn't say, and I didn't ask. Tomara, I don't mind Hoagy calling me. If it was me in his place, I wouldn't be thinking very straight. But I don't want to get involved, not that way. I don't know if they did what they're accused of doing. If I tried to help them and they were caught—I don't want to risk my future. Can you understand that?"

Tomara could. "You didn't do anything wrong by talking to Hoagy," she offered. "Even if someone finds out, and you have to testify to that, I can't see that it's your fault that you picked up the phone. What makes you think they need money or food?"

"Just the way he sounded. Ah, I asked him if they had a place to stay, and he said yes."

One of the coaches was looking their way. "Is that all he said?"

"Not quite." David glanced over at his coach. "He said— what he said was they've already looked there. They're not going to look again."

"Oh." David had to leave. If she kept him with her much longer, he might get in trouble. But there was one more question she needed to ask. "Is he going to try to get in touch with you again?"

"I don't know. It sounded like he wanted to go on talking, but he was afraid to."

David was gone. Aware that others might be watching her, Tomara kept her face impassive, but her thoughts raced. She was now convinced that the beer distributor had been wrong

and that Al and Hoagy were still hanging around Copper for
the simple reason that they had no way of leaving, and nowhere to go even if they did. There were so many things she
wanted to tell David in case Hoagy called him again. Things
that had to do with wanting to slap her father and brother
silly for breaking out the way they had, and at the same time
desperately needing to hear that they were all right.

*They're staying somewhere they think they'll be safe be-
cause the police have already been there.* That could be only
one place.

She should tell Jay. She was aiding and abetting fugitives
by remaining silent. But if she said something, David might
get in trouble.

That wasn't the only reason Tomara remained where she
was. If Jay and the state police went after her father and
brother, someone else might be hurt. Someone had tried to
kill Jay. Someone was desperate.

Tomara refused to put a name to that someone. Instead,
she listened to what her heart was trying to tell her.

She had to talk sense into her father and brother.

As soon as she could leave without calling attention to
herself, Tomara returned to Mandy's place. She quickly
threw together a backpack containing a half-dozen sandwiches, candy bars and some fruit. After leaving a note
telling Mandy that she'd gone for a drive and didn't know
when she'd be back, Tomara got into the Jeep and drove
away. She first went north, hoping that anyone who might
be watching her would think she was trying to find Jay.
Then, relying on her knowledge of the area, Tomara cut off
the main road and picked up one of the many dirt tracks
that cut through the prairie.

Hayden didn't try to analyze what Tomara was doing.
Thanks to the helicopter and a powerful set of binoculars,
he was able to take note of her progress without giving away
his presence.

She was heading east, but unless he was wrong, she
wouldn't be continuing in that direction much longer. When
she once again cut away from paved roads and started

bucking over the trail the two of them had gone over a few days ago, Hayden knew what he had to do.

The helicopter wasn't the way to go. If he got any closer, he would give himself away. But it wouldn't take that long to land, load a horse into a trailer and take off after her. The reason for the horse was twofold. The animal would be able to travel farther than the Bronco could. And Tomara would be less likely to hear him coming.

And if she was doing what he thought she was— Damn it, he'd deal with that and her deception when he had no choice.

Tomara's thoughts still weren't as organized as she needed them to be. She should be trying to amass the arguments she would use to try to convince her father and brother to give themselves up. By now they had to have had enough of running and hiding. She could tell them that their lawyer still hadn't thrown up his hands, although he was getting close to that point, and if they didn't do something positive soon . . .

The thought faded away.

She hadn't been alone the last time she was out here. Hayden had come with her, maybe simply because he wanted to keep an eye on her, and maybe because he believed her half-baked idea that the prairie might hold answers. They had found something, but that something had little to do with evidence gathering. He had touched her; she'd touched him. And what had been slumbering so deeply within her that she'd been able to deny its existence had become a living force.

A thing called attraction.

Tomara refused to call it anything else. To do so would expose her to much more than she could deal with today and probably tomorrow.

Being alone was both a comforting and uneasy feeling. She needed time with her thoughts. But what haunted and tested her today were thoughts she'd never had before. Parr had been someone to have in her life, a reason to put an end

o the dating game. Before things unraveled for them, she'd
njoyed his presence. But she'd never felt this—needing—
around Parr.

Today it was a pulsing, building storm.

A winter storm, Tomara thought with her eyes on the
flawless sky. How deceptive that incredible blue could be.
In summer the sky was her friend, a caressing presence that
allowed her to almost forget a hurricane of wind, snow that
didn't fall gently but drove its cold deep into a person. The
prairie wasn't a gentle land in the winter, not if one wanted
to survive to experience another spring.

Was that what Hayden Conover was? she asked, too deep
in her thoughts to realize how absurd it was to compare a
man with the elements. He was a chinook. A violent thunderstorm.

He could also be sunlight on a spring morning.

She couldn't drive any farther. With the pack strapped to
her back, Tomara left the Jeep and started into the rugged
hills. She might not find anything here. Al and Hoagy could
be anywhere, but she had no other place to look, and if it
were her, she probably would have gone back to the cave.

The effort of climbing kept her thoughts on the here and
now. During those short snatches of time when she was able
to concentrate on something other than her footing, she
tried to go back to the arguments she would use to convince
her father and brother that running would serve no purpose, but Hayden kept intruding.

Hayden pulled the Bronco off the highway at the spot
where the dirt road leading to the base of the hills joined the
main road. He unloaded the gelding that had become one
of the necessities of his job and set off at an easy trot. When
he reached Tomara's Jeep, he stopped only long enough to
assure himself that the engine was already cold. He shielded
his eyes against the sun and scanned his surroundings. He
felt tight, taut, and, although he didn't want to admit it,
deeply disappointed.

Tomara should be trusting him and the legal system. She should have told someone what she was doing. Damn it, she had no business presenting herself as an aider and abettor for a couple of fugitives.

But that was what she was, and no matter how much he wanted to, Hayden could think of nothing else to call her.

The binoculars were no help, but he'd expected that. The nature of the hills was such that unless she was walking on a crest, Tomara would be hidden. The route Hayden chose was longer than a person on foot would choose, but one his horse could handle. By his reckoning, he should reach the cave about the same time she did. And then? Hayden didn't try to answer the question. He also didn't ask why he carried a rifle strapped to his saddle.

There was no one in the cave.

For a few seconds Tomara wasn't sure she could handle the sense of futility that flooded through her, and then acceptance set in. Nothing had gone as she wanted it to. Why had she thought it would be any different this time? Still, she couldn't help calling out her father's name, wondering whether he'd ever hear it from her again.

And yet the trip hadn't been totally wasted. Once her eyes adjusted to the dim light, Tomara made out something in a corner of the cave that hadn't been there before. She stretched out her hand and came in contact with a soft bundle. Someone had left a sleeping bag here. Two sleeping bags, Tomara amended after crawling still closer. And several cans of beans, a half-empty whiskey bottle, an almost empty bag of stale bread.

"How long ago?" Tomara asked aloud, surprising herself with the sound of her voice. She repeated the question as if the sleeping bags were capable of telling her how long it had been since her father and brother had used them. Because they were on foot, it would take them between three and four hours to get from here to whatever telephone they'd used to call David. Maybe they were sneaking around the outskirts of town even now, looking for something to supplement their meager food supply.

Tomara settled herself cross-legged and leaned forward, her head aching. She felt insulated from the world, insulated and shut off. Had her father and brother really come to this? Hiding in a cave and stealing food?

With that question, Tomara made up her mind. She would stay here the rest of the day, and all night if necessary. She wouldn't leave until she'd talked to her father and brother, and she wouldn't stop talking until she'd convinced them that living empty stomach to empty stomach wasn't a life.

She couldn't spend the hours sitting inside the lonely little cave. Needing sunlight, Tomara backed out and stood. Though she scanned her surroundings, because she wasn't at the top of a bluff she was unable to see down to the prairie below. She was sorry she hadn't brought binoculars with her, but because she was carrying enough for three people that hadn't been possible.

Still— Half curious and half looking for a way to fill her time, Tomara started walking, not toward the side of the hills that would give her a view of her Jeep, but toward the far side where, maybe, she and Hayden had seen something.

She'd covered the better part of a mile, a slow, crawling mile, and had clawed her way to a high spot when it happened. Something loud and violent slammed into the rock no more than three feet away. The echo of a rifle shattered the air.

She dove for the ground, survival her only concern.

Hayden heard the hard blast. He knew what he had to do; he was terrified of what he might find.

With impatient feet, he pushed his horse onward, but in less than a minute the going became treacherous. With one hand he steadied himself to dismount. With the other he reached for his rifle.

Another blast. What the hell! Damn it, Tomara was out there somewhere. Unarmed.

God! Someone was shooting at her!

Hayden had always believed himself surefooted, but the jagged terrain slowed him. He wanted to cry out and let Tomara know he was coming, but he knew better than to give himself away.

He refused to accept the possibility that he might be too late.

A flash of movement. For a moment Hayden thought he might have glimpsed the rifle or whomever had fired it.

His binoculars thudded into his chest, but Hayden didn't stop long enough to use them. Instead he dropped to his knees so he wouldn't present a target and waited for the movement to be repeated.

He was soon rewarded.

Splendid hair caught in a thick braid fell to one side as Tomara lifted her head for a quick look. Hayden was crouched at least a hundred feet away behind a projecting rock, but that didn't prevent him from sensing the tension radiating out from the woman. She wasn't afraid. How he knew that he couldn't say. What he did know at this moment was that he admired her as he'd never before admired a human being.

She was in a life-threatening situation. Unarmed, and, she believed, with no one at her side. And yet she was coolly, almost dispassionately assessing her surroundings and trying to make sense of what was insanity.

"Tomara."

It couldn't be. And yet Tomara would never mistake that voice. Slowly, not trusting anything or anyone, she turned. What Hayden was doing there wasn't important. She needed to deal with the reality of his presence, and the even greater reality that someone was trying to kill her.

"Where are they?"

Tomara pointed. With the gesture she made an unconscious decision. They were together in this, whatever it was.

"Can you see them?"

Tomara shook her head. Then because whoever had shot at her hadn't reacted to Hayden's voice, she took a chance on speaking. "They're down there. Where we found the tracks the other day."

Hayden was coming toward her, reminding her of a wild animal with its instinct for survival kicked into high gear. He moved swiftly, smoothly, yet so low to the ground that he couldn't possibly be seen by anyone below them.

"You're all right?" he asked when he was close enough that she could reach out and touch him.

"Scared but all right." Tomara didn't care that she'd given away a great deal by admitting her fear. Hayden was here. Things were changing. Not only did he have a rifle with him, but he was someone she could depend on. Someone to trust.

She couldn't remember ever totally believing that before.

Hayden brushed his hand over her shoulder; the contact didn't last long enough to be anything except a promise. Now he was inching forward for a better look at the prairie below. "A truck." His voice was more vibration than sound.

"I know. I've never seen it before."

Tomara watched as Hayden lifted his binoculars to his eyes. "I can't see the license plate. Or whoever's driving it. You said 'they'. How many of them are there?"

"I'm not sure. I think three. I don't understand."

"Neither do I. But I'm sure as hell going to find out."

"You're not going down there? Hayden? No."

"No." He gave her a half smile she didn't understand but wouldn't soon forget. "I'm not that crazy. Three against one. At least three against one. I wonder what would happen if I did this." Before Tomara could think to stop him, Hayden sprang to his feet, exposing himself.

He dropped almost immediately. Another bullet harmlessly sliced the air where he'd been.

Tomara bit down a cry. Life wasn't supposed to be like this. In movies, yes, but not— She stopped the useless argument. This was her life, and this was happening. "Please don't do that again."

"I have to. I've got to get them to expose themselves."

No, you don't, she thought but knew better than to say anything.

Once again Hayden exposed himself, this time with his binoculars held in his right hand. Once again a shot was his reward. Hayden didn't seem to notice. "Yeah," he whispered after staring through the binoculars. "That's where they are."

"You can see them?"

"Not much. Just some movement. One of them's wearing a white T-shirt. Bad idea if you want to stay hidden." Hayden indicated that Tomara was to hand him his rifle. When she did, he crouched forward and then sighted. He was on his feet and firing before Tomara understood his plan. One shot. Two. Three.

Hayden was back behind the relative safety of a rock. He'd dropped his rifle and was staring through the binoculars. "They're leaving. On the run."

Despite everything that had happened in the past few minutes Tomara was aware of Hayden's impact on her senses. And yet she was thinking clearly enough that she touched the binoculars, telling him she wanted to see.

There were three men, all of them exposed as they sprinted from the rocks to the waiting truck. Tomara made a minor adjustment in the binoculars but didn't take her eyes off the action. In less than a minute they would be in the truck and gone. "I don't believe—" Tomara began. She didn't finish.

The man bringing up the rear. She knew him. Recognition tugged at her, but because the man was out of his element, it took a moment for her to put the pieces together.

"Leonard."

"What?" Hayden snatched the binoculars from her, but it was too late. The men were already in the pickup. The black Ford with a roll bar in the bed and two oversize spotlights mounted on top was pulling away. "Are you sure?" Hayden asked after he'd given up trying to read the license.

"I think so."

"Leonard," Hayden repeated. "What in the hell is he doing here?"

"Hayden?" Tomara waited until he was looking at her. "I was so sure. When I saw him running, I was positive it was him. But he was so far away, and—"

"And it doesn't make any sense. That's what you were going to say, isn't it?"

The strength was being stripped from Tomara. Except for the first unexpected shot, she hadn't actually believed that her life was in danger. The chance that a bullet would find its mark at this range was pretty remote. And yet it had happened.

What had happened to Jay and to the man Hayden had found had almost been repeated. Tomara didn't want to feel weak. She wanted to be like those female cops on TV who shrugged off gun battles and met their male partners pace for pace.

But she wasn't a cop. And she no longer believed the TV image.

"You're shaking."

That's the least of my problems, Tomara thought. "Reaction. I'll be all right."

"I know you will. I wish to hell—"

"You wish what?" Tomara asked when he didn't finish.

"Nothing." Hayden swung away from the prairie and its slowly disappearing puff of dust that was all that remained of the men who'd tried to kill Tomara. "This has to come to an end. Somehow we have to find the answers."

"We?"

"Jay and me," Hayden said. The way he was looking at her left Tomara open to a faint hope. Maybe he was including her. "Tomara? If you were in court, could you swear it was Leonard?"

Tomara wished he hadn't put it that way. "I don't know," she had to tell him. "It was so fast, and he was so far away. The truck. Did you recognize it?"

"No. But they're heading toward the reservation. If it's been around there, someone will have noticed. There's been a lot of custom work done to it."

"Should we go after them?" Tomara was glad her voice sounded steady. It might be a while before she stopped shaking, but at least she could speak without giving herself away.

"We could. But we're not going to."

Something in Hayden's tone warned Tomara. "Why not?"

"Because there's no way we can catch up with them. And because we have unfinished business up here."

Tomara waited.

"Do you have any idea what I'm doing here?"

Until now Tomara hadn't had time to ask herself that. Now the answer became the most important thing in her life. "You were following me, weren't you?"

"Do you blame me?"

"Please. Don't answer my question with another question. Why were you following me?"

"I take it you didn't find Al or Hoagy."

"No." Did she dare tell him what she'd found? There was a scratch on the side of Hayden's neck, a souvenir of what he'd risked to protect her. "But they've been up here. In the cave."

"And they might be back. Tell me something, Tomara. How did you know to come here? Did they get in touch with you?"

Tomara didn't want to bring David into the explanation. "I didn't know what else to do," she told him, hating herself for lying. "I'd heard rumors that they were trying to get to Canada, but I didn't believe that. I started thinking that this really was the only place they could come."

"So you acted on a hunch. Just a hunch."

He didn't believe her. That didn't surprise Tomara, and yet she would have given a great deal not to have things like this between them. "Do you want to see?" she asked. What she was offering wasn't enough; she knew that. But it was all she had.

"Yeah. And then we'll talk."

Everything was wrong between them. For the first time in her life she'd met a man she wanted to get close to, and now everything was wrong. It hurt. Deeply.

Hayden spent a couple of minutes inside the cave while Tomara waited outside. Finally he emerged with the whiskey bottle. "One of the mechanics at the gas station said someone had swiped a bottle from his truck. He thought it was one of his friends' idea of a joke. I guess he was wrong."

Tomara accepted this further evidence of how deeply her father and brother had dug their hole. "I can't apologize for them, Hayden."

"I'm not asking you to. What's in your backpack?"

She showed him and then waited, knowing what conclusion he would come to after seeing the amount of food. But he didn't say anything, and in the end his silence was harder to take than condemnation.

"Aren't you going to go back?" Tomara asked although she'd already posed the question once.

"No. And neither are you."

"What?"

"We're staying the night. And if Al and Hoagy come back, you're going to tell them that running is the most stupid thing they could possibly do. After that I'm going to ask them who the hell those three other men are and if they've ever seen Leonard up here."

Hayden's argument made sense. If she'd been able to dismiss the emotional component and focus on the practical aspects, she couldn't have agreed more. "What do you intend to do while I'm trying to talk them into turning themselves in? Hold that rifle on them?"

"If that's what it takes."

"You really don't know what you're asking of me, do you?" Tomara asked.

"What I'm trying to do is give you the time to talk sense into those two. Time you didn't have out at their place the other day."

"That's not what you said," Tomara pressed. She wasn't sure why this point she was trying to make was so important, but she couldn't stop, not with so much still unresolved between them. "You said that what they're doing is stupid."

"Yeah."

"That's all it is to you, isn't it? An irrational act by two irrational men. But, Hayden, those irrational men are part of my life."

They'd touched on this subject before. Hayden tried, honestly tried to put himself in her position, but he had nothing to draw on. If it had been his family he probably wouldn't be up here. The reason was simple; they wouldn't have done the same for him.

"If you're asking me to try to see this from their side of things, I'm sorry, but I can't."

"I know you can't." Tomara sounded sad. "And maybe I know why. Oh, Hayden, what does it matter? I feel as if half of me is out there hiding, sneaking around in the shadows—"

"Running from a dead man? Shooting at a police officer?"

Tomara almost hit Hayden. "Don't say it! Damn it, don't say that!"

"Why?"

"Because it isn't true." When he stared, she forged ahead, emotion guiding her words. "I know what you're thinking. I'm hiding from the facts. But Hayden, there aren't any facts. Nothing you can point to that says without a doubt that they're guilty of what you're accusing them of." Why was she trying? They'd had this argument before.

The rock she'd just collapsed on was rough enough to serve as a necessary distraction from the emotional turmoil she was feeling. She didn't want to go on looking at Hayden, especially not with him standing over her, reminding her of which of them had the ultimate control. But dropping her eyes was impossible. "I want you to promise me something."

"Promise?"

"That you won't shoot them."

I can't make a promise like that, Hayden almost said. Tomara's eyes stopped him. Asking him that had taken a great deal out of her. She'd been shot at today. She'd learned that he'd stalked her up here. She'd crawled into a cave hoping to find her relatives and come up with nothing. He'd have to be blind and unthinking not to realize what the day had done to her.

And Hayden wasn't blind or unthinking. In fact, at the moment, he believed he knew more about what was going on inside Tomara than he'd ever known about anyone before.

He took a step closer, his weapon forgotten. "I promise," he told her softly.

"You mean it?"

An answer wasn't necessary, at least not one that required words. Because she hadn't drawn away from him, Hayden took her hand and brought it to his lips. She'd spent the day clambering over rocks yet the flesh on her knuckles remained soft. "We've been fighting for a long time, Tomara. I can't deny that. But when I heard that shot, when I realized it was you who was being shot at, the only thing I could think of was making sure you were alive. When I saw you move—"

"You risked yourself for me."

"Yes."

"You didn't have to do that."

"Yes, I did, Tomara."

He wanted the day to be over. He wanted the night to begin. And he didn't want anyone coming up here to disturb them.

Tomara was saying something about Al and Hoagy not having any weapons. Her voice was losing strength. Her eyes were on him; her incredible eyes were on him, reaching his soul. Instead of hearing her out, Hayden ran his hands up her arms and pulled her close. She stopped in midsentence, her lips parted.

The message was there.

"I'm glad I came," he told her.

"Hayden?"

"No one knows I'm here," he went on. The sound of his voice reminded him of reality, but he wasn't sure how much longer that would go on. "What about you?"

"No one."

"Then we could stay the night."

"Yes."

"Waiting for Al and Hoagy. Doing what we came up here to accomplish."

"Yes." *All night. We won't rejoin the world until morning.*

Chapter Thirteen

For dinner they had sandwiches washed down with water. Afterward Hayden and Tomara sat on separate rocks and watched the shading of the landscape and talked about rodeos. Both of them had been to the Wild Horse Stampede in Wolf Point—Hayden as temporary help hired to deal with crowd control, Tomara as a child sneaking in when the ticket taker wasn't looking.

"It was another world," Tomara said with the setting sun turning her hair gold. "So much was happening. There was so much excitement. I remember feeling as if I was part of something larger than myself. I was afraid of all those people. I guess I thought someone would ask me to prove I had a right to be there. At the same time I wanted it to go on forever. Life seemed so ordinary when it was over."

"I hope I don't get asked to work this year." Hayden hoped his words would form themselves without conscious effort from him. The sun on her hair was doing incredible things, releasing her from the earth's ties and turning her into a spirit, a wild bird with its wings spread in flight. "I want to sit in the stands and watch those crazy men pit themselves against bulls and broncs.''

"Have you ever wanted to compete?"

"And wind up with a broken neck? No, thank you."

Tomara took her eyes off Hayden long enough to lock on the rifle propped nearby. "Every year I told myself I wouldn't do it again. It was too much, and going back to my routine was always so hard. And then the time would come, and I'd go again."

"Would you do it now?"

Tomara couldn't imagine herself being anywhere except where she was tonight. It seemed that she had always been here trying to work through what was going on inside her. And like the rodeo, Hayden was drawing her.

"Oh, yes." Strange. She couldn't do more than whisper. "I'd like to learn whether the appeal is still there. I was always intimidated by those cowboys. They seemed so brave. So strong." Tomara leaned forward and cupped her chin in her hands. "I wonder if I'd still feel that way."

"They aren't any braver than you are."

Her body might be sagging, but nothing about her felt relaxed. "Once someone said I should try out for the Olympics. Distance running. I didn't take the suggestion seriously, and yet I've always wondered what it would be like. If I competed, would I feel the way those cowboys do when they come out of a chute? Are they scared, or are they so well trained and so sure of themselves that all they feel is a sense of anticipation?"

"Do you think you could have made the Olympics?"

Dark. Hayden's eyes were dark. In an attempt to counter their effect Tomara tried to remind herself why they were here; it didn't work. They were going to spend the night here. That was the only reality.

"I didn't have the dedication. I run because it's something I need to do, not because I want to pit myself against someone else."

Hayden was saying something about a childhood friend who'd tried out for a professional football team. When he didn't make the cut, the young man had gone through a long period of depression. "I don't know. Dreams are fine. We all need them. But our dreams have to be realistic."

"What are your dreams?" Tomara asked, without knowing the question was in her.

Hayden leaned forward. Tomara took the gesture as a blending of a man both at peace with his body and yet ever alert. "I'd like to build my own home. With a shop for woodworking and a garage large enough to house a vintage car. Someday, when I'm rich, I'm going to buy an antique vehicle and restore it."

"That's your dream?"

"Part of it. The other is children. I'd like to be a father. To see if I could do a better job than my parents did."

Tomara didn't need to see Hayden. What he'd just told her said more about him than his physical image ever could. "Those children will need a mother. What do you want her to be like?" she asked boldly.

"I don't want her to be like anything, Tomara. I don't believe in trying to fit people into molds."

"But—" Thank God he was far enough away that she couldn't touch him. "The two of you should have certain things in common."

"Understanding. I guess she'd have to be understanding. I'd like her to see what I do is important to me. And material possessions shouldn't mean too much to her."

"Except for a vintage car?"

Hayden chuckled. "Except for an old wreck of a car strewn all over the garage."

"You didn't say anything about what you'd like her to look like."

"No. I didn't."

He hadn't because physical appearance wasn't important to him, Tomara thought. She guessed that this mythical woman would have to have the stamina to survive Hayden's outdoor life-style. She couldn't see him being happy with someone who relied on beauty parlors and cosmetic counters.

Someone like me, Tomara almost allowed herself to think.

"What about you?" Hayden was asking. "What are your dreams?"

Tomara thought that maybe she was living one of them tonight. Despite what had brought them here, and what might happen if her father and brother showed up, she relished every moment she was being allowed to spend with this man who was, finally, giving her something of himself.

"I'd like to build my own home, too," she answered although she was barely aware of what she was thinking. "I like where I'm living now. It's a challenge. But I don't know how much longer I'll feel that way. Once I have it fixed up the way I want it, I guess I'd start looking for a new challenge."

"That's the only thing you want?"

Hayden had asked a dangerous question. He might feel free to tell her about his dreams for a family, but she wasn't sure it was safe to give away that much of herself. Still, he deserved more than he'd been given. "I'd like to become very good at photography. To win prizes. To see my work in *National Geographic*."

"Why not aim for the top? You haven't said anything about the people you want in your life."

"I know." He hadn't been fooled; he was trying to draw her into that dangerous territory. "One thing at a time, Hayden. Until there's no longer a reason for me to be here, I can't think beyond that."

"You must have had those thoughts before all this happened."

Hayden was right. She had dreamed—about a baby in her arms, and a man to share the wonder of a new life with. Someone to share her days and nights. "They're not going to come," she said as the last of the sun dropped below the horizon. "They won't try to get up here after dark."

"And we can't go down."

They continued to talk, only this time Tomara was careful to keep to safe subjects. She learned that staying in college had taken a great deal of discipline on Hayden's part; in turn she told him that she'd regretted not taking more history courses. He was satisfied with the Bronco the Fish,

Wildlife, and Parks Department had supplied for him but preferred to use the helicopter whenever possible. Tomara volunteered that she hadn't learned to swim until she moved away from Copper and that she'd never seen the ocean.

"I think I'd rather sleep outside."

The sudden change in conversation caught Tomara off guard. She couldn't say how long it had been dark and didn't care what time it was. Her body was trying to tell her that it needed rest, and yet she knew that sleep would be elusive at best. "You can use one of the sleeping bags."

"You pick. I don't care which one I have."

Tomara wished they'd settled this issue before it had gotten dark. Even more she wished the issue never had to be brought up. Still, she made a show of crawling into the cave and dragging out the two bags. They weren't what could be called clean, but at least they were serviceable. Somehow Tomara found that comforting.

"I wonder where they are tonight?"

Tomara realized she'd gone the better part of an hour without thinking about her family. "I don't know."

"Tomara?"

Somehow she had to convince him not to say her name like that. The tone was turning her toward him. The breath expelled at the end of the word was cutting through a thousand layers.

"What?"

What was he going to say? That separate sleeping bags weren't going to work, and he would give up a great deal in life just to spend the night making love to her? That he needed to know if she felt anything of what he was feeling? But Hayden couldn't ask those questions. He could only act. She was on her knees, pulling off her shoes. He dropped soundlessly beside her.

She wasn't drawing away. Not yet. Because he was aware of nothing else, Hayden was able to find her in the dark. He felt newborn. There was no past to him, no future. He'd never been anything except this wanting. This needing. Everything would come unraveled if she pulled away, but until she did that, he would do the only thing that was in him to do.

A touch shouldn't have such power over her.

The black of night was so intense that Hayden was little more than a presence. The world had closed itself out, a nothing punctuated only by stars so distant that they made almost no impact. The moon was a sliver. Tomara was locked into herself. There was nothing to turn to, nothing except this place, and this time. And then Hayden touched her and gave her access to another world.

Tomara gave back. She found his cheek with the back of her hand and ran over rough stubble. His hair was coarse, his jawline hard. His size had intimidated men; it intimidated her. His size also drew her. If she was reckless enough to give herself to this man, would she never again be a woman standing alone? This night might mean nothing in the morning. They had no guarantees against that.

But Hayden was strength and an end to being alone. And tonight she needed to know what that felt like.

Touching became everything. Because there was no relief from the night, everything had to come through her fingers. Tomara felt his hand moving slowly down her arm, circling her wrist, slipping out to the end of her fingers. Now it was fingertips against fingertips.

She felt ignited. Quick shafts of something she dared not put a name to shot through her and made her unmindful of the hard ground, the long hours since morning. It was her turn to move. She ran her fingers over the back of his hand, feeling bone and flesh and hair. A sound; one of them had sighed.

"Tomara?"

"Don't," she told him with greater wisdom than she'd ever possessed. "Don't talk. Don't think."

"I can't think. I haven't been able to since the day I met you."

He was giving her so much of himself. Giving back became essential. "I'm afraid of you," she whispered. "Afraid of what you do to me."

"I won't hurt you."

"Oh, Hayden. You can't make that promise." They weren't speaking of physical pain.

"That's the hell of it, isn't it?" he asked with his fingers laced through hers. "Neither of us can promise anything."

"Except tonight." How had she found the courage for this? "We can promise tonight."

"You want—?"

Oh, God. "I want."

Silence. Silence except for the sound of his breathing and her heart beating a cadence it had never beaten before. Fingers embracing fingers was no longer enough. She had to come closer. To feel his heat. To understand his strength.

They had yet to kiss, but Tomara couldn't wait. Hayden's powerful, roughened hand was on her throat. She felt utterly, completely safe. She was glad nature had made her flesh soft. It was a gift she wanted to give him, just as she wanted to take his masculine gifts. Satin and leather. Lower; his hand was moving lower. Tomara leaned closer, but their bent legs kept them apart. It wasn't enough. She needed more of him, and yet the promise of what was to come kept her still. She would experience this moment, feel him and wait for what was to come.

Had she always wanted him to touch her breasts? The answer came almost as soon as the question was asked. Oh, yes! A lifetime.

Command. He was taking command. There was no force, no surrender, only an igniting, an awareness of her body that she'd never dreamed possible. She wanted everything, every touch, every whisper, every second of this night.

And she was being given her wish.

Hayden's fingers were rough, and yet not too rough. Before tonight Tomara had believed she understood the meaning of the word *need*, but nothing, no goals, no desires had come close to this. She needed him inside her, becoming her, turning her into something new.

The power of her desire didn't shock her. She'd gone beyond that. From the moment their fingertips met, she'd stepped outside what she'd always been and entered a new realm.

In this realm there was no hesitancy about pulling off her blouse and unsnapping her bra. If he'd wanted to do that for her she was sorry, but urgency had become too much a part of her makeup for her to wait. He was forbidden fruit. Mostly he was danger.

And she was giving herself to that danger.

Hayden stood. She looked up, confused. In answer he covered her shoulders and drew her up against him. Now his breath was in her hair and on her shoulders, and the ache inside her slid lower and became more primitive. In blind desire Tomara reached for the buttons of his shirt, but Hayden stopped her.

He wanted to touch, to bring himself to believe that this incredible woman was truly giving herself to him. She was silk. Despite her life-style she was silk. Those warm and ready breasts, the long sheath of her arms, the fine ripple of ribs—those were the gifts she was offering him.

Hayden kissed her. He wanted their kiss to be gentle. He wanted his lips to let her know how precious this moment was for him. But there was nothing gentle in Hayden tonight. His hands might be giving pleasure—he hoped it was like that for her—but the moment he found her mouth, he knew how much of himself he would be giving away.

The urgency was there, driving their kiss. It wasn't just that there hadn't been any woman in his life for a long time. It wasn't that she was the last woman on earth he should be with. It was— Hayden refused to attach the word *love* to what was happening. He couldn't possibly be in love with someone he hadn't known existed a few weeks ago. But it was more than lust. Oh, yes, it was much more than lust.

She was giving back as much as he offered. There was insistence in the way she pressed her breasts into his chest and arched her back and dug hungry fingers into his flesh.

There wasn't going to be a morning, Hayden told himself. This night would last forever. Then with his vow echoing through him, he ripped off his shirt and drew her heat into him.

It was happening so fast and yet not fast enough. There should be a slow dance, a tasting of textures, a building.

Time. But Tomara wanted him in a way that was primitive and powerful. She had no choice but to part her lips and invite him in. Her hands restlessly ran up and down his exposed back and absorbed the fever of him. She pressed and dug, bringing him closer, revealing everything about herself.

The sleeping bags. With her swaying over him, Hayden quickly spread them. For a half second Tomara drew back from the reality of what he'd done, but hesitancy had no place here tonight.

Tonight might be the only night they would have.

Tomara allowed her legs to give up their burden and sank to her knees. Hayden was already waiting for her. Once again his fingers and palms were everywhere.

Their jeans were an encumbrance. Still touching, first Tomara and then Hayden cast the rest of their clothes aside. The wind spun a cold web down the small of Tomara's back. For a moment the chill warred with the heat inside, warred and lost.

"I've always wanted to do this," Hayden whispered.

He was releasing her braid. Tomara felt the freed mass slide over her naked shoulders and threw back her head so it sleeted down her back. With a tenderness that served as the perfect contrast for their previous frenzy, Hayden slipped his fingers through her hair. His breath was on her throat, and her body ached for more. It was all Tomara could do to restrain herself as he explored what she'd always taken for granted. "Why don't you ever wear it loose?" he asked.

"Why? I told you. It isn't practical."

"But it's beautiful. So beautiful."

As he'd done when they were clothed, Hayden let his fingertips make the exploration that would turn her body into his possession. Tomara clamped her hand over his wrist, not to restrain him, but because she couldn't not touch him. The sway and dip of her waist fascinated him. Again and again he ran his fingers from the edge of her breast, down her side, and up over her hipbone. With every inch he covered, Tomara was taken further into herself. She should be giving him pleasure, and yet, for a few seconds, she would think and experience nothing except what he was capable of giving her.

Her breasts felt heavy. Somehow he must have known that. He cupped one so it was angled toward him. And then he leaned toward her and took her breast into his mouth. Tomara couldn't wait any longer.

"Hayden." *Hayden.*

"Now?"

"Now."

He was rolling her onto her back. Yes. And she was spreading her legs. Yes. And then, oh, yes, then his hardness slid down and in and she lifted herself up to meet him. This time it was her tongue probing his open mouth. Once again her fingers dug into his flesh. Her breath came in great gasps.

Why was she crying? Tomara thought. The thought didn't stay. He was taking her, and she was allowing herself to be taken. She was trying to give pleasure as she'd never tried before and sending out prayers of thanks to the night that cradled them.

And for a little while, Tomara forgot what it meant to be alone.

She was trembling a little in her sleep, but for a long time Hayden simply lay with Tomara's back pressed against his cheek, his fingers trailing over her exposed breasts. They'd made love so quickly. Not enough had been said. Not enough experienced.

The moon was little more than a promise, and there wasn't enough strength in the stars to slash away the night. He wanted to see her. He wanted to ask her to turn toward him and look at him with honest eyes. Hayden had tasted her tears at the moment of lovemaking; that scared the hell out of him. There was no explanation except that, no matter how much they'd shared, how good making love had been, he'd given her reason to cry.

Hayden wasn't used to seeing people cry, or, the truth was, when he had, he'd hidden behind the mantle called "policeman" and viewed tears in a dispassionate way. Because of the way he'd been raised, it had been easier for him than for some of his fellow workers. In the process of becoming a man, Hayden had learned how flawed his family had been, but when it came to doing his job in the face of humans in crisis, being dispassionate had served him well.

Or had it? Hayden asked as he wrapped his leg over Tomara to keep her warm. He'd been proud of his ability to keep himself removed from the storms of those he came in contact with. And yet he'd turned his back on his former career and come to this lonely country because—Hayden didn't try to complete the scenario. It was enough that he could now admit that the lessons of his childhood hadn't been as deeply ingrained as he once believed they were.

Now, thinking about Tomara's tears, Hayden was able to be more honest than he ever had before. It wasn't enough that he understood that people sometimes had no defense against tears, that sometimes what was going on inside them was too powerful to be locked away. Tonight Hayden needed to know what Tomara was feeling.

He wanted to understand.

She was still shivering. He would like to believe he was capable of keeping her warm, but that wasn't possible. "Tomara." Her name belonged out here where the wind could temper and mold it. "Tomara. You need to get under the sleeping bag."

Waking up took a long, long time. Tomara was in a place where there was nothing except floating and feeling. She resisted coming back to that reality where thinking was required. But because it was Hayden who was showing her the way, she reached out for him. "I'm cold."

"That's why I want you to cover up."

She could deal with that. "The ground's hard."

"I thought you were used to that."

"I thought I was, too." Hayden had started to move away, but Tomara found him and pressed her palm along his shoulder. "You have goose bumps."

"So do you. Are you going to get up?"

Hayden's question brought her fully into the present. She let him help her to her feet and stood there feeling the wind on her exposed body as he rearranged the sleeping bags.

They had become lovers. Tomara felt no shock, no surprise. Not long ago she believed it was impossible, but a great deal had happened in a short time. She'd learned about her father and brother from David. Worried about them, she'd thrown together some food and had come up here trying to find them. There had been the strangers, one of whom might have been Leonard Barth, shooting at her, and Hayden had shown up and saved her life.

But most important of all, she and Hayden had stayed here while the day died and something else came to life.

"Tomara? Come here."

Teaching herself about his body hadn't taken away any of the mystery. He pulled the sleeping bag over them and wrapped himself around her to keep her warm. In some way she felt trapped, but she accepted this confinement.

She wasn't going to fall back asleep. Hayden had only to cover her leg with his for her to know that. Her mouth was only inches from his throat. Her tongue slid out to taste him and found what was maybe the only soft thing about Hayden Conover. His pulse was throbbing just below the surface and vibrating against her tongue. With a soft childlike cry, Tomara slid closer so she could run her teeth and lips over his flesh. His reaction was what she expected, what she needed.

"You know what you're doing to me, don't you?"

"Yes."

"And you like having that much control over me, don't you?"

"Do I?" Tomara asked. The power was with him and not her. "When it comes to you, I don't have that at all."

"You're wrong. Believe me, Tomara, you're wrong."

She was no longer trembling, at least not from cold. He was so much a part of her; there was no part of her he hadn't touched in one way or another. "Does anyone know we're here?"

"No."

He knew as well as she did that tonight might be all they had. All they would ever have. The knowledge hurt. Frightened, she cast it aside. Tomara sought blindly until their mouths met. He was waiting for her, less frenzied this time but still with a message that needed no explanation. Tomara surrendered to the message.

A long time later Hayden asked her why she'd cried the first time, but by then Tomara couldn't remember that it had happened.

Chapter Fourteen

Jay met Tomara and Hayden on the country road before they could return to town. One look from Jay let Tomara know that he wasn't going to ask questions about what had happened in the hills last night.

The police chief's reason for being out was simple. Hayden's horse had somehow found its way back to the Bronco and had just escaped being run down by a half-awake trucker a little after four in the morning. "Your horse is back in its pasture, thanks to an obliging farmer with some room on his cattle truck. Now what if you tell me what this is about?"

Hayden kept his explanation terse and simple. He would be mighty obliged to Jay if Jay could find out anything about the distinctive black pickup that the three men had taken off in. But first Jay and Hayden should drop by Leonard's office and drag some answers out of the lawyer.

There was little for Tomara to say. Although she carried with her a small sorrow, she wasn't surprised by the ease with which Hayden changed from lover to professional. They might have held hands most of the way down this morning, but last night had begun to evaporate even before they left the hills. It hadn't taken any words. The truth was, Tomara had no words in her. She had come closer than she'd ever been with another human being. She'd never forget that, never turn her back on the magic. But what they'd shared had been incredibly fragile. The morning had put an end to that time away from reality.

Tomara didn't know how to tell Hayden that. And, she suspected, he felt the same way.

"I want to go with you," Tomara told the men after they'd made the decision to pay an unannounced call on Leonard.

Jay had no objection, but he wanted to be the one to ask questions. "I still don't understand something, Tomara. No one's seen Al or Hoagy for days. Those so-called sightings, all they are is gossip. And yet you know to go back up to the cave."

Tomara nodded.

"How'd they get in touch with you?"

"They didn't," Tomara answered. She needed to weigh every word first to be sure she didn't somehow implicate David. "It was just a hunch."

"I don't think so."

Last night was something separate from today. Tomara read the unarguable message in Hayden's terse statement. "What don't you think?" she asked.

"That it was a hunch. I watched you take off in one direction and then cut cross-country. A person doesn't do that unless they don't want anyone following them. Unless they've got a reason for wanting to be alone."

"Think what you want." Hayden needed a shave. His shirt was wrinkled. He reminded her more than a little of a wolf just coming out of hibernation. "You don't have any right to interrogate me."

"Interrogate? Is that what you think this is?"

This was the man she'd made love to? If Tomara had been anyone else, the hard question might have undone her, but Tomara had no illusions. She would deal with reality and place her emotions in a tight, dark compartment. "I don't know what it is. I had every right to go up there. You had a right, I guess, to follow me. Let's leave it at that."

It wasn't until Tomara had fallen in line behind the Bronco that she became aware of her hands. The tips that had made that first electric contact with Hayden ached. She understood what was behind the sensation. No matter what they'd just said, if the time was right, she would reach out and repeat what had led to a night of lovemaking.

Only, that wasn't going to happen.

Leonard wasn't in his office. His secretary didn't know what to do. Mr. Barth had several appointments set up for the day, but when she got to work this morning there'd been a message on the answering machine that an emergency had come up and he wouldn't be in. No, she said in reply to Jay's question, he hadn't been in the office yesterday afternoon, either. There was, however, a perfectly good explanation for that. His business then had been in Sidney.

Jay didn't think it was going to do any good, but as soon as he'd put in a phone call to the reservation, he'd drop by Leonard's place. Hayden was on his way to work; otherwise he would go with Jay. When both men turned toward her, Tomara met their eyes. "I have to talk to Mandy," she said.

"What are you going to tell her?" Hayden asked.

"I don't know." Tomara felt as if she'd been dismissed. Neither Hayden nor Jay needed her today. Maybe, she told herself, it was just as well. Otherwise she might never be able to put last night into perspective. Never understand what had happened. And she needed to come to grips with the possibility that it might never happen again. "I haven't thought everything out yet," she went on. "But I don't want her to hear anything from someone else."

Mandy was opening for the day when Tomara pushed open the tavern door. "The prodigal daughter," Mandy said by way of welcome. "I won't ask, but if you want to tell me where you were last night I'll listen."

If it had been anyone else, Tomara would have changed the subject. But this was the one person in the world she could be honest with. "In the hills. Al and Hoagy have been staying in the cave there."

"You saw them?"

"No." Tomara reached for a handful of peanuts to quiet her rumbling stomach. Thoughts of a shower threatened to distract her. "But, Mandy, someone suggested I might go back up there. When I did, I found evidence that they'd been there."

"And that's where you were all night? Waiting for Al and Hoagy to show up."

"That was part of it. Hayden followed me."

Mandy had been placing chairs around a table. She stopped in midmotion. "You and Hayden. As in you and Hayden?"

Tomara took over the chore Mandy had forgotten. The silence stretched out, not because Tomara had anything to hide, but because she needed time to deal with the emotions stirred by her friend's question. "It happened."

"You don't sound particularly happy."

Was she that transparent? "I don't know how I feel. Maybe it was just that we had the hills to ourselves. And the stars. And it was so dark."

"Bull. It'll never be like that with you. When you sleep with a man, it's because something feels damn good between the two of you. Tell me it felt right last night."

There weren't any more chairs to be arranged. "You know me too well."

"Maybe. Maybe not. What I think I see is a woman who doesn't know what she's feeling other than if he walked in the door this minute she'd have a hard time telling him no."

Tomara didn't blush. Instead she met Mandy's eyes. "How did you get so wise?"

"You have to ask?" Mandy laughed. "You're talking to a woman who's been married too many times. It's the pits, isn't it? Feeling like there's a storm going on inside you and you don't have any way of getting out of it."

If she hadn't been so right, Tomara might have laughed at the picture Mandy was drawing. She wanted to tell her friend what it had felt like to forget who she was and what Hayden represented. To let needing and wanting and falling in love rule everything. But that wasn't why she'd come in here.

Mandy had started to take inventory of the liquor supply when Tomara told her about a rifle bullet just missing her. "No."

What was it Mandy had called herself? A warhorse. Tomara hoped she was enough of one. "Hayden shot back. There were three men, so far away we couldn't read the license number of their truck through binoculars. One of them— Mandy, he looked like Leonard."

No. Tomara felt the unspoken denial. Mandy was frozen. Her jaw sagged and, for once, her age showed. She seemed to be shrinking. "You saw?"

What did Mandy need? A touch? To stand alone? Because last night Hayden had taught her something magical about what a touch could do, Tomara took Mandy's fingers and brought them to the side of her neck to warm them. "I can't be sure," she said, and then because she didn't want Mandy to find hope and then have that hope dashed, she told her about being with Jay and Hayden when they'd gone to Leonard's office.

"I haven't seen him since yesterday morning." Mandy's words were cold and too controlled. "He said he had to go to Sidney. I thought he might be back last night but—"

"I don't understand it, either." Tomara drew Mandy over to a chair and helped her sit down. "None of this makes sense. I wish I had some explanation, but I don't."

"Tell me."

The two women didn't break apart until the first of Mandy's customers arrived. By then Mandy knew as much as Tomara did. Tomara told her friend that she was going upstairs for a shower, but she'd be back before long so they could talk some more.

Mandy had gone shopping. There were fresh eggs in the refrigerator and bananas on the counter. Tomara grabbed a banana, but fixing anything that had to be heated would call for more concentration than she was capable of.

The shower was a welcome release. Warm water seeped into Tomara and left her feeling as if she'd been wrapped in sheep's wool. She heard nothing except water hitting her flesh. She smelled nothing except soap. Once, while she was shampooing her hair, she almost thought of what Hayden had said about her hair down, but she refused to give the thought life.

It wasn't until she was back in jeans and a loose blouse that Tomara faced the rest of the day.

She couldn't go back into the hills. She would have to be stupid not to realize that Hayden and Jay would be watching her. Maybe it was better this way. Her father and brother would return and see that someone had been in the cave. Maybe they would bundle up their belongings and put the county behind them.

Tomara almost wished they would—even if it meant going the rest of her life without seeing them. At this moment all she wanted was to have them out of her life.

She had too much to think about; Al and Hoagy would have to wait their turn. There was the question of Leonard, the reality of a rifle aimed at her. And through, and above, and around that, there was Hayden.

He'd said he had to get back to work today. Had he first gone to his house for a shower? Had he used the shower to scrub her memory from his body, or like her, hadn't soap and a rough towel done the job they should have?

I've been made love to. That was the message her body and heart continued to give out. *No matter what happens now, we made love.*

Mandy couldn't talk. A group of vacationers in RVs had taken up every available space. Tomara helped out until Mandy declared that she had things under control. Then Tomara left, telling her friend she'd be back later.

Outside, she noticed that Leonard's car still wasn't in its usual parking place. Maybe Jay would talk to her.

Jay was on the phone when Tomara entered his office. He didn't smile at her, but neither did he make her feel as if she was the last person he wanted to see. "Interesting," he said as he hung up the receiver. "That was my uncle over at the reservation. A cop should always have a relative who owns a gas station."

"He knows something about the truck we saw?"

"Yeah. He remembered gassing up that particular truck earlier this week. The driver used a credit card. From that my uncle was able to get a name."

"Is that going to do you any good?"

"It is with this particular name." Jay handed Tomara the piece of paper he'd been worrying. Although he'd traced over it several times, Tomara read Bradley Wisdom.

"Bradley Wisdom." Jay spoke the name as if it belonged to something he'd found under a rock. "If he hadn't been so damn arrogant, I might not have remembered it. He was here in the spring. Him and some other guy. They knew where there was some petroleum out on the prairie. By God, there wasn't anyone going to follow them out there. It was up to me to make sure they were left alone. I figured as long as they kept their mouths shut, no one would give a you-know-what about what they were doing. Unfortunately, they bragged, and then when they came up empty-handed they had to eat a little crow."

"Petroleum? Jay, that's what the geologist had been looking for."

"That's what I was thinking. And don't ask me if I think there's a connection, because I don't believe in asking myself questions I can't answer. That's for Bradley Wisdom and his friends to say."

"You know where they are?"

"My uncle knows where they've been camping. Just north of the reservation. Like I said, there's nothing that's more help than a nosy relative."

Tomara smiled for Jay. "You're going to look for them now?"

"Not by myself. I'm not that much of a fool. First I'm going to find out when Hayden can knock off work, and then we're going to ask some questions."

"Jay? What if Leonard's with them?"

"Then we ask him some questions, too."

"I told Mandy."

"Mandy." Jay frowned. "This is going to be hard on her. I've never cared for Leonard much one way or the other, but I don't want to see Mandy hurt. Tomara, I can't make any promises about how this is going to turn out."

"I know you can't." Tomara reached out and covered Jay's thick hand with her own. "You'll take care of yourself, won't you?"

"I'll try to, but thank you for asking. Tomara, Hayden didn't say anything, so I'm going to ask you. Things changed between the two of you last night, didn't they?"

Changed? What a simple word for something that wasn't simple at all. "Yes."

"I thought so. It complicates things, doesn't it?"

"I don't know what to say."

"Don't say anything. It's none of my business."

"I appreciate that. But I just wish I wasn't who I was, and he hadn't been the one to find the body."

"I think it's more than that, Tomara."

"What do you mean?"

"This is between you and Hayden," Jay told her gently. "You two are the only ones who can work it out."

"I know."

Tomara stayed while Jay put in a call to Hayden. The game warden explained that he would be by in a few minutes. The two men could make their plans after that. "There's nothing you can do," Jay told her after hanging up. "I wouldn't be asking for Hayden's help if he wasn't a cop. And there's no way I'm going to let you go with us."

"I didn't ask," Tomara reminded him. She decided to leave before Hayden showed up.

She hadn't gotten back to Mandy's place before she thought back to her denial. Maybe she hadn't asked in so many words, but Jay had been right in guessing that she wanted to be part of whatever was going to happen this afternoon.

Maybe they wouldn't find answers. Maybe there would be a logical explanation. Maybe they were in no way connected with the geologist's death, and the search for her father and brother would begin all over again.

The thought sickened Tomara.

"I can't stay here," she told Mandy after passing on the essence of her conversation with Jay. "I don't know what I'm looking for. I don't know what I expect those men to say, or if Leonard's with them, but this involves me. Somehow this involves Al and Hoagy and me. And you."

"I wish I could go with you."

Dirt in the gas tank. That was Jay's uncle's simple explanation. "They're not going to get a mile," he said when Jay and Hayden dropped by the service station that stood in the middle of the reservation. "I figured you wanted them to hang around, and when they came by for gas just after you and I got off the phone, it was obvious they had other plans."

Jay's uncle was right. Less than ten minutes after taking off in the direction the black pickup had gone, Hayden and Jay found them off to the side of the road. Because a low profile made the most sense, Jay drove his own truck. Neither he nor Hayden wore clothing that identified them as members of law enforcement agencies although both of them carried pistols tucked in the small of their backs. Their quarry, two bearded, disgusted men, were leaning over the truck's engine when Jay got out and walked casually toward them. Hayden hung back, watching.

The conversation didn't last long. Hayden saw Jay step back, his hand moving slowly to where his pistol was hidden. There wasn't time to think. Hayden acted automatically; he picked up the rifle Jay had left on the front seat and aimed it at the two men who were in the process of ducking away from the hood.

"I wouldn't do that," Hayden ordered. "I'm not that bad a shot."

The warning stopped them. Their looks of confusion amused him but not enough that he dropped his guard. It was possible that they'd done nothing more than fire warning shots at Tomara yesterday. It was also possible that they were responsible for a great deal more.

"Suspicion of attempted murder," Jay snapped in response to the taller man's demand for an explanation of why they were being handcuffed.

"The hell! What's the proof?"

"That's what a trial is for," Hayden answered. "You know what you two need, don't you? A damn good lawyer."

Hayden was rewarded. The two suspects exchanged quick looks. "Unless of course," Hayden went on, his tone deceptively casual, "the lawyer you know is in as much trouble as you are."

"What are you talking about?" the shorter man asked. "Look, we don't need to say a damn thing."

"You're right." Hayden turned toward Jay, who was sizing up the expensive, inoperative pickup. "They don't have to say a thing, do they, Jay? There's no reason for them to tell us who the third man is. Of course that way these two are going to take all the heat, but if that's what they want to do, who are we to argue? If it was me, though, I wouldn't take it too kindly if I was the one doing hard time while the man who got me into this walked."

"What are you talking about? You don't have proof of anything."

Hayden forced out a hard laugh. Right now he didn't care whether he was stretching things or not. The way he looked at it, this was the time to hit the men with everything he had and watch what way the cards landed. "You don't know that. What you're about to find out is that we aren't the backwoods bumpkins you think we are. This whole damn thing's tied together, and we know it. What happened yesterday, that murdered geologist, attempted murder of a police officer—if it was me, I'd at least be smart enough to know what kind of a hole I'd dug for myself. I sure as hell wouldn't be looking to make it any worse.''

That was all it took. Although the taller man, the one who'd been identified as Bradley Wisdom, didn't want to say anything until he'd thought it over, his partner had no qualms about telling everything, as rapidly as he could get the words out.

None of this had been his idea, he said, his tongue thick, his eyes darting everywhere and nowhere. Oh, yes, he'd gone along with trailing the geologist, but as things had been laid out to him, the plan had been to stick on his tail until McDonald had either proven or disproven the existence of petroleum around Copper. Kirk Morgan had the look of a man who knew he was in deep. ''We figured, knowing how slowly the government works, even if McDonald found something big, Barth could pull some strings and buy the land before the feds knew what was happening. No one said anything about killing McDonald.''

''Shut up!'' Wisdom hissed. ''Will you shut the hell up?''

''You shut up!'' Morgan snapped back. He took a half step toward his partner and almost lost his balance in the process. He groaned. Hayden could smell the alcohol on his breath. ''I'm not about to take all the heat.''

''Damn.'' Wisdom sagged against the truck. ''You fool. Why I ever hooked up with you—''

It was too late for regrets. Leonard Barth was implicated. Hayden and Jay had real suspects in the government geologist's murder, and, although nothing had been said, maybe Jay's wounding as well.

Jay ordered the two suspects to stand beside his pickup and then pulled Hayden aside. ''This is big,'' he whispered. ''Big and dirty.''

''You know what I'm thinking?'' Hayden's tone was grim. ''I'd say if the government could get another geologist to come out here, they're going to find something that's going to put Copper on the map.''

''I'm not concerned with who does or doesn't get rich off this,'' Jay pointed out. ''We've got a way to go before we can put this mess to rest. So far all we have is one man's word, but if we can come up with enough evidence for a charge that'll stick—''

"We will."

"We?" Jay questioned. "I thought you were a game cop."

"I am." Something had knotted itself up inside Hayden. He didn't yet understand, only that what he was feeling was somehow tied up with Tomara and what she'd been going through. "I'm also personally involved in this. I was shot at, too, remember."

"So was Tomara. That's what this all boils down to, isn't it?"

"Maybe."

"No maybe. Someone shoots at the woman you're falling in love with, and you want to know who, and why."

Falling in love with. "Don't put words in my mouth, Jay."

"I don't think I am. Look, you know I can use your help. The only thing I ask is that you remain objective."

That, Hayden admitted, might not be possible. He was angry, and his anger might become fury if he didn't contain it. He suspected that when he finally sorted it out, he might not have enough control over his feelings.

Hayden drove. Jay sat in the back of his pickup with the two handcuffed prisoners. From the size of the crowd that had gathered around the gas station, news of why Jay Eagle had come to the reservation had spread quickly. It took Hayden a few minutes to realize that Tomara was among them.

She walked slowly toward him, her arms wrapped tightly around her slim waist. She was in jeans. Her shirt was clean. Her hair was back in its braid. She looked like someone who'd forgotten what sleep felt like. Her eyes darted to the prisoners and then stayed on Hayden. "They're the ones?"

"Officially we can't say that yet. But, yeah, they're the ones."

A soft sigh told Hayden not enough of what was going on inside her. He wondered if she felt somehow vulnerable around the two men, but that didn't add up with what he knew of her. "What are they being accused of?" she asked.

"Right now? Trying to kill you."

"And you."

She had to stop whispering. If she didn't, he might forget what he was out here for. "Yeah. Me, too. But there's more."

Tomara waited.

"Leonard's been implicated. And it looks like it's more than just a case of attempted murder."

"Murder." Tomara tried the word and found it nearly impossible to say. "Is that possible?"

"I can't say that. Right now it's one liar's word against another's."

"Don't play games with me, Hayden. You know what I'm talking about. Does this have something to do with that man, McDonald?" Hayden didn't say anything, and Tomara plunged on. "Why are you making me drag this out of you? It's a simple question. Is it possible that they killed the man my father and brother are accused of murdering?"

"It's possible."

Tomara's second sigh in less than a minute was more ragged than the first, but she didn't care. Hope, the first real sense of hope she'd felt in weeks, flooded her. "What happens now?" she asked the stony-faced Hayden.

"What happens is we get these two to jail and give them access to a lawyer. And then I'm going to tag along while Jay talks to Leonard. When Leonard hears that I was up there with you, he's going to have a hell of a time talking himself out of this."

"I want to go with you."

"No. Damn it, Tomara. You weren't supposed to come out here."

"Did you really think anything would stop me?" Tomara was trying to remember why it had been so easy to bury herself in this man last night. With the world pressing around her, last night simply no longer existed. "Hayden, you have no right to tell me what I can or can't do. Only Jay can tell me whether I can go with him.''

Jay put off giving Tomara a yes or no, but she could be patient. The first order of business was to make sure the two suspects were taken to Sidney. Jay hoped to be back in a couple of hours, and then they would talk.

Hayden would go back with Tomara. If Leonard was around, Hayden wanted to be able to keep an eye on him.

"We don't really have anything yet, do we?" Tomara asked after Hayden joined her in the Jeep. "The word of one man isn't going to be enough. We have to have more.''

"What are you looking for?"

Tomara couldn't believe he'd asked that question. Surely Hayden knew what was on her mind. "They didn't do it," she said over the sound of the Jeep. "My father and brother, they didn't kill anyone.''

"Don't. Don't make something out of nothing. What you have so far is nothing.''

"How can you say that?" Tomara challenged. "Those were the men who shot at me. And at you. If they were responsible for one act of violence, then they're capable of others.''

"Capable maybe. That Morgan guy was scared. And it's a fair bet he was pretty drunk. Don't try to take what he said to the bank. Damn it, Tomara. I know who was out there with McDonald. Al and Hoagy, not anyone else.''

This was insane. Arguing would solve nothing. Besides, it was up to a court of law to determine a person's guilt or innocence. But didn't Hayden understand how much she needed this kernel of hope? "What are you saying?"

"I don't know what I'm saying.''

Tomara didn't believe that, but she knew enough not to press the issue. It was too emotional, too loaded with danger. She wanted Hayden with her in this. Nothing much, just a belief that her father and brother were incapable of murder. More than innocent. More than cleared. Incapable.

But he couldn't, or wouldn't give her that.

* * *

Leonard was in his office. Although Tomara believed he should be confronted right away, Hayden remained firm. If this was to be a legal investigation, they had to wait for Jay to return. In the meantime both of them were to go about their routines.

And that meant Tomara had to let Hayden off at his place and then drive back to town without him.

It was almost nightfall before Jay returned. By that time Tomara was taut with tension. No matter how much she tried not to, she had pictured everything unraveling in Sidney. Jay wouldn't have enough evidence against the men to keep them in jail. The man who'd implicated them in McDonald's murder would change his story.

And Hayden would demand to know how she could possibly go on defending her father and brother.

"I'm sorry. I know this has been hard on you," Jay told Tomara when she followed him into his office. "Let me call Hayden, and then we'll talk."

Tomara couldn't wait for Hayden. As soon as Jay hung up the phone she started shooting questions at him. Yes, Jay assured her, the two men had been formally charged with attempted murder and were in jail. At least that charge was a start. "Hayden's going to have to go to the D.A. in the morning and make a statement. You, too."

"Is that it?" Tomara managed. "That's all you have against them?"

"No. That's why it took me so long. I was putting some pressure on them. But I'd like to wait until Hayden gets here, so I only have to go through this once. I take it Leonard didn't leave his office this afternoon."

Tomara explained that she'd kept an eye on Leonard's car. It had been all she could do to keep from going to see the attorney, but she'd forced herself to remain in Mandy's apartment. She hadn't even let her friend know where she had been. "I couldn't trust what I might say around her. And if I said anything she might pass something on to Leonard."

"Good thinking. This has been hard on you."

Tomara didn't have time to give Jay an answer. The sound of the vehicle pulling up outside was unmistakable.

"Took your own sweet time, didn't you?" Hayden grumbled as he came in the door. "Next time I'm coming with you to make sure things get done." He didn't look at Tomara.

"Sit down," Jay ordered. "There's something both of you need to hear."

Booking the two prisoners hadn't taken long. From then Jay had gone over to the crime lab with the rifle he'd confiscated from the black pickup. He'd had to make a pest of himself, but he'd managed to get the crime lab to run the necessary tests.

"Funny thing. They hadn't been able to make a match between the bullets dug out of McDonald and me and Al and Hoagy's weapons. But when I gave them something new to work on—"

"Jay." Tomara felt light-headed. "Are you saying—"

"Am I saying the rifle I brought the crime lab fired those bullets? You're damn right I am. That's when I decided it was time to go back to the jail. Wisdom, he still wasn't talking. But Morgan— They're an odd pair. One cold as ice. The other so nervous he was about to embarrass himself. What they did to McDonald. Tomara, it wasn't pretty."

Tomara took a deep breath. What was one more shock? "Tell me."

If one was to believe Morgan, and Jay had no reason not to, the two men had known that Al and Hoagy were out on the prairie with McDonald and had been for several days. Apparently McDonald had work to do that kept him in one place. Al and Hoagy had wandered off and wound up shooting the antelope. "Don't ask me why Al and Hoagy took off after they bagged the antelope. Maybe they knew someone was watching them. Anyway, a couple of hours later, McDonald showed up. That's when our suspects decided to talk to him. A little friendly persuasion."

Tomara moved uneasily in her chair. She felt Hayden's eyes on her but refused to be sidetracked.

"It sounds like Wisdom was trying to strike a deal with McDonald. For a share of the profits, McDonald would forget he worked for the government. I guess McDonald had scruples, and I think you can pretty much figure out the rest."

"They killed him."

"In cold blood. I guess they didn't see Al and Hoagy coming back for their antelope. Wisdom and Morgan decided to cut out."

"And when I came by, Al and Hoagy panicked."

Jay nodded in response to Hayden's terse comment. "Apparently McDonald was pretty tight-mouthed about the exact location of the find. That's why Wisdom and Morgan have been hanging around all this time. They knew that McDonald had centered his exploration on the hills. I was shot because greed and nerves do crazy things to some people. They wanted those hills and the land between the reservation and the hills to themselves. They didn't know I was a cop. At least that's what they said."

"What were they trying to do?" Tomara asked. She felt numb. Numb and yet alive. "Kill everyone who came close?"

"Kill or scare them off. They didn't know about the cave so they didn't know where Al and Hoagy were hiding. Not that that bothered them. Wisdom and Morgan had heard that Al and Hoagy were on the run. That your brother and father were being accused of McDonald's murder. They figured any 'accidents' would be blamed on them. All Wisdom and Morgan had to do was wait for Leonard to put his plan into operation."

"Which was?"

"That's where the hang-up is," Jay said in response to Hayden's question. "Leonard isn't a fool. Wisdom and Morgan do the dirty work. Leonard works behind the scenes. All Morgan knows is that Leonard was working to get the land in question put in his name. After that everything would be nice and legal. With McDonald dead, there was no way of proving that Leonard had done anything more than make an extremely profitable real-estate deal."

"That's it. Just like that?" Tomara's head throbbed. Maybe later she would try to sort through everything Jay had told her. Right now all she could do was react.

"Just like that. The bullet in the antelope was fired by your father's rifle. They're guilty of hunting out of season and breaking out of jail. But that's all."

Tomara struggled to remain seated upright. Jay's words were so simple. There should be more to it, some sense of drama. But maybe all that mattered was that her father and brother had been cleared. "I have to tell them. They need to know."

Hayden grunted. "They'll find out soon enough, Tomara."

"Is that what you'd do?" Tomara asked. His words had turned her cold, but she didn't know how to insulate herself against that. "Wait until they run out of beans and come back to Copper? Maybe they'll read it in the newspaper. Of course. That's good enough for Al and Hoagy Metcalf."

"I didn't say that."

"Yes, you did." Tomara was on her feet. She felt strong. And weak. Incredibly weak.

"Maybe I did." Hayden placed himself between Tomara and the door. "Where are you going?"

"Where do you think?" She could shove him aside. Surely he wouldn't stand in her way if she insisted on leaving.

"Don't. Do you hear me? You're not going after them by yourself."

He shouldn't have said that. She might be in love with him; that didn't mean she wasn't capable of feeling the opposite emotion. "Why? Because they're scum? Don't mince words, Hayden. You can't tell me anything I haven't heard already."

"Don't put words in my mouth." He was so large. And he was standing too close to allow her to forget last night. "I thought you wanted to be with us when we went to talk to Leonard. Damn it, Tomara. It's almost dark. You can't be thinking of going back into the hills."

"You don't need me when you talk to Leonard."

"We'll go after them tomorrow. That's all I'm saying. Wait until tomorrow."

"Maybe I don't want you with me."

"You're waiting for me to say it, aren't you?" Hayden challenged. "All right. They're not worth it, Tomara. You've allowed those two losers to put you through hell. It didn't have to happen. They could have waited for me to land. If they hadn't run off, if they'd cooperated— But that's not the way they see things. It never has, and it never will be."

Tomara pushed her way around Hayden. He was an obstacle, nothing else. Maybe one thing. He was capable of hurting her in a way those years of growing up as a Metcalf had never hurt.

"Don't do it, Tomara," were the last words she heard. "They're not worth it."

Chapter Fifteen

Tomara thought of nothing. Or maybe the truth was that she was thinking of too many things. She fought to concentrate on what needed to be done. She had to run back to Mandy's long enough to change into hiking boots. Water, binoculars, food would have to be taken for what, hopefully, would be her last trip into the hills. If it took a week, she would wait there until her father and brother showed up.

And then they would come down and try to go on with their lives.

She would go back to Idaho Falls. There was nothing left to keep her here.

Nothing except Hayden Conover who'd killed everything she felt for him with his condemnation of her family.

And Mandy. Mandy was here.

No matter how much Tomara needed to get into the hills, Mandy had to come first. She had no idea what Jay and Hayden would say to Leonard, or if there was a way to tie him in with murder and attempted murder. What she did know was that Mandy deserved to know everything, from her.

When Mandy's eyes met hers across the dark tavern, Tomara read hope and pain and confusion. Ignoring her customers, Mandy drew Tomara into a far corner of the room.
Mandy spoke first. "He came to see me this afternoon. He
said he'd had an emergency this morning and that's why he
wasn't at work. When—when I asked him where he'd been
yesterday he gave me this."

Mandy held out an engagement ring. Tomara stared, her
heart breaking for her friend. "He asked you to marry him?
Oh, Mandy, what did you say?"

"Nothing." Mandy's voice was lifeless. "He can't do that
to me. There's never been any talk of marriage and then
this."

Tomara wished Mandy was more of a drinking woman.
This was one time when something to take the hard edge off
her emotions might help. "Did you say that to him?"

Mandy nodded. "I told him I needed time to think. And
I needed an explanation. Do you know what he said?"
Mandy didn't wait for a response from Tomara before going
on. "He started talking about his life. About wasting himself out here. About spending all his life having dreams and
not having those dreams realized. He's ambitious. More
ambitious than I knew. He should have left Copper, he said.
But he kept thinking that if he worked hard and made a
name for himself, maybe he'd get a political appointment.
He knows all the politicians in the state— It didn't happen.
And now—"

Taking Mandy's dry hand, Tomara squeezed it in an effort to give her friend the strength to carry on. "When he
gave me the ring, he said if he can't have those other things,
maybe at least he could have a marriage."

Tomara wanted to believe Leonard. Despite everything
she'd heard from Jay, she wanted to believe that Leonard
had honest feelings for Mandy. But life was more complicated than that. "You didn't say yes. Was it because his
proposal was unexpected?"

Once again Mandy shook her head. "After you told me
he might be involved with those shots that came so close to
you, that was the only thing I could think about. I kept

looking at him, hoping to find something to cling to. But the whole time he was proposing, he didn't look me in the eye."

"Mandy."

"He did that once before. A couple of weeks ago when he tried to buy some property that belonged to my third husband. I didn't want to sell. He said I was just being sentimental because that land isn't good for anything. I've never seen Leonard angry before, but I knew he was then. He didn't say anything. That isn't his way. But he wouldn't look me in the eye."

For maybe three seconds what Mandy was saying didn't make enough sense. "Property," Tomara made herself say. "Where?"

Mandy waved vaguely. "Not that far from the reservation. Tomara, I feel terrible about this. When my husband died, I became the owner of the prairie near the hills where Jay was shot, where Al and Hoagy have been hiding."

The same land that had held Wisdom and Morgan. Land that might hold a huge petroleum deposit. Land Leonard could get his hands on by marrying Mandy.

"What are you going to do with the ring?" Tomara asked gently.

"Give it back to him. Tomara, I've had enough marriages for any woman. Even if you hadn't told me, you know, about what Jay suspects, I wouldn't want to get that involved with another man."

"I thought you were happy with him," Tomara said gently.

"I was. It was exciting having someone care about me. But Tomara, I think Leonard asked me to marry him because he's restless or dissatisfied or something. I don't want to be responsible for filling up the holes in someone's life."

That wasn't the whole story, but maybe that was part of it. Tomara hoped it was. She could have told Mandy about what had probably been Leonard's ulterior motive in asking her to marry him, but that could wait. She wanted to find her father and brother. And she wanted to get out of Copper before she had to face Hayden again.

The lights were on in Jay's office when Tomara drove out of town. She wondered if Hayden was taking note of what she was doing, not that his reaction mattered, she told herself. She would think of only one thing at a time.

It had been dark for well over an hour by the time Tomara, with the help of a powerful flashlight, neared the cave. She called out her father's and brother's names, hoping against hope that their running and hiding could end tonight, but no one answered.

The cave was empty. There was no way Tomara could be sure whether anyone had been in there since she and Hayden—

Biting down her disappointment and the dangerous emotions she was trying to deny, Tomara ate half a sandwich before climbing into the sleeping bag. She held out no hope that she would be able to sleep, but the emotional and physical exertion of the day caught up with her. With the howl of a coyote for company Tomara fell asleep.

It was still night when she woke.

Hayden. No! He was back in Copper. She would think about what she wanted to say to her father and brother, the questions that still needed answers such as who had given them the pistol they'd used to make their escape. She would try to make them see the consequences of their actions. She would—

What did she have to do that for? Hayden and the rest of the town, too, would be only too happy to hold low opinions of her relatives. What was it he'd said? That they weren't worth her time.

But they were because they were all she had.

That's what Hayden didn't understand, and what she hadn't been able to explain. Maybe if she hadn't been so emotional—

No. If Hayden didn't have the capacity to accept her brother and father for what they were, then too much stood between them.

The night seemed endless. Tomara thought about getting up and going to sit out where she could watch the stars, but it was cool enough that she would have to bring the sleeping bag with her, and if she did that, memories of the night they'd spent together would be even stronger.

If that was possible.

One night of lovemaking shouldn't mean that much. Tomara didn't doubt that Mandy and Leonard had been lovers, and yet Mandy had been able to see the flaws in Leonard without being devastated. Tomara could certainly learn from her friend. She would go back to Copper, pack her belongings and leave the small town without feeling as if she was leaving a large part of herself behind.

But she couldn't. That reality kept Tomara awake.

"He isn't going to say anything. Nothing more than he's said already, which is damn little."

Hayden stared bleary-eyed at his best friend. According to Jay's living-room clock, it was a little before two in the morning. They'd confronted Leonard, and after talking themselves into the ground without getting anything approaching a confession, they'd gone into Mandy's for a drink. Mandy had virtually ignored them, and when Jay—Hayden wasn't going to do it; he'd told himself Tomara would wait for him—asked Mandy if she knew where Tomara was, the older woman's answer was the one Hayden hadn't wanted to hear.

She was gone. She didn't need or want him.

The two men had somehow wound up at Jay's place for barely cooked hamburgers and more beer. Somehow the time kept passing. Yet all Hayden was aware of was how long it had been since he'd seen Tomara.

Jay spoke as if he hadn't heard Hayden. "What we need is more than just Morgan's word against Wisdom and Leonard," he said.

"You said that," Hayden responded, "at least a hundred times."

"All right, we both know the D.A.'s probably going to be able to make a case out of this, but it's going to take a lot of work. You sure you couldn't tell a jury there's no doubt it was Leonard you saw?"

"It wasn't me. It was Tomara."

"So get Tomara to do it."

"She won't listen to anything I say."

Jay grunted. His eyes were reddened but focused. "So you're finally going to admit that."

Hayden wasn't sure how they'd gone this far without talking about Tomara. "This isn't any of your business."

"Sure it isn't. You've been bending my ear for hours, getting me to drink too much, not going after her because I'm fascinating company. Admit it. Rehashing this case is easier than talking about what's happening between you and Tomara."

"Nothing's happening."

"The hell it isn't. I was there, remember."

Hayden remembered. Not a half second had gone by that he didn't remember. "I'm not going to apologize about what I said. I'm right. They're not worth it."

"Did I ask you to? Besides, your quarrel is with Tomara, not me."

Hayden didn't like the word *quarrel* but he didn't know any way around it. "Why'd she take off like that? You'd think she'd be sick of making that climb up there. And there's no way she could get there before dark." Suddenly the hours of holding his thoughts at bay caved in around him. If he wasn't careful he'd wind up spilling his guts. "They aren't worth it."

"That's what you said."

"You don't agree?"

"That isn't the point. Look, I've known her a lot longer than you have. I have a pretty good idea how badly she wanted out of here all those years ago. But she stayed. Because she didn't want them to starve. Because she wanted to make sure Hoagy stayed in school. Maybe because they meant something to her. Then you came around trying to tell her they aren't worth her time. How do you expect her to react?"

Hayden had been sitting too long. His spine ached, and his legs were going to sleep. In his stocking feet he paced to the window and looked out. He couldn't see a thing. He didn't need to.

Somewhere out there a woman was sleeping. Maybe she'd already found her father and brother and was waiting for daylight before returning. And maybe she was alone.

The thought of Tomara being alone tore a jagged slice through Hayden. He'd never known anyone who would take off in the middle of the night for some rugged hills that might or might not be providing shelter for the two biggest fools in the county. She should be here with him tonight. They would go over the events of this remarkable day, and then he would reach for her, and she would respond. One of them would lead the way into the bedroom. One of them would make the first move that would lead to lovemaking.

And they would spend the night together.

It wasn't happening. Tomara was miles away.

Hayden groaned. "I need a vacation. Once hunting season is over, I'm going to get out of here."

"Where will you go?"

"Anywhere."

"Right. Who will you go with?"

Two figures. From this distance, even with binoculars, it was hard for Tomara to make out who they were. Should she stand up and expose herself?

She wanted it to be Al and Hoagy.

She needed it to be Hayden. Only Hayden.

Five minutes later Tomara had her answer. Hayden walked with power and purpose. Neither of the men scrambling toward her carried themselves with that undeniable sense of pride.

Waiting was hard, and yet Tomara made no effort to meet her father and brother. She didn't know whether she wanted to hug them or kick them. The question remained unanswered until she saw that they hadn't shaved for at least a week.

Hoagy spoke first. "You're looking good, sis."

"You aren't," Tomara countered with her emotions in check. "You came walking right up here. How did you know someone wasn't waiting for you?"

"We saw the Jeep."

It should be easier to find something to say, but Tomara needed time. It was more than their not having shaved. Her father looked beaten, her brother exhausted. Some of what they were feeling was being transferred to her. Tomara sat back down.

"You alone?" her father asked.

"It's just me." *Hasn't it always just been me?*

"What are you doing here?"

The telling took longer than Tomara thought it would. She studied her relatives' faces carefully for signs that they truly understood that everything had changed. The looks came, but slowly, as if they too needed time to comprehend that the nightmare was over.

"Do you think they'll charge us for poaching?" her father asked.

"I don't know. Good God, Dad, next to everything that could have happened, this is nothing. Pay your fine. Plead guilty and get it over with."

"We don't have any money, sis."

"All right." Tomara closed her eyes, willing to continue to accept responsibility for them. "I'll pay it. But this is the last time. The last time."

"I know."

Her father's tone took Tomara out of herself. "I've heard that before," she said warily.

"I 'spect you have. Only this time I mean it."

Hoagy filled in the blanks. The two men had had a lot of time to think, too long, but that was beside the point. They'd done a lot of talking. And most important, some decisions had been made.

"You're going to laugh. Go ahead. I don't care," Hoagy said. "But when David came to see us, he started me thinking. Do you know where he's going? San Diego. To college on a baseball scholarship."

"I know."

"The whole time he was talking, I wanted to be him. Dad said, well, he said if we ever got out of this mess that's where we'd go."

"To San Diego?" Tomara fought back disappointment. If this was yet another of their pipe dreams—

"They've got colleges there. Trade schools that don't cost much. I bet I could make it in one of those."

"College? Hoagy, what are you saying?"

Her brother looked as if he hadn't slept for a week, but he kept his tired eyes on her. "I'm saying David Kemper isn't the only one from Copper who can go on with his schooling."

Tomara was slow to absorb and believe what her brother was telling her, but the determination in his eyes finally made its impact. During those days and nights of hiding, Al and Hoagy Metcalf had made what might be the first truly intelligent decisions of their lives. They were going to sell the house and the land down by the river. It might not bring much, although if this petroleum talk turned out to be more than talk, buyers might come looking for them. The money would be used to get them to San Diego. Hoagy would apply at a trade school. Al figured he could get a job.

"A job? You'd work for someone else?"

"It beats running. Anything beats running."

Tears. Tomara had tasted tears the night she and Hayden became lovers. Today's tears were for an entirely different reason. One she could handle. Al and Hoagy still weren't particularly focused or practical about their plans, but Tomara felt a sense of purpose in them that she'd never felt before. She offered them some of the food she'd brought up and then sat back while Al described in more detail his plans for turning their lives around.

When he finally finished, Tomara was left with only one question, one that had nothing to do with San Diego.

"Who helped you escape?"

Father and son exchanged glances. "Leonard. It had to be him."

"You're sure?"

Al couldn't swear to it in court, but they remembered Leonard's last visit to the jail. The picture he painted for their chances with the legal system was nothing less than terrifying. According to Leonard, who had to know such things, the evidence was piling up against them. There was Hayden Conover to testify that he'd seen Al and Hoagy standing beside a body, and with their reputations... Leonard didn't want to second-guess the courts, but unless things turned around, he wanted his clients to prepare themselves for the possibility of lengthy prison terms.

"I was scared," Hoagy admitted. "I've never felt like that before, like everything was being pulled out from under me. Leonard walked out of the room. One of those little interviewing rooms. There were papers on the floor. Newspapers. I thought, I figured I'd grab them so I'd have something to read. Underneath was a gun. Hell. Anyone could have put it there. It was a real madhouse at the jail that day. People in and out all the time. I grabbed it. I didn't even think about it until we were out."

"And then?"

"And then I remembered that Leonard was already in the room when the jailer led us in."

Tomara pulled a crust off her sandwich and tossed it as far as she could. "You'd testify to that?"

Hoagy nodded. "Never figured it'd come to that, but yeah. If it'll do any good."

Sleep. What was that?

Hayden had found his way home a little before dawn. There was at least a half hour of the previous night he couldn't account for. Hayden's body let him know it needed something it wasn't getting. Unfortunately sleep wasn't on the agenda if he was going to go on earning a salary. A shower and shave plugged him into the routine, but when he went into the kitchen he found that he was out of coffee.

He'd drop by the grocery store on his way to work. Then he'd push himself until dark, and then, maybe, he'd be able to sleep.

Hayden had pulled out of his driveway when he spotted Mandy's car. When she gestured to indicate she wanted to talk to him, he backed up and turned off the engine.

Mandy looked the way he felt. "I wanted to talk to Jay," Mandy said almost before she was out of her car. "But he isn't at his house or the office. Do you know where he is?"

"He was going to talk to the D.A."

"About Leonard?"

"I'm afraid so. Mandy, I'd invite you in for coffee, but I'm out."

"This isn't a social visit, Hayden. I think you know that. Last night when you and Jay came into the tavern, I wasn't ready to talk to either of you. But I am now. I need some answers."

"I kind of thought you did."

"Will you give them to me?"

"If I can." Hayden wanted to tell Mandy how much he admired her guts, but that could wait. Instead he climbed into the passenger's side of Mandy's car and stretched his legs as far as he could. "I think you understand the ground rules," he started. "There are certain things you should hear from Jay. But you've been through a lot. If there's anything I can do—"

"What I've been through is nothing compared to what Tomara's faced. I figured, if she can do what she's done, then I better by God face everything that needs facing."

"Are you sure you want to do that? It isn't going to be pretty."

"I've figured that out."

"Leonard isn't the man you thought he was."

"You don't know what I thought he was. That's for me to work out. I think I understand why he did some of the things he did. At least I'm trying to. But Hayden, I don't want to sit there in court and hear things I haven't prepared myself for. Can you understand that?"

"Yes."

"I think—" Mandy looked down. "I guess there's really only one question. Do you think he did it? Pulled the trigger that killed that man. Put a bullet in Jay."

Because he'd guessed that the question was coming, Hayden was ready for it. Mandy was strong. As strong as Tomara. He didn't have to soft-pedal anything he said around either woman. "No. I don't. I think it's going to come out that his business practices were less than ethical. That he wasn't really trying to defend Al and Hoagy. But I can't believe Leonard is capable of violence."

A long, low sigh was Mandy's only reaction. "That's what I thought. I'm glad to have it come from you, though."

"Mandy?" Hayden glanced over at the woman. She looked exhausted, and yet her inner strength would see her through this. "Why did you come here this morning? I mean, wouldn't it have been easier if you just turned your back on Leonard?"

"Maybe."

"But you didn't do that."

"No. I didn't."

"I'd like to know why. If you don't mind telling me."

Mandy smiled. It was a forced gesture and quickly gone. "I think you've asked me a harder question than the one I asked you. Oh, Hayden, how can I explain it? Leonard's been part of my life for years. An important part recently. I think in some ways I'll always be emotionally involved with him. He might be scum. Once he's charged and the trial starts, I think I'm going to find out that there's always been a dark side to him. But turning my back on him? I can't do that."

"Why?"

"Why? Because he's a human being. Because I'm a human being."

"And that's the only reason?" Hayden was reaching for something. He couldn't put a name to what that thing was, only that he knew he was asking the question for himself.

"Does there have to be another reason? I feel sorry for him, Hayden. I'd like to know why he turned out the way he did. Maybe I'll find out that the bad in him completely outweighs the good. And maybe I'll learn that he's nothing more than a complex human being who somehow got twisted in the wrong direction."

"And that's why you'll be at the trial?"

Mandy nodded. "Life would be easier if people wore white or black hats, wouldn't it? If we could say this person is good and that one bad. But it doesn't work out that way. We can't simply turn our backs on those whose hats are more black than white. At least I can't."

Tomara was tired of herself. Her body hurt from lack of sleep. Her head ached as a result of the conversation she'd had with Al and Hoagy. She'd taken them back to the house, and then because she needed time alone, she'd parked the Jeep by the side of the road and gone for a run that lasted the better part of two hours. The run should have clarified her thoughts; it had always worked before.

But the only thing she knew as she made her way back to the Jeep was that she was hungry, and her muscles ached and she was tired of herself.

She didn't want to be Tomara Metcalf. She didn't want to have taken on the responsibility of helping her father and brother turn their dreams into reality. She didn't want to have to decide when to leave Copper.

And she didn't want to see Hayden again.

Or maybe the truth was that she wanted to see him too much.

"Tomara."

Wrinkled shirt. Red-rimmed eyes. Boots that received more attention than the rest of his wardrobe put together. He was leaning against her Jeep, his hand held to his forehead to ward off the sun. Behind him a hay truck chugged past while its driver stared at the two people standing at the side of the county road.

"What are you doing here?"

"Looking for you. You've been running."

"Yes."

"You found them. Al and Hoagy?"

"Yes."

"Damn it, Tomara. You aren't making this easy for me."

"What do you want me to say?" Her body was heat. Heat and ice.

"I don't know. Tell me what they said. What they've been up to."

"Why don't you ask them yourself? No. You won't do that, will you? They aren't worth the time. Yours or mine."

"Stop it, Tomara."

She was pushing him. Too bad. She'd been pushed, too, pushed enough that she'd gone for a two-hour run and felt a breath away from needing to do it again. "I'm not going to stop it, Hayden. I'm not made the way you'd like me to be. I'm going to be helping them put their lives on track.

Yeah. I know it. They aren't worth it. Not to you, but they are to me.''

"You aren't going to let me talk, are you?" Hayden pushed away from the Jeep. Dust had made its imprint on his thigh.

Talking hadn't gotten them anywhere. Lovemaking had taken her too far into love. She didn't know how to get out. Despite everything, she didn't know how to get out. "Hayden, I spent hours talking this morning. I did the same with Mandy last night. And you. I tried to talk to you."

"But did either of us listen?"

He was too damn close. She'd told herself she'd be leaving Copper tomorrow. Now she had no idea how she was was going to accomplish that. "I can't answer that," she told him sadly. Warily.

"I didn't."

Tomara waited.

"Not the way I should have," he went on. "Tomara, I just didn't want you hurt. I have a pretty good idea what Al and Hoagy had been putting you through for years. I didn't want that to happen again. I just wanted you out from under."

"Life doesn't work that way. At least not for most of us."

"I know that. Now."

"Now?"

Hayden moved. His muscles bunched, relaxed, bunched again. "You know what my upbringing was like. The distances—the lack of caring. That's the background I came from. I grew up thinking it was easier that way. If you didn't care too much. If you didn't invest too much of yourself—"

If you didn't receive or give too much love, Tomara thought. She felt sorry for Hayden, for the boy who'd never really had a mother and a father. "If we don't invest ourselves in people, what's the purpose?" she asked.

"I don't know, Tomara. What is the purpose?"

At first Tomara thought Hayden was throwing up yet another wedge between them. But he didn't know what to do with his hands, and his apparent nervousness made her listen to what he was truly saying. "Hayden? I was going to leave Copper tomorrow."

"You were?"

His hands had been moving restlessly along his thighs. Now they were hooked over his front pockets. They wouldn't stay there long. "I told myself there wasn't any reason to stay," she said. "I could go back to my job, my house, deal with my father and brother's affairs from there."

"You said 'were'."

"I did. But—" Tomara slid her hands into her back pockets. She knew what she was doing; she just didn't know how to still her own restlessness. "It would have been a cop-out."

Hayden touched her. His fingers, his leathered, prairie-tempered fingers were on her forearm. "I was tired, Hayden," she went on. "Of everything I've been through. Of having to deal with the town, my father and brother, Leonard, Mandy. You. Mostly I was tired of having to deal with you."

"Because I was putting you through hell."

"No." She wanted to touch in return. She needed. And yet— "Because you were another layer. The most important layer. I could deal with everything except what I was feeling for you."

"Tomara? I don't know where this conversation is going."

Tomara didn't, either. She suspected that they would have to come back to it many times before the elaborate jigsaw was solved, before they truly found the right pieces and put it all together. But he'd come out here to find her, and she knew she wasn't going to leave Copper tomorrow and that was a start. "I need some sleep," she told him. "And a shower."

"Come back to my place. You can use the shower there."

Somehow Hayden's offer had made perfect sense. She'd followed him back to his place, her mind strangely empty. She had been aware of nothing except the shadowy outline of the man driving the Bronco and the feel of his fingers on her arm. The shower hadn't taken away that feeling. And she hadn't been able to sleep because he was in the next room.

Now, clad in Hayden's shirt, Tomara was sitting on the side of his bed, wondering what they were going to say to each other. Tomara felt her braid hanging heavily down her back and wondered if they would need words after all. Slowly, feeling like a nervous bride, she undid the braid and shook out her hair.

He was sitting in his living room. He held a newspaper in his hands, but he was staring straight ahead. When she walked into the room, he turned toward her.

Would he want her? Tomara had never asked herself that question before. "I couldn't sleep."

"I tried to be quiet."

She wore nothing except a soft, old shirt that smelled and felt of him. Half of her wanted him to tell her that he was aware of her legs, hips, breasts. The other half wanted his eyes to remain locked with hers. Somehow he managed to do both. "You were reading the paper."

"I made some phone calls while you were in the shower. Leonard has been arrested."

"Oh."

"Mandy wants you to call her."

"Oh."

"Aren't you going to say more?"

They'd had this conversation before. The difference this time was that Tomara was ready to have it moved forward. She felt her calves, taut and muscled, as she closed the gap between them. "I told you something while we were standing out there. About planning on leaving Copper tomorrow."

"Don't do it."

God! He'd said what she needed to hear! "The town's going to be on the map soon. Not just because of the trial. The petroleum. Mandy's going to wind up a rich woman. And maybe other people. Farmers who'll lease their mineral rights."

He was on his feet. When Hayden took her loose hair between his fingers, she believed that now he knew exactly what he was doing with his hand. "I don't care about petroleum or oil rights."

"You don't care that I think I can make a living here? Being part of the expansion?"

"I love your hair down."

"I love you."

Strength. The word did more than describe Hayden. It was him. He was like the land, strong and undefeatable. But the prairie was more than sage and dust, rocks and a winter wind that could bring a man to his knees. It was also where antelope played out the cycle of their lives and where she'd learned how to run. Where her roots were. She was in his arms now, breathing him in, hearing his heart, hearing his words.

"I love you, Tomara."

Sweet. His lips, the lips that had said the most wonderful words she'd ever heard, were sweet and soft. Tomara tightened her calves and brought herself up and close until Hayden was all she was aware of. She was surrounded by him. It felt wonderful.

"When?"

He was asking a question. "When what?"

"When did you fall in love?"

"I don't know, Hayden. I don't know. Does it matter?"

"I don't know," he whispered with his lips molding to hers and a hand pushing into the small of her back, making Tomara understand why she hadn't been able to sleep, and why she wouldn't until he'd taken her need and turned it into a song.

"You love me?"

"Yes. And it scares the hell out of me."

Thank heavens he'd been the one to say that. Now all she had to do was tell him she felt the same way. Later. After they'd made love. After the night was gone and they'd been given a new day.

* * * * *

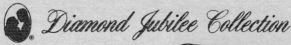

Diamond Jubilee Collection

It's our 10th Anniversary... and *you* get a present!

This collection of early Silhouette Romances features novels written by three of your favorite authors:

ANN MAJOR—*Wild Lady*
ANNETTE BROADRICK—*Circumstantial Evidence*
DIXIE BROWNING—*Island on the Hill*

* These Silhouette Romance titles were first published in the early 1980s and have not been available since!

* Beautiful Collector's Edition bound in antique green simulated leather to last a lifetime!

* Embossed in gold on the cover and spine!

This special collection will not be sold in retail stores and is only available through this exclusive offer.
Look for details in all Silhouette series published in June, July and August.

DJC-1

Take 4 bestselling love stories FREE

Plus get a FREE surprise gift!

COMING SOON...

For years Harlequin and Silhouette novels have been taking readers places—but only in their imaginations.

This fall look for PASSPORT TO ROMANCE, a promotion that could take you around the corner or around the world!

Watch for it in September!

★